About the Author

Elizabeth Quincey started writing many years ago but only decided to publish after she retired from a long and successful career as a business woman. She is a graduate of the University of Exeter and lives with her family in Surrey, England.

Please visit her website at www.elizabethquincey.com

The Lyndhurst Affair

Elizabeth Quincey

Grosvenor House
Publishing Limited

This book is published by
Grosvenor House Publishing Ltd
Link House
140 The Broadway, Tolworth, Surrey, KT6 7HT.
www.grosvenorhousepublishing.co.uk

A CIP record for this book
is available from the British Library

ISBN 978-1-78623-858-0

Dedication

*To all women who are trying to find themselves and
to those men who are trying to help us.*

Acknowledgments

To my husband and my two children. Thank you for putting
up with the madness.

To all those friends in the Claygate Writers Club who encour-
aged me to write this book.

Special thanks to Susannah Rickards, a great teacher, whose
faith never wavered.

PART 1

JANUARY 1819, NORTHUMBERLAND

CHAPTER 1

The duo stared in awe at the vivid glow on the horizon. The scarlet-streaked sky resembled gashes of blood, splattered against a vibrant blue canvas. Neither man had ever seen such a dramatic sunset and the picture laid out before them would burn into their memories forever. As they rode on, dark towers rose from amongst the trees in the near distance. Eventually, a narrow, snake-like path guided them onwards and the smell of cedar settling into the twilight was a warm invitation to come closer.

On inspection the vision was, at its heart, a Norman castle, richly ornamented and extended over the years. Stained glass windows twinkled in the dying light of the sun.

Count Nikolaus Andrassy whistled in appreciation. 'I do believe, dear friend, that we have just ridden into a Mrs Radcliffe novel. *The Romance of the Forest*, perhaps.'

William Fitzalan, Earl of Lyndhurst, could not answer. His heart pounded in his eagerness to get closer. In his wildest dreams he had never imagined such a magnificent sight, and to think that this was now his. Despite the misdeeds that had led to this inheritance, its beauty overwhelmed him. The soft thud of hooves landing on velvet moss hardened as they rode across the bridge that arched over the refracted lilac water of the moat. The clattering horses' shoes echoed loudly around the cobbled courtyard, announcing their arrival. Immediately, men came running from the stables to help them dismount. A man the size of a mountain stood in a doorway, filling the frame. Then he walked towards them, eyes darting between the two aristocrats, as if trying to work out who was the new lord of the manor. William read the signal and stepped forward.

'I am the Earl of Lyndhurst,' he declared.

'Lord Lyndhurst, I am Eric Sweyne, steward of the house-hold. Welcome to Northumberland, and to Goldsborough Castle.'

William took stock of the man. Eric Sweyne looked like a latter-day Viking, he thought, with a vigorous titian beard and wayward blond hair that should have faded years ago, but had steadfastly refused to do so. This was definitely the sort of man he would want on his side in battle.

'Ah, yes, Mr Sweyne. Thank you for your letter. You clearly know everything there is to know about the estate.'

Eric Sweyne bowed his head respectfully, but without a hint of humility, William noted.

'My family has been part of the estate for generations, my lord. Nobody could know more except the Goldsboroughs themselves.'

William nodded approvingly before looking up at the mag-nificent towers. He turned on his heel to take in the splendid sight. The light was fading fast, but he could still make out some of the features of the stonework. Narrow lancet windows with no decoration signalled that this was the oldest part of the castle. As he turned full circle, he spied a candle in one of them and a face watching him, before whoever it was disappeared swiftly out of view. A servant, no doubt, he thought. Then, William caught the steward appraising the heavy horizontal gold braid on the jacket of his travelling companion.

'This is Count Nikolaus Andrassy,' William said. 'A Hungarian Hussar, if you're wondering about the uniform.'

Sweyne looked none the wiser for the explanation, but swiftly ushered the two gentlemen into the castle. They walked through one room after another, all filled with ancient furniture. As they moved through to the more recent east wing the rooms became lighter and airier, and it became obvious to William that parts of the building had simply been added on over time, spreading the castle along either side of the courtyard. The place smelt old, not unpleasant, but of leather and wood smoke. Eventually, they came to a large drawing room at the end of the building. William tried to look out of the window, but it was too dark to see anything. He would have to wait until the morning.

'Who managed the land for the Marquess of Goldsborough?' he asked, 'An agent?'

'No, there is no agent,' Sweyne replied, somewhat hesitantly, as if surprised by the question. 'The marquess and his daughter have always taken a keen interest in the running of the estate.'

That was a pleasant surprise to William, gentlemen did not usually concern themselves with such things and it was something he had never understood. Land was a precious commodity to be nurtured and cherished, not just for future generations, but also for the people who worked it. *Noblesse oblige*, something most of his family would have scoffed at, was a notion that was very important to him. Then he registered what Sweyne had just said.

'Daughter?' William swung around to face him. 'You never mentioned a daughter in your letter.'

'Well, no, I did not, my lord, but that is because I assumed Mr Tobias, the solicitor, had informed you.'

'Where is she now?' demanded William.

'Here,' answered an assured female voice.

Sweyne stood aside to reveal a vision in powder-blue silk. The vision glided across the room and came face to face with William.

'I am Lady Angeline Goldsborough, daughter of the late Marquess of Goldsborough.'

She was extraordinary: tall, elegant and swan-necked, she was blonde, with silver-grey eyes, and an ethereal quality that caused William to peer over her shoulder. It would not have surprised him to see gossamer wings.

His stare did not unnerve the lady. In fact, despite her obvious youth, he watched the aristocrat in her rise before his very eyes. William composed himself and bowed deeply.

'I am the Earl of Lyndhurst. I am honoured to make your acquaintance.' Why did he sound so pompous all of a sudden? 'Lady Angeline, I am so,' William searched for the right words, 'so very sorry. I… I was unaware there was a daughter. Please may I pass on my sincere condolences to you and the marchioness.'

Lady Angeline swallowed hard. 'My mother died over a year ago, sir.'

William felt Nikolaus' quizzical gaze burn into him. Of course she had, he knew that. It was what had driven the marquess to excessive drinking and gaming, leading to the fateful night when he had met George, William's elder brother, the 7th Earl of Lyndhurst. The appearance of this previously unknown daughter really had unsettled him. William cleared his throat.

'Of course, please forgive my error.'

Lady Angeline inclined her head slightly, barely accepting the apology and William studied her closely. How much did she know about the circumstances surrounding her father's death? She would surely know that his brother had been the victor in that last disastrous game of cards. Did she know George's reputation as a libertine? Would she assume that he, William, was the same kind of man? Or did she think he was George? Perhaps she knew nothing except that the Earl of Lyndhurst was now the Lord of the Manor. He looked deeply into her eyes but she was giving nothing away. She was young and all alone in the world, but, he could see, she was brave. Glancing down, he caught sight of the black sash around her waist and realised that they were both in mourning for two people. Lady Angeline for her parents, and William for his brother and mother, for his mother had died soon after George, the favoured son, from the shock or from a broken heart. They shared a common bond in their grief because they were both now orphans, and although William was much older than the lady, even at the age of thirty, it was a terrible thing. He, too, was alone in the world. A wave of empathy for the young Lady Angeline washed over him, but there was nothing he could say or do to ease the pain.

'Please let me introduce to you my very good friend, Count Nikolaus Andrassy,' he said.

Nikolaus clicked his heels and bowed deeply. William observed Lady Angeline take in the visual feast. It was obvious she had never seen anyone quite like him, with his green and gold jacket, red trousers and long hair braids that hung down on either side of his face. Rather than being dazzled by Nikolaus, as most women were, she seemed to find him a curiosity. It entertained William to see the puzzled expression on Nikolaus' face. He was not used to being looked up and down in such a fashion, particularly by a woman.

Eventually, Lady Angeline managed to tear her eyes away and say, 'Gentlemen, you must be tired and hungry. We did not know when to expect you, so we have prepared a light supper only. I hope you will find this adequate. Please follow me.' Lady Angeline led them back through the rooms, giving gentle orders to scurrying servants as they went. 'The footman will take your luggage up to your bedchambers.'

'It's obvious who is the chatelaine of this household,' Nikolaus whispered to William with wry amusement. 'You're going to have trouble wresting control from that one. "Frosty" is the word that springs to mind.' Mesmerised by their new surroundings, the two men found themselves falling behind as Lady Angeline and Mr Sweyne marched onwards. There was so much to look at: the paintings, the armoury, the mounted stag antlers.

'Plenty of good hunting around here, by the look of things,' Nikolaus said.

They just about managed to keep track of the forward party by catching sight of the powder-blue skirt as it swished around the corners. 'She is rather imperious, don't you think? Doesn't she realise that if you were a different kind of man, William, this could certainly end like a scene from a novel?'

'What do you mean, Nikolaus?'

'The new lord, discovering an unwanted daughter, turns her out in the middle of the night, in the pouring rain, with nothing but the clothes she is standing in.'

William gave him a withering look.

'It's not as far-fetched as it sounds,' Nikolaus said, laughing.

'Perhaps not in the Carpathians,' William replied, 'but this is England. Even this far north, English sensibility prevails. Besides, it's not raining.'

Although he would never admit it, William saw that Nikolaus had a point. The servants looked understandably fearful of their new lord. They had no idea what this new regime would bring. Mr Sweyne knew his place, but was clearly the type of man who would only be deferential up to a point; to where his self-respect would allow. Lady Angeline, however, was either naïve in the extreme, or her confidence came from some source as yet unknown to him. She certainly intrigued him.

William and Nikolaus found Lady Angeline and Sweyne waiting for them in the small entrance hall that led to the dining room. As they came together, a door flew open from under the stairs and a thunderous explosion could be heard from the darkness within. Instinctively, William braced himself as eyes coloured by fire locked onto his. A huge, four-legged monster, covered in coarse, ash-hued fur, came bounding over to Lady Angeline and jumped up at her, demanding her full attention.

'Down, Odin!' she said with mock sternness. The monster obeyed immediately. 'Gentlemen, let me introduce you to Odin, my Irish wolfhound.'

William held his hand out to the dog, who went willingly to sniff and become better acquainted, but the moment was broken by heavy laboured breathing, coming from the darkened doorway.

'That dog will be the death of me!' rasped an apparition wreathed in indeterminate layers of brown and grey taffeta covered in a film of cobwebbed lace. She hung onto the ancient door handle, catching her breath.

'Nan, our guests have arrived,' announced Lady Angeline. Then she coloured. 'I mean, the new lord has arrived.' She glanced at William through lowered eyelashes.

At last, the lady understands, he thought.

Warily, the old woman moved into the light, then curtsied badly. William observed someone who could only be described as a butterball: she was completely round. Dark grey hair that curled around the ruddy orb of a face, perched on top of a rotund body with saucer-like eyes that looked as if they had seen too much.

'So, the travellers have come then, just as I said they would a twelve-month ago.' She had a thick local accent that William could barely understand. 'I've glimpsed the future, yer ken. You've been called here for a reason, but there's trouble ahead for all of us,' she warned, her voice surprisingly strong as she delivered her premonition,

'Nan, stop that immediately!' demanded Lady Angeline.

'But I tell yer, I ken the future. I've seen it,' insisted the old woman.

'What have you seen?' Nikolaus asked nervously.

She did not answer but gingerly walked towards him placing her hand over his heart, her eyes peering into the distance.

'Yer carry a heavy heart, sir. Yer time here will be hard. Summat in the dark chases yer. I cannot see it, but it will nae rest until it hunts yer down.'

The blood drained from Nikolaus' face and his body, shivering, vibrated against her fingers. As if in accord, Odin released one long, mighty howl into the night.

Eric Sweyne tried to lead the hound away, but William stopped him.

'Mr Sweyne,' William raised his voice above the din, so that the servants could hear clearly, 'please ensure that fresh horses are made ready for us. Count Nikolaus and I will be riding out early tomorrow morning to view the estate.'

Sweyne's eyes flickered momentarily towards Lady Angeline, but he quickly corrected himself as she turned her head away and fiddled nervously with her black sash.

'Aye, my lord. I will see to it immediately,' he replied. Everyone knew that the new lord of the manor was staking his claim.

CHAPTER 2

'The events that have brought us on this journey are so extraordinary, there must be a higher authority at work,' Nikolaus said solemnly as he sat down to eat.

William raised his eyebrows. 'Believe what you like, my friend, but you will never get me to subscribe to such a notion. It's a twist of fate that has brought us here, nothing more.'

A servant boy delivered their food, then left the two men alone.

Nikolaus shook his head. 'Our destiny is mapped out for us. Despite the tragic circumstances that prompted our journey, something or someone has called us to the north country.' He lent over the table. 'You heard the old woman. She knew we were coming, even before we did. She has the sight.'

William threw him a sceptical look. 'Surely you didn't believe any of that prattle?'

A shadow fell across Nikolaus' face. 'You must not mock, William. There are forces at work in this world that the likes of you and I will never understand. She reminds me of the gypsies at home in Hungary. They have great powers, too.'

'Superstitious nonsense!' William replied as he tucked into the pie, 'but what exactly was it that convinced you to come on this journey with me?'

'Ah,' Nikolaus said, 'something told me to come along and watch your back,' he wagged his finger at William, 'as I have had to do so many times before.'

'Really?' William huffed as he poured himself a drink.

'Oh in truth, I was becoming bored with all the delights that London has to offer.'

'The delights of the fairer sex boring a rake like you, Nikolaus? I find that hard to swallow.' William took his first gulp of ale.

'Believe me, William, it's not easy living with a reputation like mine. Sometimes it feels like every widow in town is in need of my services. Honestly, have you any idea how dull it becomes when one's appetites are constantly satisfied down below but never up here?' Nikolaus tapped his skull vigorously. William shook his head in disbelief at his companion's complaint, for he suspected a more sinister reason. Count Nikolaus Andrassy was an opium-eater. Ever since they started their journey from London, William had noticed recurring bouts of anxiety in his friend. The nearer they got to Northumberland, the more erratic his moods had become. William hoped above hope that Nikolaus was using this adventure as a way of ridding himself of opium's shadowy malice.

'So what do you think of the local delicacy?' William asked. 'Ox-tongue pie.'

'With brown sugar and sultanas,' Nikolaus remarked. 'A surprising combination.'

William watched in amusement as his friend picked the offending fruit from his mouth with great aplomb. Count Nikolaus Andrassy always cut a dash wherever he went. *A typical Hussar show-off,* was how Wellington had described him – unruly and swashbuckling. Andrassy usually wore the short dolman jacket the Hungarians were so famous for, teamed with colourful trousers and gleaming black boots.

Like all hussars, he wore his hair long – just like the Huns used to. It made him look wild and dangerous and so very irresistible to women. Except Lady Angeline, William noted.

'Well, I have never tasted anything quite like that.' Nikolaus dabbed his mouth delicately with a napkin. 'But at least the local ale is palatable.'

'What do you make of her?' asked William.

'Who, the old woman?'

'No, Lady Angeline.'

'Ah, there's blood and fire underneath all that ice, I'm sure of it,' Nikolaus replied. 'But the real question is, what are you going to *do* with her?'

'I have absolutely no idea,' William admitted, and a silence filled the room.

After a while, Nikolaus stretched out in boredom. 'Well, as there is nothing else to do, I think I will take myself off to bed.'

William toyed with his jug of ale. 'I'll stay up a bit longer. I have some thinking to do.'

With that, his friend gave a casual salute and left the room.

William glanced around the oak-panelled room. Paintings of Goldsborough ancestors looked down on him disapprovingly as he mulled over recent events. It was a long and sorry mess that had brought him here, to Goldsborough Castle, and he would have to live with the guilt for the rest of his life.

When William had become the 8th Earl of Lyndhurst, only a few months earlier, he was sure he would have to sell off what was left of the Lyndhurst estate to pay off his brother's debts. George had inherited the family traits of recklessness and self-indulgence and had spent years gambling away the family fortune and drinking himself into an early grave. However, by a quirk of fate, George had won a substantial estate in a game of cards the night he died. William suspected that George had been so deep in his cups at the time that he never really comprehended what he had won. If he had, he would never have embarked on the chain of events that finally led to his death.

As it was, the incident had saved the family from ruin. It was not a respectable way to inherit land, especially as the loser of the game, the Marquess of Goldsborough, had shot himself afterwards, this being the only honourable avenue left open to him. If William had known about the game sooner, he was sure he could have come to some arrangement to help Goldsborough save face, but he did not discover what had happened until days after the untimely demise of both his brother and the marquess. Perhaps the most tragic aspect of all was that, seemingly, gambling was completely out of character for the marquess. The recent death of his wife had hit him so hard that those who knew him, and there were precious few who did, said that he plunged down into a state of utter despair. By all accounts, Goldsborough had been of upstanding character, an intensely private man, very rarely seen in London, preferring to stay on his beloved Northumbrian estate.

All in all, it had been a terrible state of affairs, but as a result, William was now in Northumberland, with his very good friend, to explore his new lands. The adventure would begin in earnest tomorrow.

CHAPTER 3

William came downstairs just before daybreak, but he found Nikolaus already pacing the floor.

'Tell me you heard it last night,' Nikolaus said.

'Heard what?'

'All that hauling and grating, as if...' Nikolaus could not find the words he was looking for, 'as if bodies were being dragged along the floor.'

William's eyes widened. 'I'm afraid not, my friend. I had the most restful night, even though this is the coldest castle I have ever tried to sleep in.'

'How many castles have you slept in?' asked Nikolaus waspishly.

'Hmm, this is the first I believe.'

'I thought so. Trust me William, I have lived in castles all my life. This one is positively tropical.'

'Well then, you must be used to the noises that castles make. The howling of the wind, the groaning of the ghosts,' William teased, gesticulating wildly.

'Howling and groaning I am familiar with, but not the constant dragging of dead weights. No, something very peculiar was afoot last night.'

William frowned. 'It's not like you to leave a mystery unsolved. Why did you not go and explore?'

Nikolaus shook his head. 'William, you never explore a castle you don't know well in the dark. First, you won't find what you're looking for, and second, you will end up sleeping in an uncomfortable chair in a draughty corridor because you can't find the way back to your bedroom.'

William laughed loudly and slapped him on the back, eager to get on. 'Come on Nikolaus, let's go. The fresh air will revive your spirits.'

They saddled up their horses in the pre-dawn dark and rode out from the castle to watch the sunrise break through the morning mist hovering over the distant hills.

'My skin is crawling,' said Nikolaus, 'not with the morning chill but with something beyond my imagination. Everything is different up here: the land, the people.'

'Explain,' William said.

'It could be a different country. The people, they look like have just fallen from Valhalla – all wild and windswept, like the landscape. It's as if they are one and the same.'

'Maybe,' William said. 'It's nothing like Hampshire, of course.' He vaulted off his horse, knelt down and plucked out a great clump of clay that he crumbled between his fingers. 'Clay is heavy soil. It needs to be ploughed deep so the frosts can break it up over the winter. It's difficult to work. I will ask Sweyne if they add a mulch.' He looked out towards the sea. 'They could spread seaweed, of course. That would help.' Talking faster with excitement, he said, 'They need top-quality heavy horses, too, in order to maximise the yields. We need to check on them when we get back.'

Nikolaus, bored with the farming talk, grunted in mild agreement. 'But things do not sit well here, William. Have you not noticed the relentless melancholy that hangs over the place?'

'Oh, come now, Nikolaus. I've rarely seen you so rattled. Surely the wild ramblings of an eccentric old woman hasn't done this to you?'

Nikolaus did not reply, but sulked in silence. William remounted and they rode on for some time. Eventually William said, 'Nikolaus, what is wrong with you?'

'I'm tired and hungry.'

'You've been tired and hungry before.'

Nikolaus shifted his weight in the saddle. 'There is something about the place that makes me uneasy. I can feel strange forces at work here.'

'It's just your imagination,' William cajoled him.

'Ah yes, it's always my imagination.' Nikolaus clamped his lips together.

William knew there was no talking sense to him when he was in this mood, so once more there was a stony silence.

They had been riding for a couple of hours when suddenly Nikolaus sat bolt upright in the saddle.

'We've been out for an age. I'm going back to the castle to sleep off my mood. Are you coming?'

William guessed Nikolaus was going back to the dreaded opium. He hesitated, looking around him; there was still so much to explore. 'No, I think I'll carry on.'

'Suit yourself.' Nikolaus kicked his horse into a gallop and rode hard, back towards the castle.

Watching him disappear over the horizon, William worried for him. Count Nikolaus Andrassy, full of charm and bonhomie, rich beyond the dreams of avarice, and the delight of London society, especially the women, appeared to be blessed. As the nephew of Princess Eszterházy, one of the grande dames of the *haut ton*, a sparkling lifestyle was assured for him, but his addiction made him mercurial, and his moods could change like the wind. Sometimes, a darkness would come over him that was more than the ennui of a jaded sophisticate. He would disappear into the cesspools of St Giles, to drink and whore himself into oblivion for weeks on end. William had learnt long ago that to try to help Nikolaus during these times was pointless, even dangerous, and that the madness had to run its course. He feared that one day his dearest friend would be discovered lying dead in a gutter somewhere. But coming from a long line of dissolutes himself, William knew that often it was in the blood, and nothing could be done to save a person from himself.

Perhaps this was why they had become such good friends, because they recognised something of the darkness in each other. William had always known that he must manage his own demons with iron control. He could all too often taste the blood of excitement which, if set free, would enslave him to the same wildness and pleasure that had devoured his father and brother. He could never let that happen – there was just too much at stake. He was the last Earl of Lyndhurst. The Fitzalan family could trace their ancestry back to the Norman Conquest, but they would disappear forever unless he secured the future with money and an heir.

William wiped away the mud from his cheek that had splashed up when Nikolaus galloped off. He looked at the smear on his hand and it reminded him of *her*.

There had been one time, once only, when he had let go of the reins and loved with abandon, concealing nothing of himself. But that had been different. They had both known that it would be fleeting, so they grabbed what the other had to offer with a ferocity that had ensnared them completely. The Marqueza Theresa de Moronha e Mendonça e Almada had danced her way through life with an exuberance that astounded him. He felt her warmth radiate inside him whenever he remembered her. She had heightened his senses, making him see sensuality in every little thing. The way she swung her glorious chestnut tresses from side to side when she was being haughty. The golden, honey-rich brown of her eyes that twinkled like stars when she was teasing him. Her luscious, lusty laugh, which cascaded from those full red lips that he would kiss until they were sore.

All of this, mixed with the smell of gun smoke and polished leather as they moved behind enemy lines together, caked in mud, sabotaging Napoleon and his army. The marqueza had been a vigilante, hiding in the Portuguese mountains with her band of men, menacing the French. Wellington had instructed William to find her and coordinate her activities with English attacks. They had made a great team, living and loving to the full, but her life had been so brutally cut short and he still ached with the longing for her.

She had been so vivacious, so full of colour. Very different, he realised, from the pallid, icy Lady Angeline. He knew he would never love like that again, but his title and lands must pass down to the next generation; to be the last of the line was a thought too awful to contemplate. To that end he knew that he must find a wife soon. It was expected. So, he would sort out his affairs in Northumberland and then head to London for the season, where he would find a suitable wife. He understood his affairs in Northumberland now included a rather frosty young lady, but he was at a loss to know what to do with her, or what she expected of him.

As he contemplated the conundrum that was Lady Angeline, William, compelled to see the farthest reaches of his new estate, decided to follow the course of the river inland. Some forty minutes later, the river became a stream and he sensed he was nearing its source.

William's eyes followed the river's length until he saw something in the distance that looked like a gravestone, though it was not on consecrated ground. A second look suggested that it must be a boundary marker, but how could this be? Surely he was still on his own land? He tried to recall the maps he had been studying in the library, late last night. What lay beyond the boundary on this part of the estate? He could not recollect. As he moved nearer, he saw another marker, and then another, all of different shapes. They seemed to sweep around a wooded copse.

He rode closer and could hardly believe his eyes when he read the worn inscription on the first stone: IMP MC PIAVONIO VICTORINA AVG

For the Emperor Caesar Marcus Piavonius Victorinus Augustus. From his time reading Classics at Oxford, William knew that Victorinus was a short-lived Emperor of the Gallic empire from around the year 270 AD. He rode on to the next marker, which was tall and thin, but found he could not decipher it. The symbols looked like Viking runes: sharp, angular lines cut into the stone. He continued to arc around the copse until he came upon another. This one was squat and square and read: *Cursed be he that removeth his neighbour's landmark. Deuteronomy 27:17.* To find three such markers, spanning hundreds of years, standing together to protect whatever was in the woods was extraordinary. As lord of the manor, William had to know what lay beyond. He was sure his land extended to the woodland. These markers were an encroachment. So he rode on. A path meandered through the trees, following the trickle of water, which by now was a brook. It took him deeper into the thicket, which became darker as the branches of the trees hung densely over the path forming a canopy. Not a sound could be heard, except the soft snorting of his horse. Stillness enveloped him, as if all the world were dead.

His mare began to prance and William could feel the animal's unease building. Her ears constantly twitched, searching for a familiar sound. William looked around and his heart missed a beat at the sight of two amber eyes staring at him from the undergrowth. Unblinking, they followed him until, in a flash, they darted away. Spooked by the fox, his horse spun around, snorting madly now and desperate to bolt. It was only with supreme effort that William managed to control the mare and urge her onwards.

As they rounded the bend, the horse stopped dead in her tracks, ears flat back with fear. William stared in horror, his heart pounding so hard he could feel his pulse throbbing in his neck. Hanging from every branch spreading above them were strange looking amulets: animal horns, antlers and skulls, none big enough to be human, or not so he could see, but it was a gruesome sight. This was a godforsaken place. His sense of dread grew stronger by the second.

Soapy foam began to build up around the horse's neck and steam rose high off her liver-chestnut coat. William heard his own breath, ragged and frayed, and realised that the horse could sense his tension, so he relaxed his seat in the saddle and his hold on the reins. He nudged the animal forward, gently coaxing her on, passing under the relics. Although he prayed for this journey through perdition to end, he never once contemplated retreat, doggedly soldiering on until, at last, a clearing could be seen through the trees. Relief overwhelmed him. He could not remember ever feeling such morbid terror before, not even in battle. A well-kept thatched house came into view, and then he spied a smaller cottage, far away, on the other side of the land. He stopped at the edge of the wood and observed the scene for a time, before riding out into the open. Eventually, he ventured out into the sunlight and immediately the atmosphere seemed to change. This was a pretty place, with drifts of snowdrops carpeting the glade. In the forest, terror hung in the air, but here there was peace and tranquillity.

William rode up to the house and tethered his horse. He knocked forcefully on the front door, but no one answered, so he walked around to the back of the house, then stopped and stared, open-mouthed, at what lay in front of him. Scattered throughout the long grass were Roman ruins. They could not be real, could they? Of course they could. There were, he knew, many ruins in this part of the country; he had just not expected to find them in a field. He walked past a broken, smooth column that stood some four feet high. He was studying it so intently that he tripped over the foundations of an ancient floor that revealed fragments of mosaic. In the middle of the field was a statue on a plinth. William walked towards it and saw that it stood at the source of the river. He watched the light rise and fall on the water's flow as it ruffled to the surface. On inspection, he saw the statue was a classical Bacchus and satyr composition, with Bacchus holding up a dish to the gods while the satyr sat at his feet, playing with bunches of grapes.

This mysterious place fascinated him. He walked back to the house and looked through the windows. He wandered around to the front door again and, when he hammered on it once more, the latch opened, almost inviting him in. It seemed too easy. Hesitating, he looked around: nothing. He decided to step inside. He was no intruder, but he needed to find out who was living here, convinced as he was that this was his land.

William walked softly into the house and found himself in the living area. It was a cosy, if old-fashioned dwelling. Straight in front of him was the hearth surrounded by chairs and a winged settle, clearly the heart of the house. On the left was the kitchen and on the right was the only other door. He surmised that behind it lay a bedroom. But it was the painting on the right wall that commanded his attention. A huge blue and gold mural covered almost the entire wall. In the middle of the mural was the face of a beautiful woman with long flowing strands of golden hair. William lurched back, holding onto the door to balance himself. He knew that face. Lady Angeline! He walked up and examined it closely. The mural was obviously very old because the paint flaked off in his hand when he touched it. What intrigue was this? That face had been there for perhaps one hundred years. But it was her face.

He could feel irritation rising. Setting his jaw, he spun around the room, searching for answers. He found none. He did not like anything that he could not understand logically, and none of this made any sense. Looking back at the aged picture, he saw that the golden strands of hair divided the painting into a wheel of eight parts. He identified the vital elements of fire, water, air and earth, and he also made out the sun, moon and stars, together with something that looked like a spirit. At the top of the mural, the words, 'Lady of the Source' were clearly visible. What could this possibly mean?

A decorative wooden altar of dark oak stood against the wall below the mural. The carving was skilled and intricate, showing scenes from nature: birds, bees, and fruit-bearing trees. A rope had been placed in a circle on the surface of the altar. Inside the circle sat a goblet and a dagger. Both were made of the purest gold and were so beautifully decorated that William almost gasped.

The hilt of the dagger was studded with tiny garnets, cut to catch the light perfectly. They looked like tiny specks of blood encased in fine gold lattice. The goblet was adorned with filigree: delicate ornamental work which looked like lace, studded with large precious stones – sapphires, rubies and pearls. Captivated by its beauty, it struck William that this goblet was exactly how most people would imagine the Holy Grail to look. He picked up the dagger, touched the tip and flinched: it was so sharp it pierced his skin and a trickle of blood flowed.

Both goblet and dagger were exquisite. Moreover, they looked priceless. Whoever lived in this house was very, very sure that people would be too frightened of the consequences to attempt to steal these fine pieces. William was determined to find out exactly who the occupant was.

CHAPTER 4

The winter sun had burned off the early frost by the time Nikolaus returned to the castle. He made his way to the kitchens and went in search of food. He was starving, for supper last night had been scant and William had allowed no time for breakfast that morning. He might be aristocracy, but he was Hungarian aristocracy. He did not stand on ceremony like the English. If he wanted something, he would go and get it, not wait for a servant to offer it.

Once again, Nikolaus felt himself seized by the old angst that so often haunted him. His agitation mounted as the desire for all his passions to be sated bubbled up from within. He would find it increasingly hard to resist and in the end, he knew, he would have to resort to opium to help him manage the torment. The old woman and her vision were the cause of this bout of suffering, he was sure of it.

He walked through the kitchen garden, ignoring the gardener who doffed his cap to him, churning over in his mind the old servant-woman's prediction. She had reminded him of the gypsies back home in Hungary. The story went that, many moons ago, one of his ancestors had defiled a gypsy queen and in revenge she had sent a ferocious wolf to savage him. Although his ancestor had survived the ordeal, he lived out the rest of his life horribly disfigured. Legend had it that he was so badly maimed, people could not bear to look upon him, so he became as ugly on the inside as he was on the outside. From that day forward, Nikolaus' ancestors carried a curse, a darkness of the mind that would pass down the Andrassy line for eternity. The previous night it was as if the old crone had penetrated deep into his soul and seen everything. He had felt horribly vulnerable and exposed.

There was nobody in the kitchen, so Nikolaus walked into the pantry and helped himself to bread and cheese. That would satisfy him until luncheon. He was eating, instantly feeling happier, when someone walked into the kitchen.

'Now, yer do as I say, do yer hear me?'

He knew that voice. It stilled his breath and chilled his bones. Nikolaus peered around the door and caught sight of the old woman called Nan talking to the young boy who had served them their supper last night. She put her hand into a deep pocket and pulled out a phial made of dark brown glass.

'Yer put this in. Only a few drops at a time, do yer hear? But it must be done at every meal.' The boy nodded his head enthusiastically. 'We'll get rid of this blight once and for all, ye and me, shan't we?' Nan tousled the boy's hair and he looked up, smiling warmly. 'Now, yer mustn't tell a soul.' The boy's expression changed as he glanced down at the phial, looking worried. 'Do yer promise, Jack?' The boy thought for a moment, then gave one last affirmative nod before running out into the garden as fast as his legs could carry him.

Nan turned around to watch the boy out of the window, so Nikolaus stepped out into the light.

'Shall I also not tell a soul?' he asked.

Nan swung around and held her hand over her own heart. Nikolaus could see he had frightened her witless and smiled at the irony.

'Oh, yer scared the life out of me, sir.'

'Not quite, alas. Fear gives a curious feeling of delight, no?'

'No, it does not, my lord,' she answered, looking at him strangely.

'Tell me, old woman, what was going on here?'

'Nothing to concern yerself with my lord, a simple errand for the boy, nothing more. How was yer morning ride, sir?'

He strode up to her and stared directly into her face. She stepped back, wary.

'What secrets are you hiding, old lady?'

Nan reddened as she vigorously wiped her hands down her apron.

'I don't know what yer mean, sir.'

'I think you do. Tell me, what was abroad last night?'

'I have no idea what yer talking about, my lord.' She tried to walk around him, but Nikolaus blocked her path.

'I heard strange noises in the dark.'

'Castles always make strange noises' she said, trying to get past him once more. Again he blocked her.

'Yes, but not like this. Deep thumps in the night. Heavy objects being scraped along the floor.'

'It must be your imagination, sir.'

He finally let her pass. 'Ah yes, of course, my imagination. Believe me, old lady, reality is far more macabre than anything this paltry imagination of mine can come up with. Let me tell you about my ancestor, Elizabeth Bathory, who was known as the Bloody Lady of Cachtice. She was an exceptional beauty, but her narcissism drove her to such depths of depravity that even our imaginations could not conceive such evils.'

Nan stopped what she was doing and turned to look at Nikolaus with apprehension. She backed into a corner as he approached her in a menacing fashion.

He dropped his voice into a ghoulish whisper. 'She would kidnap beautiful young virgins and spirit them away to her mountain fortress, where she bled them, and bathed in their blood, while they watched her as they slowly died. Poor Elizabeth believed she could regain her youth and radiance by performing this perversion.'

Nan's mouth dropped open and her eyes bulged.

'When they finally broke into the castle, they discovered hundreds of mutilated female bodies in the dungeons, half-eaten by dogs and rats. They say she had bled and tortured over six hundred victims in her lifetime.'

Nan swallowed hard.

'Do you know what they did to her?'

Frozen with fear, Nan managed, very slowly, to turn her head from side to side.

Nikolaus moved in so close he could smell the herbs on her breath.

'Elizabeth was found to be insane, so they imprisoned her in a tiny dungeon and walled it up, so there was only the smallest hatch, where the guards could pass food to her. She stayed there until she died. Can you imagine it, old woman? It must have been like being buried alive.'

He moved away just far enough so that there was space for Nan to expel the air she had been holding in her lungs, then he jerked forward again. Instinctively, she tried to jump back, but the wall behind her prevented it.

'However, the fate of her servants was worse,' Nikolaus said, 'because without their help, she could never have carried out her dreadful deeds.'

A small whimper emitted from Nan's mouth.

'They had their fingers ripped off their hands, one by one, with red-hot tongs, before they were finally burned alive.'

Nan looked like she was about to faint, so Nikolaus decided he had toyed with her long enough. He started to walk out of the door into the garden, when he stopped and looked back at the old woman who was still pasted to the wall.

'So don't tell me it was all in my imagination, old lady. I will find out your secrets.' Flamboyantly, he pulled a silk handkerchief from his pocket and patted his mouth with affectation. 'By the way, I have many more grisly tales, just like that one, about my family,' he drawled. 'Remind me to tell you about my great-uncle, the man they called the "Terror of Transylvania".' He smiled winningly and, with a flourish, closed the door behind him and was gone.

CHAPTER 5

William returned to the castle by mid-afternoon, much later than he had intended, but he was thankful to be back to some sort of normality.

He watched the estate workers move in harmony, like ants, busy for the greater good of the community. The blacksmith was replacing the handle of a cooking pot between one horse leaving with a brand-new set of shoes and another horse arriving to receive the same. A milkmaid, carrying churns, made her way towards the kitchens. In the distance, men could be heard hollering at a bull who had escaped into the cows' field, and nearby, carpenters were sawing a felled oak. The estate day continued as any other day, as it had for centuries, and it pleased William to see that the chain of unity had not been broken, despite the change of ownership.

He ran up the stairs two at a time and crossed Lady Angeline in the hallway. Looking past her in the direction from which she had come, he realised her rooms must be situated there, right over the courtyard. The perfect vantage point to keep an eye on the comings and goings of castle life. She nodded briskly to him and quickened her pace.

'Lady Angeline.'

Stopping sharply, she kept her back to him and turned her head only slightly.

'I would be pleased if you would join me for dinner tonight.'

'I prefer to eat alone,' she replied coolly.

William smiled at the snub.

'I'm sure you do, but I insist. I have some questions I would like to ask you about the running of the household.' He could tell from the movement of her body that she had bristled at his insistence.

'Very well, Lord Lyndhurst. If you insist,' she said, and with her head held as high as it was possible for it to go, she continued on her way.

Nan served the food. William was sure this was not part of her normal duties, but rather, she was acting as chaperone to Lady Angeline, who sat opposite him at the other end of the long table. William had, without even thinking about it, assumed the position at the head of the table, where her father would have sat, and fleetingly he felt awkward. He observed that she would not look directly at him but sat sullenly, awaiting the soup.

Nikolaus' brooding appearance made it obvious that his mood had not improved any. He seemed to be fixated by the old woman, never taking his eyes off her, following her around the room, watching every move she made.

The soup was placed in front of Lady Angeline. William studied her. The mural he had seen that morning was an uncanny likeness. The painting was far too old for the woman to be her. It had to be an ancestor, he concluded, but the bloodline was unusually strong.

'What is this?' Lady Angeline demanded.

'Chicken soup,' replied Nan.

'But we always have mutton broth.'

'Yer've got venison next,' Nan retorted.

'What's going on?' Lady Angeline looked around the room, waiting for an explanation.

'Ah, I took the liberty of changing the menus,' William said, the memory of ox-tongue pie flashing through his mind. 'I'm rather fussy about what I eat. I have certain tastes.'

Lady Angeline's eyes flickered. 'Yes, yes, of course. This is your home now. You must change things as you see fit. She pushed the soup aside. 'Take it away, please, Nan. It is not to my liking.'

A bowl was placed in front of Nikolaus, which caused his morose silence to be broken. Jumping up from his seat, he flung the soup bowl the length of the room. 'William, do not eat the soup! The old crone has poisoned it!'

'Nikolaus, what on earth is the meaning of this?' William demanded.

'I caught her this morning, giving a potion to the kitchen boy. She told him to add a few drops to our food. Then she swore him to secrecy.'

Nan shook her head. 'I did no such thing. It was medicine for the boy's mother.'

'You can't trick me, you old witch. All this is a ruse.' He pointed to Lady Angeline. 'No one dislikes chicken soup.'

'For goodness sake, man, get a grip,' William implored him, noting that his friend's eyes were sunk deep into his skull and that his skin was sallow.

Lady Angeline had not flinched once, but sat throughout the drama with poise and self-control. Her composure was impressive, William had to admit.

'Nikolaus, please sit down,' William urged. Reluctantly, the Hungarian obeyed, staring at William as he picked up his spoon and began to eat. Three pairs of eyes watched him in silence as William supped the bowl dry. A frisson of expectation filled the room. 'Mmm, my compliments to the chef,' William said. 'Now, Nan, I think I will take a little more, please.' Nan gently took the bowl from him and began to refill it. The new lord had publicly demonstrated his trust in her and she was humbled.

Lady Angeline now met his gaze squarely. 'Nan, I have changed my mind. I will also take some soup.'

William knew she was showing her gratitude to him for declaring his faith in her maid, and in that moment something passed between them; he could feel it. Turning again to Nikolaus, he said, 'Think logically, man. Poisoning me would serve no purpose whatsoever. Lady Angeline would not get back the estate. My cousin, Simon, would inherit. And after all, better the devil you know, eh, Nan!' William winked at her, and in return she giggled like a young girl.

'Victims are always unconscious of their own doom,' Nikolaus replied cryptically, as he rose and bowed solemnly. 'I think I have outstayed my welcome this evening, so I must take my leave.' He walked towards the door.

'Have courage, my friend,' William called out to him. 'This is just another battle you have to win.' Nikolaus hovered for a few moments as if he was contemplating saying something more. Instead, he nodded curtly and removed himself from the room.

'You must excuse my companion's ill humour,' William said to Lady Angeline as he stroked the grain of the wooden table. 'He is not well, and in some distress, I think, but I trust he will improve with time.'

'I hope so, for all our sakes,' Angeline replied.

William studied the lady sitting in front of him in more detail. She was exquisite. 'Most ladies seem to find the Count's charm irresistible, despite his ill humour,' he said.

'Really? How peculiar!' She frowned with incredulity. 'I find him rather odd, but perhaps that is because we are simple people here in Northumberland. We like things to be straight-forward and matter-of-fact.'

William raised his eyebrows. Things did not appear straightforward and matter-of-fact to him, not since his journey into the forest. He wanted to question Lady Angeline about the boundary land but he had to be careful. He did not want to upset her. He needed her as an ally. It would make the transi-tion of the estate so much easier.

Lady Angeline watched the new lord of the manor warily. Despite his kindness to Nan this evening, she needed to be on her guard. She tried to appear outwardly relaxed, but she felt trapped in unfamiliar territory. She should not trust this usurper, and yet she thought she saw something special in those intelligent eyes. Count Andrassy was obviously more dashing, but the earl was quite nice-looking; handsome, in fact. Especially when he flashed her a smile that reached his eyes. His mahogany-brown hair was cut short, in the modern style, but it looked dishevelled and untamed. He was athleti-cally built, so wore his clothes, which were elegant and beauti-fully cut, exceedingly well. They clearly came from the hands of a master tailor.

Angeline pulled herself together. He was a blackguard, she remembered. He had taken what belonged to her: Goldsborough Castle.

'Do you know where the boundaries of the Goldsborough Estate lie?' she heard him ask. Her breath quickened. Why would he ask her such a thing?

'The maps in the library have them clearly marked,' she replied curtly.

'Hmmm, I'm not sure how accurate they are.'

'They are very accurate indeed, I can assure you. They will show you everything you need to know.' She hoped the sharpness in her voice would stop him from pursuing this line of enquiry. She had secrets to keep.

At that moment a flash of Nikolaus on horseback was seen through the dining-room window.

'Where the devil is he going?' William shouted.

'Fleeing the castle for an evening in the local town of Thornby, I expect,' replied Lady Angeline, pleased that something had distracted the earl. She took this opportunity to bring the evening to an end, not relishing the thought of being interrogated further.

William escorted Lady Angeline to the foot of the stairs. 'Good night, my lady, and please remember, I am not your enemy. Despite the circumstances, I hope one day we can be friends.'

She reflected on Lord Lyndhurst's words as she walked to her rooms, but her heart was hardened to him. He could not seduce her that easily with his fine manners and even finer words. He was a master trickster. He was responsible for everything that had happened to her and she could not so easily forgive or forget.

CHAPTER 6

'So, yer out of bed then?' Nan scolded as she walked into the bedroom.

Lady Angeline stood by the window, brushing her hair absentmindedly.

'There is nothing to get out of bed for. I no longer give the orders in this household. Or have you not noticed?' she replied churlishly.

Nan tsked in response as she got on with her chores.

Lady Angeline watched the Earl of Lyndhurst walk across the courtyard. He had a long, easy stride, unhurried and self-assured. She had never seen him walk any other way. He had evidently just returned from his daily ride, surveying his newly acquired estate. She observed that he always rode out early in the morning, but was always back by noon, for luncheon, obviously a man who liked to keep to a routine. How dull!

Nan came up behind her and peeked out of the window. 'He has a kindness in him, that one,' she said, 'not like most of the fancy. I can see it in his eyes.'

'They're blue,' Lady Angeline replied and could have kicked herself as soon as the words popped out of her mouth, angry that she had even noticed.

'Mind you,' Nan continued, 'that friend of his is a strange fish. The only things not dark about him are the clothes he wears. I suppose that's what comes with being foreign.'

'Nan, really!'

'But as far as his lordship is concerned, I have to say, we're all very pleased with him.'

Angeline turned on her, fury dancing in her eyes. 'How can you say such a thing about the man who has ruined our lives?'

Nan moved away from the window and carried on making the bed. 'I speak the truth. All the servants say he's a true gentleman, very chivalrous in his dealings with them. They're all greatly relieved, I can tell yer. Things could have been a lot worse.' She picked up a shoe, stopping to look over at Lady Angeline. 'And I think yer like him a little.'

'I loathe him!' Angeline spat. 'I loathe everything he stands for.'

'So why are yer still here then?' Nan threw back. 'We all told yer to leave the castle before he arrived. It would have been easier for everyone. Yer should have gone to live on your mother's land. Whatever possessed yer to stay?'

Lady Angeline turned her back on Nan to look over the courtyard again because she could not answer. She should leave, she knew that, but the truth was, she was finding it harder than she cared to admit to tear herself away from her family home. This land and the people who toiled it meant everything to her. All that she knew of the world was rooted in Goldsborough dirt, but the sins of the father had expelled her from Eden. Once she left this place, she knew that something vital would have slipped away. The natural order of things and the security that this brought would be replaced by turmoil and heartbreak, she felt it in her bones. She already sensed that Lord Lyndhurst would turn her world upside down. From the moment she stood face to face with him on that very first evening and observed his finely developed patrician air, she could tell that this was a man who took responsibility effortlessly and who was used to getting his own way. A man born to command. Perhaps such a man could triumph over those lurking in the darkness. Like the man lurking in the library at that very moment, waiting to pounce.

CHAPTER 7

'I'm Viscount Elewald, your neighbour.'

William's hackles rose immediately, but he crossed the library to shake the man's hand. He had expected it to be limp and damp; instead it was a bone-crusher of a shake, a ludicrous attempt to assert authority.

Although they had never met, William knew the Elewald family by reputation. After all, there were only three hundred peers in all England and the seats of Lyndhurst and Elewald were amongst the oldest. Unfortunately, the Elewalds' reputation was tarnished. Historically, they were known as being troublesome meddlers, with a streak of cruelty, men who would switch allegiance at the drop of a hat if it advanced their cause.

'Luck of the devil, Lyndhurst, acquiring this pile,' Elewald barked. 'A real honey fall, certainly saved your bacon.' William realised with some discomfort that Elewald was equally familiar with his own family's reputation and circumstances.

'Yes, it was surprising,' he answered politely as he watched Elewald draw the silver handle of his whip across some books on a shelf.

'All on the turn of a card, eh, the night your brother died? More than surprising, astounding, I would say.'

William did not take kindly to the insinuation in Elewald's voice but decided to let it go.

'How can I help you, Elewald?' William asked. He turned his back on him and walked over to the bureau to study the local maps that he had left there.

'Ah well, you see, I've come to help you. I've a little proposition for you.'

'Really – and what might that be?'

Elewald stood tall and pulled the bottom of his waistcoat down with a quick jerk, as if preparing himself for a very important speech. 'Well, must be hell of an inconvenience discovering that old Goldsborough had a daughter, so I'm prepared to take her off your hands. My wife died some years ago. I need another as I have no heir. What d'ya say if I take her as my bride?'

William turned and stared at Elewald in utter disbelief. He had to be fifty if he was a day and there was something very odd about his appearance which William could not put his finger on, when suddenly it came to him. Elewald was grey. His hair was grey. It matched his complexion, which was like dried-out parchment and he had bulging, water-coloured eyes that made him look like a fish on dry land. He looked fit enough, but his teeth were stained and his breath was rancid.

'You can't be serious, Elewald,' William replied.

The viscount puffed out his chest.

'Deadly serious; I don't mind admitting that the filly has rather caught my eye. In fact, I'll pay you a pretty penny for her.' Elewald made no attempt to disguise the lust in his eyes. 'Name your price, Lyndhurst.'

An image of this man forcing himself on Lady Angeline flashed through William's mind and his stomach churned, acid racing up to hit the back of his throat.

'Out of the question, I have officially made Lady Angeline my ward. She will be coming to London with me for the Season. I have already made the arrangements,' he lied.

Elewald blustered at the rebuff. 'How much do you want, Lyndhurst? I know you need the money.'

Propriety demanded that emotion be kept tightly controlled in public, but William could feel his blood rising.

'She is not for sale,' he spat.

Elewald cracked his whip on the floor in frustration. The sound rang out, bouncing off the walls. William noticed that it was one of those vicious ones with sharp barbs on the end, intended to inflict maximum pain.

'Oh, I see how it is – you want the virgin beauty for yourself,' Elewald sneered.

Clenching his fists tightly, William could feel his nails cutting into his skin. Keeping his voice dangerously quiet, William said, 'I think you should leave now.'

'All right, Lyndhurst, I'll do you a deal,' Elewald ran his tongue over his grey-green teeth. 'You can have her first, then you can pass her on to me when you're done. I don't mind soiled goods.'

Silent fury filled the room.

'Get out, Elewald, before I call you out.'

Elewald hesitated for a moment, wondering if he should rise to the challenge, but thought better of it. 'You'll regret this, Lyndhurst,' he blurted as he backed out of the room. 'The women from that clan are pure trouble, born and bred for scandal. She's headstrong, that girl, just like her mother.' Elewald slammed his whip across a bookcase. 'She'll need firm handling, if you get my meaning.' He cracked the whip again, as if to leave his meaning in no doubt.

As soon as she saw Viscount Elewald scuttle away from the castle, Lady Angeline left her bedroom and went in search of

Lord Lyndhurst. She needed to know what had just happened between them. She was sure her future depended on it. Elewald was a cad, just like the Earl of Lyndhurst, who had stolen everything from her. She did not feel safe with either of them, so she had to tread very carefully and be prepared to flee, if need be, to her mother's land beyond the boundary.

She found Lyndhurst in the library, bent over the bureau, holding onto it for dear life. He glared at her as she tiptoed into the room. Fear gripped her. She could not imagine what had happened to make him look like that: as if he could kill someone.

'Viscount Elewald came to ask for your hand in marriage,' he said through gritted teeth. Her hand instinctively rose up to protect her neck and he saw the colour drain from her face. 'I took the liberty of judging your reaction, so I sent him away with a flea in his ear.'

'Thank you.' He heard palpable relief in her voice. 'I'm not exactly surprised, though,' she whispered. 'It was only a matter of time before he came calling. It's not me he is interested in.'

William gave her a peculiar look. Reading its meaning, she blushed. 'Not really,' she stammered. 'It's my land he's after.'

'Your land? What land? I'm afraid I now own your land, and I certainly have no intention of marrying Elewald.' He was pleased to see her smile at the quip.

Lady Angeline took a deep breath and moved further into the room, trying to decide how much to reveal.

'My mother's family, the Bernicians, hold a small piece of land at the source of the Rivendor, the river that divides the Elewald and Goldsborough estates. We've owned it for possibly a thousand years. It passes down the female line. That is allowed in Anglo-Saxon tradition.' She said the last sentence forcefully, anticipating his reaction. 'But the Elewalds and the Goldsboroughs have fought us for it for generations.'

'I see,' William said. 'The land must be important due to its location.' He made the connection between Lady Angeline's land and the house in the woods. 'He who owns the source of the river, holds the power.'

'Exactly,' Lady Angeline replied, pleased that William was no dullard. 'My family have always managed to hold onto the land.' She faltered for a few seconds but finally said, 'By various means, but mainly with the help of the local community.'

William laughed out loud. By scaring people out of their wits, he said to himself, as the image of the amulets hanging from the trees jumped into his mind. Her raised eyebrows told William that his reaction had shocked her. 'I suppose the locals knew that it could be disastrous if either the Goldsboroughs or Elewalds got hold of the source and then decide to cut the water off or divert it,' he said.

She answered on a long breath. 'Yes, the two families were always trying to wrest land away from each other. If one side controlled the source, they could have destroyed the other, but it would have been the people who suffered most.'

William thought for a moment. 'But once your mother married the marquis, all her possessions would pass to him. That is the law.'

'Indeed it is. My mother was the first of her clan to marry. It was tradition for the women in my family to choose their mate, a mate for life. They would have children, but never marry, in order to keep control of the land. Then it would be entailed to the eldest daughter. It was best for everybody who lived hereabouts and needed the river for their survival.'

As the story unfolded Lady Angeline realised that she was wringing her hands. It was a difficult tale to tell an outsider, especially a lord of the realm, because it was so unusual, even strange. Yet something compelled her to tell him, gratitude perhaps. She prayed she was not making a schoolgirl error. 'My mother,' she swallowed hard, 'my mother married on the condition that my father grant back the land to her and that in turn she be allowed to bequeath it to her daughter. He readily agreed. It was a love match, you see.'

'Oh, I do see. Being a marquis, he had to marry and bear legitimate children.'

Lady Angeline nodded. 'My mother refused to be his mistress. She did not need to marry, but she did need to be the only one.'

'So, who are your mother's people? William asked. 'I have never heard of the Bernicians.'

Lady Angeline's heart sank as she lowered her gaze to the floor. This was the question she had been dreading. William read the signs.

'Your mother's people were not gentry then?'

A flush rushed up her neck to her cheeks, and she slowly shook her head. She knew the aristocracy could be ruthless in excluding from its ranks those considered to be of inferior birth. It could take generations before the descendants of a commoner became an accepted member of their number.

'Ah, of course.' William's face lit up as comprehension dawned. 'That is why your father had not been seen in society for years and why you have never made your debut.' And why so very little was known about the marquis, William realised, when he had made enquiries about him after his suicide. He had married far below his station, which, twenty years ago, would have meant immediate ostracism from society.

Lady Angeline continued to stare at the floor while William looked out of the window. He was profoundly shocked by what he had just heard, though he desperately tried not to show it. Good God, Lady Angeline was descended from bastards. She was the first legitimate offspring and there was only one generation of aristocratic blood. Not only that, but from everything he had seen at the cottage, she appeared to come from a long line of pagans.

Something deep inside William counselled him not to reveal his hand to her yet. Not to tell her where he had been and what he had seen there. He was sure she had not told him the full story, but she would do eventually, he would make sure of that.

Finally, Angeline heard his steps move around the bureau, then she saw the tip of his boots. She felt his finger fit under her chin and draw her face up so that her eyes met the peacock blue of his own. She felt her stomach leap, something akin to a somersault.

'Things are not how they used to be,' she heard William say kindly. 'I have made my decision. I am making you my ward. You will come with me to London where you will have a season. Under my protection you will make a suitable match.'

These days money could buy almost anything and he now had Goldsborough wealth. With the right dowry, and with her beauty, her lack of breeding would be overlooked.

The feeling in Angeline's stomach turned to fear. Horrified, she pulled away.

'No, no that will never do!' she said. 'I do not need your protection. I plan to leave the estate and go to live on my own land. There is a house there and I have a stipend, a legacy from my mother. I can support myself and a small staff.'

'Don't be ridiculous, Lady Angeline! A chit of a girl could never manage alone.'

'I am twenty, sir, not such a chit, and the chits in my family have always managed alone.' Angeline's voice rose. 'My mother prepared me well. I will not go to London with you, sir. I don't want to make a suitable match, thank you very much. As I told you, the women in my family have always chosen their own mate.'

'Chosen their own mate?' William repeated, placing his hands on his hips and pushing his face nearer to hers. 'What century do you think you are living in? We are not living in a gothic novel, my lady. You can't frighten off the likes of Elewald with a bag of moonshine like sorcery and witchcraft, which is what I suspect has been going on here for the past few hundred years. Nonsense, created by your family and maintained with the help of the locals, to keep the source of the river in the right hands.'

Angeline's mouth dropped open. She could not believe that he had worked it out.

He read her expression and hoped that he had not revealed too much of what he knew. 'Did you really think that I would be fooled by that little charade the other night, from 'Nan, the soothsayer?' Popping out from under the stairs. All that nonsense about something chasing us in the dark. She may have fooled Nikolaus, but not me, I'm afraid. What did you think I was going to do? Hightail it back to the south as fast as I could, find a local agent to run the estate, and never step foot on it again, as long as I was receiving a regular income?'

Angeline felt the floor fall away from beneath her feet. He had seen right through her and right through hundreds of years. He seemed to understand everything in an instant. She was speechless.

'Life is not how it used to be, my lady,' he said sharply, 'not even up here. Your tricks will no longer prevail. We live in tumultuous times. The old order is under threat. There is radicalism and sedition in the air. Heavens above, people are rioting in the streets of London.'

'That will never happen here,' she said.

'You have no idea, my lady, how fast things travel these days. It's like lighting a touchpaper. No, whether you like it or not, you do need my protection.'

'I do not!' Lady Angeline stamped her foot as she spoke. She knew it made her look like a child having a tantrum, but she did not care. He had made her furious.

'Yes, you do,' he replied. He knew she was trying to goad him, and she was succeeding.

Lady Angeline opened her mouth to say something more.

'Enough.' William raised his hand in the air to signal that she had pushed him as far as he was prepared to go. 'I have made up my mind.' He was livid with her. 'How ungrateful can you be? I have just saved you from a fate worse than death with Viscount Elewald and you are refusing my protection. How dare you? I am the Earl of Lyndhurst. Most sane people would not believe their good fortune!'

She was being outmanoeuvred. She scowled at Lord Lyndhurst, who seemed to take some satisfaction from her reaction. He was highhanded and pompous but she reluctantly admired his intelligence and his sense of duty. He had surprised her. She had begun to believe that her land, her people, would fare well under his protection. But would she?

CHAPTER 8

Strategy was everything with this particular female, William decided, so he needed a diversion while he reined in his temper. He could not believe he had allowed her to get under his skin. She had made him raise his voice and he never did that. He walked to the back of the library and picked up one of the books that had been lying on an occasional table ever since he arrived.

'I am assuming these are the books you are reading at the moment,' he said. Lady Angeline nodded. 'It's a very eclectic choice, my lady.'

'I like to read widely,' she said, unwilling to give ground.

He read out the title of the one he was holding. *'A Vindication of the Rights of Women.'*

'Any female alone sympathises with Mary Wollstonecraft's views on female education and rights,' she stated firmly.

'I agree with her notion that women should not be measured by men's standards and that we should honour women's natural talents,' William said.

'You have read it?' She could not disguise the surprise in her voice.

'Yes indeed, I found it most interesting. In fact, I agree with almost everything Miss Wollstonecraft has to say.'

'You do?' Her surprise turned into incredulity.

'My lady, in many respects you will find me a thoroughly enlightened man.'

'I will?'

'Indeed. I, too, read widely.'

'Really?'

William straightened the pile of books 'Yes, in fact I was planning to become an academic, but decided in the end to go into the army.' He did not bother to explain that it had been a request from Wellington himself.

He picked up the next book. *Lovers' Vows*, a play by Elizabeth Inchbald. 'Doesn't she write about high-spirited heroines, struggling against society's restraints?' William asked.

'Perhaps.' Lady Angeline pouted, in response to the sarcasm in his voice.

'*The Mysteries of Udolpho*, by Mrs Radcliffe. Now, why am I not surprised to see this here?' He raised an eyebrow, daring her to comment.

She refused, but looked down her nose at him with as much haughtiness as she could muster.

'And, lastly, Byron, such romantic nonsense. In London, I've seen women literally throw themselves at him. I told him the last time we met...'

'You know Lord Byron?' Lady Angeline ran towards him, animated with anticipation.

Ah, got you! he thought, feeling rather pleased with himself. 'Yes,' he said carelessly, 'we're members of the same club. Although he has been travelling on the Continent for some time.' He did not feel the need to tell her that Lord Byron's rakish lifestyle meant that society had turned against him years ago, prompting the poet to leave England, probably never to return. 'Perhaps you will meet him at one of the balls,' William told her, feeling a little guilty at the white lie, but needing to press home his advantage as he sensed his goal was in sight.

Lady Angeline gasped, wide-eyed and artless, and he melted slightly. In that moment her guard was down and he saw the innocent young girl who lay so close to the surface.

'You will enjoy London, you know. Every girl should have at least one season. It's your birthright.' He watched her wrestle with her thoughts for a few moments before she replied.

'Very well.' She fixed him with a steady stare. 'But you must promise not to try to organise a match for me.' William sighed with relief, surprised that her acquiescence had meant so much to him.

'Be assured, Lady Angeline, you will be allowed to choose your own mate, as all the females in your family have done for generations,' he replied, smiling warmly, 'as long as he is acceptable, of course. And willing. No dragging the gentleman of your choice from the ballroom by his hair.' Once again, it pleased him to see her laugh at his joke. Finally, they had come to an agreement.

William took the opportunity that this truce facilitated to ask Lady Angeline to give him a tour of the castle and tell him about the family history. They spent the next few hours walking and chatting amiably. He heard how the Norman Baron, Richard De Goldsbourg, had been given the land by William the Conqueror and it was he who had built the original castle. The focal point of the sprawling buildings was now the Tudor Great Hall where they stood, which featured a spectacularly high arch-braced timber roof. Lady Angeline showed him the original refectory table made of solid oak, the top of which could be reversed to provide a clean surface in the morning, after it had been danced on all night. She explained that this was where the expression 'turning the tables' came from. Although impressed by everything Lady Angeline had shown him, William could see that the place was in dire need of renovation and remodelling. It was cold, draughty and bits of it were falling down, not to mention the lack of modern amenities, like a bathroom and a water closet.

William had spent hours studying the accounts. The estate had been extremely well managed by the late marquis and as a result was very wealthy. However, he had not moved with the times, his practices were old fashioned and the castle itself had been sorely neglected. William was under no illusion. He would have to manage the income from this estate very carefully. He had two large properties to renovate, Goldsborough Castle and Lyndhurst Manor, which was also in a state of disrepair due to the profligate behaviour of his family.

He was starting to formulate a plan when he was distracted from his thoughts by Lady Angeline who was keen to show him a great secret, so they walked to the end of the Tudor Hall and stood in front of a dark oak dresser. She asked two servants to move it, which they managed with a huge amount of effort. A secret door was revealed, which led to a hidden chapel that had been built during the reign of Elizabeth I. During this period the Goldsboroughs had been a Catholic family.

They lit candles as they moved reverently through the room. It was long and narrow and could only take four people wide, but perhaps twenty deep, if they were standing. At the far end, the flickering candles warmly lit a pretty little makeshift altar with hand-painted scenes of the baby Jesus and Mother Mary. At the back of the room stood the confessional. Lady Angeline gently sat inside, where the priest would normally be. Something drew William to sit on the other side of the lattice frame that divided them. They sat together, very quietly. He could see the outline of her body, silently moving in and out to the rhythm of her breath.

William still had the thought of Lyndhurst fresh in his mind, which finally prompted him to ask her a question.

'Lady Angeline, how much do you know about the circumstances surrounding your father's death?' You could have heard a feather fall in the silence that separated them at that moment.

'As much as I need,' she eventually answered.

'Tell me what you know. It's important to me.'

'Why?'

He could not answer. He did not know why, it just was.

'For your salvation perhaps?' she quizzed.

'Yes, perhaps.'

She thought long and hard. She did not want to reveal any more to him and yet she felt an obligation to do so. Ever since he had rescued her from the clutches of Viscount Elewald, she felt somehow beholden to him. 'My father left me a note.' More silence filled the air.

'What did it say?'

'Only that he was truly sorry; that he loved me and he hoped I could forgive him, but to salvage what was left of his reputation, he had no choice but to take his own life.'

'Have you forgiven him?'

The truth was she had not, but she knew that it was the Christian thing to do, so she must try.

'Barely. Not because he lost the estate, but because he abandoned me.' After a few more moments of reflection she said, 'There was something else. He wrote that he was afraid for me. That the earl who had won the estate had a terrible reputation as a rake and a blackguard. He begged me that if I should ever find myself in danger, I must throw myself on the mercy of his brother – Lord Fitzalan. Although my father had never met him, by all accounts, he was very different from the earl and had a reputation for being a thoroughly honourable gentleman.' She heard him inhale deeply. 'So you can imagine we were all expecting the worse. Everyone on the estate is relieved beyond words that you seem to be nothing like your reputation.'

William felt as if he had swallowed a very large stone, which had just reached the pit of his stomach. She had never known the earl's Christian name before William arrived at the castle. Clearly, she thought he was George. 'Lady Angeline, I have a confession to make.'

'Sir?'

'I am not the man you think I am.'

'You're not the Earl of Lyndhurst?' she whispered through the latticework.

'Yes, yes, I am now, but I am William Fitzalan, the brother your father referred to in his letter. George, the man who won the estate from him, died in tragic circumstances on that very night. I knew nothing about the card game until days later, when I discovered that, as the new Earl of Lyndhurst, I had inherited extensive lands in Northumberland.'

The next few moments were vast and empty.

'I'm glad,' Lady Angeline finally said.

'You are?'

'Yes, I'm truly glad that you are here and not your brother. I confess, I loathe him for what he did to my father.'

'I understand,' William replied. He hated to think ill of the dead, but the consequences for Lady Angeline and the entire estate, if his brother had lived, were not worth thinking about. George would probably have agreed to Eleward's proposition. Once again, he was surprised by his reactions to her. For some reason, he wanted her to approve of him very much indeed. 'I give you my word, my lady, I will never abandon you, and your father was right about me. You will always be safe under my protection.'

They walked out of the little chapel together, and something new, almost undetectable, had passed between them.

Strolling past the buttery and Jack, the servant boy, who was busy there, they walked along the passage, only to hear two very familiar voices arguing with each other. Following the sound of the commotion that was coming from an antechamber at the end of the cellar, they walked past numerous barrels of brandy. William registered that he had yet to study the cellar inventory. Entering the chamber, he was dazzled by the sight before him. Everywhere he looked there were bottles, hundreds of them: green, blue, brown – all different shapes and sizes lining the walls. Strange plants were placed around the room, some under glass. Dried herbs and flowers hung from racks suspended from the ceiling, which was painted cobalt blue and dotted with gold stars. He inhaled their rich, earthy scent. It looked like a wizard's apothecary William thought. His eyes moved down the long refectory table, just like the one he had seen in the great hall. At the end stood the infamous Nan, busy with pestle and mortar, while Nikolaus loomed over her, bombarding her with questions.

'What is going on here?' William demanded.

'You may well ask,' Nikolaus replied. 'We ran out of brandy upstairs, so I took the opportunity to review the cellar, which is superb by the way, only to find the old woman here, making up some foul-smelling elixir, but she won't tell me what it is. For all I know, she is planning to poison us with it.'

'Oh don't be ridiculous!' William shot back, but he turned to Lady Angeline searching for an explanation.

The two women shared a glance and said nothing.

Very slowly, William walked around the room, smelling various bottles – they all smelt vile. He pointed to one of the plants under glass.

'Mandrake,' Lady Angeline said.

'Also known as Satan's Apple,' Nan barked. 'It wards off demonic possession.'

Lady Angeline threw her a stony stare. 'The leaves are boiled in milk and used as a poultice. The roots are purgative,' she explained.

William pointed to another.

'Monkshood,' stated Nikolaus, 'also known as Wolfsbane. Some people believe it can transform a human into a wolf.'

Both women were clearly impressed by Nikolaus' knowledge.

'But in reality, it is used to break fevers and helps with chronic pain,' Lady Angeline replied serenely.

William stood in front of another plant and waited.

'Belladonna,' continued Lady Angeline, 'used for disorders of the internal organs.'

'Bowels!' screamed Nan before howling with laughter.

Lady Angeline flinched. 'Nan, stop that!' she demanded. 'It also helps with childbirth.'

'And this one is hemlock,' William said with certainty.

'For swellings and skin disorders,' Lady Angeline explained.

'They are all poisons!' Nikolaus shouted.

'Yes, but they are also medicines if handled correctly,' Lady Angeline retorted.

'I'm telling you William, this one is a witch,' Nikolaus pointed accusingly at Nan.

Nikolaus' penchant for melodrama was starting to irritate William.

'You know I caught her in the kitchen giving the servant boy a potion and swearing him to secrecy.'

'It was medicine, I told yer, for the boy's mother. If yer don't believe me then ask him yerself. Jack! Jack!' she shouted. The boy came running in. 'Jack, what was it I gave yer in the kitchen the other day?' The boy's eyes darted nervously between the faces staring at him. 'It's all right, Jack. Tell the truth.'

'It's medicine for me mam,' he said. 'She's sick, see. She's been sick for ages.'

Nikolaus leapt forward and bent down very close to the boy. 'So why did Nan here tell you to keep it a secret?'

'Because, because.' Jack's eyes started to well up with water.

'It's all right, Jack, love.' Nan coaxed him on.

'Because me mam don't believe in medicine, she only believes in God.' He choked as the tears fell. 'She'd be mad if she knew, but she's been sick for so long and getting worse. Please, please don't tell her what I've done."

'Is that the truth, boy?' Nikolaus barked.

'I swear it, on the bible, sir,' Jack answered.

Nikolaus slowly stood upright, patting the boy awkwardly on the shoulder, 'Thank you, Jack. Thank you for telling the truth,' he said softly. 'I promise we will all keep your secret.' He tossed the boy a shilling to ease his conscience, then looked back at Nan. 'There are still strange forces at work here. I can feel it.'

William realised he had made the right decision not to tell Nikolaus about what he had discovered in the woods. Nikolaus' belief in the supernatural and the dark arts would have condemned Lady Angeline, too. William did not believe in anything that could not be explained by rational thought or natural law, so there was no such thing as witchcraft as far as he was concerned, just superstition, but Lady Angeline was keeping secrets, all his instincts told him so, and he intended to find out what they were.

William walked over to Nikolaus and placed a hand on his shoulder.

'My friend, there are no witches here. This is the nineteenth century. You have such a vivid imagination. Almost as vivid as the clothes you wear.' This comment on his appearance made Nikolaus laugh out loud and the tension was broken. 'Personally,' William continued as he looked around the room, 'I prefer a glass or two of brandy for my ailments.'

'Ha! Indeed!' Nikolaus boomed, slapping his old friend affectionately on the back.

Seizing the moment, Lady Angeline suggested the three of them return upstairs and she would arrange for brandy to be brought up immediately. As she manoeuvred the two gentlemen out of the room, she gave Nan a knowing look, who in return, gave an almost imperceptible nod. They must both leave the castle undetected tonight. For this night was Imbolc.

PART 2

IMBOLC

CHAPTER 9

The night was dense with the familiar. A soft, fat moon belied the cold, but the bonfire kept the winter chill away.

Flickering tallow candles, staked into the ground, stood to attention, proudly encircling the source of the Rivendor and the flames of the beacon. Snowdrops, bathing in the light, appeared to tinkle like tiny bells in the breeze.

Imbolc was one of the more serene seasonal ceremonies. Only the Lady of the Source and the Guardian were needed to perform the ritual this night, marking the beginning of Spring. Some of the others, like Beltane, were much more raucous affairs. Angeline had always suspected there was a very practical reason why this ceremony was so sedate. It was far too cold for people to venture out at this time of the year.

Angeline prepared herself. She stood quietly, with eyes closed, going through the service in her mind. The words must be recounted perfectly. Only when something was said in the right way would it come true. People believed this wholeheartedly. Nan certainly did. Angeline was not so sure; even so, she did not want to make a mistake.

She stepped forward, standing almost on top of the bubbling water of the source, next to the statue of Bacchus, and presented the golden chalice to the heavens. The wood from the pyre cracked and spat in anticipation, as misty smoke rose into the air. The land was alive and full of knowledge.

'To the Goddess of the source
I give thanks.
Gentle Mother, I light this fire as the flame of purification to
Banish winter for another year.'

In that instant, the pungent aroma of the crackling wood filled Angeline's nostrils. The fire had been made from nine sacred woods: birch, ash, alder, oak, hazel, hawthorn, rowan, holly, and willow. The smell was intoxicating. She heard the clanging of a bell and turned to watch Nan, through the flame light, bringing an impressive pregnant white ewe with a swollen udder into the ring.

Taking the chalice from Angeline's hand, Nan placed it under the ewe, then massaged the velvety teats, squirting the warm liquid into the bejewelled goblet. The white food gushed forth from the bursting teat and quickly the cup was overflowing.

The Guardian handed the goblet back to The Lady, milk dripping down her arm as she did so.

'Tender Goddess, Coventina, provider of plenty,
Whose protection is great,
I call upon you, my lady,
The weaver of fates and
The bringer of dreams to
Grant a full belly in the season to come.'

Slowly, Angeline raised her other hand and the tip of the dagger glinted in the firelight as she turned it downwards and thrust it into the goblet: the receptacle of feminine energy.

'As the light lengthens, so the cold strengthens.
Be nourished, strengthened and sustained.'

Then she tipped the cup and allowed the white fluid to flow
freely to the ground, which seemed to drink it thirstily.

'Welcome the growing of the light,
Welcome the new cycle of life,
Coventina, tender Goddess,
Nourish, strengthen and sustain
Until we meet again at Ostara,
Blessed Be.'

CHAPTER 10

'Women of such beauty provoke feelings of great responsibility in men like you, William,' Nikolaus teased as they mounted their horses. 'So you have made her your ward now. Have you the faintest idea how to organise a young lady's first season?'

'Of course not,' replied William curtly, 'but Aunt Vivian will be beside herself at the thought of it. I have written to her today with the news.'

'Oh my goodness, once she informs my Aunt Maria, and she will, there will be a frenzy of social activity. I shudder at the thought of what you have unleashed.' Nikolaus quivered, and Zoltan, his horse, pranced wildly on the spot in response.

It had taken them two full weeks to transverse the entire estate, mostly through remorseless rain and savage winds, but today the weak sun rose on a clear, almost warm day and William began to appreciate just how splendid his new land really was, particularly in the early morn.

He discovered from Mr Sweyne that the castle had been built originally to guard the crossing over the Rivendor against Scottish invasion, but that it had been founded on the site of a much earlier Viking fort, which had guarded against a very different kind of invasion. Sweyne had told him that the Vikings believed the bridge across the river connected the land of elves to the world of man. More superstitious nonsense, William thought.

The borders of the estate were marked by a deep ravine to the south, and the river to the north, which could be easily followed as it meandered down towards the sea and Blackrock Bay. The bay belonged to the Goldsboroughs, but the land beyond was Elewald land.

'The sun rarely shines up here in the north country,' William said as they neared the bay, 'but when it does, this land is glorious to behold.'

'Grudgingly, I agree with you,' replied Nikolaus.

'I don't suppose you heard the sound of horses' hooves leaving the castle late last night, did you?' William asked as nonchalantly as possible as he checked his horse's girth. 'Or was I dreaming?'

Nikolaus could not disguise the roguish twinkle in his eye. 'I'm afraid not. Surprisingly, I heard nothing last night. Now, if I were a Viking I would say it was probably the elves.' He laughed out loud. 'Even I find such stories hard to believe.'

William raised his eyes up to the sky in response, relieved that his friend's humour had improved. The Northumbrian air was doing him good.

The two men rode up onto a cliff in order to take in the view. This was nature at its most bewitching. A vast expanse of sand swept around the bay, which was surrounded by craggy outcrops, known as the Needlepoints, looming from the sea. The red and gold rays from the dawn sun bounced off the black, wet stone and skirted across the shimmering ocean, to produce a kaleidoscope of coloured lights resembling tiny enchanted nymphs dancing on the water. William instinctively understood why the ancients had worshipped Mother Nature.

She was so beautiful, she could reduce a grown man to tears of wonderment. He could hear the echo of the sea crashing into the caves along the seashore, a deafening noise that sounded like it came from the very centre of the earth.

Who has the power? he could almost hear the sea ask. The ancients had understood that when Mother Nature reared against them, even the mightiest overlord would fall.

William looked behind him and saw to his right, high on a cliff, the ruins of an old abbey hanging precariously over the caves from the precipice above. It could have taken fifty years to build, but as time eroded the soil, it would eventually crash into the sea and simply be washed away in a fraction of the time.

He looked back out onto the horizon and imagined Viking longboats, sailing in from the top of the world, manoeuvring deftly between the Needlepoints. Marauding warriors landing on the beach, sacking the abbey, as they moved inland, ferociously claiming new territory. William allowed his imagination to wander until he heard Nikolaus' voice over the breaking waves.

'Do my eyes deceive me?'

William came to and recognised the horse instantly because it came from his estate stable. It was a stallion, named Cherub: Northumbrian humour William assumed, because it looked like the devil himself. Jet black and beautiful, a mane like the finest silk, it had a manic look in its eyes. He had been told very clearly that the horse belonged to Lady Angeline. Then he saw her atop, galloping across the sands, her cloak swirling around like a giant moth, with Odin faithfully following. William could see that shockingly she was in a state of undress underneath, wearing only a white chemise-like flowing gown. She was barefoot, her ivory skin contrasting starkly with the rich, ox-blood brown of the leather sidesaddle.

Her long blonde hair tantalised the wind as it ran free behind her.

'Magnificent!' cried Nikolaus in ecstatic appreciation. William turned sharply and glared at him with challenge in his eyes. Nikolaus responded by laughing raucously. 'Oh, come now, William, even I would not stoop so low as to seduce an innocent, especially if she is the ward of my very best friend.'

William harrumphed loudly, but had shocked himself at the strength of his reaction. He looked back.

'Where on earth has she gone?' In the time it had taken to respond to Nikolaus, she had disappeared from view. His eyes scanned the length of the pale gold sand, the cliffs, the rocks, but she was nowhere to be seen.

The two men adroitly manoeuvred their horses down to the beach, trying to follow her trail, but the sea was washing away her tracks faster than they could ride. There were no paths, no exits on the northern side of the bay: she had simply disappeared. And that was not possible.

William tried to think clearly. Had she doubled back? Perhaps they had missed her? No, that could not be, but there had to be a logical explanation. He was racking his brain, trying to solve the puzzle, when he heard the distant ringing of a bell. Nikolaus looked around nervously. The bell seemed to be calling for the clouds to draw in and they were obeying rapidly. Something was stirring around them.

'It's coming from the Abbey,' Nikolaus shouted.

'The tide's coming in and there's a storm brewing,' William replied. 'Angeline will be cut off if we don't find her.' He looked around again. 'Why is that damned bell ringing?' he roared.

'I don't know,' Nikolaus bellowed over the rumblings of the sky, 'but I will find out.' He half turned his horse and then called back, 'William, you cannot stay here. You will be cut off yourself. You must trust Lady Angeline. She knows these shores better than you. She will be safe.'

A strong blast of wind broadsided them both and William hesitated for a moment. 'I will take one last look up at the headland. You go to the Abbey, I will follow.'

Nikolaus threw him a doubtful look, but reluctantly agreed. He turned his horse on a sixpence and rode straight up the side of the cliff. He had no need of the paths. William watched Nikolaus pick his way through the rocky cliff face as it crumbled dangerously beneath the hooves of his horse, which seemed to dance to his master's commands. The Hungarian Hussars were light cavalrymen, trained for scouting and skirmishing. They had a reputation for being notoriously impetuous and flamboyant, but also skilled, daring and brave. William knew Nikolaus to be all of these things.

The waves roared in his head as William galloped to the end of the beach. Discovering he was blocked by high, heavy rocks looming over him, he braced himself. There was no way out.

The sea lapped around his horse's hooves. The animal could sense danger and reared up, trying to break free from the spume that stuck to its legs, then William registered that the bell had suddenly stopped ringing. The sea spray flew into his face and the horse reared again as the waves came crashing in. It was becoming perilous. William had been beaten by the elements, so unwillingly withdrew.

Working his way back and finding the Abbey path, he ascended at full speed. Minutes later, William was navigating his horse around the ruins. The old Abbey walls gave some shelter from the impending storm. He could hear the bell vibrating in the whipped-up wind. William found Zoltan grazing peacefully on the grass growing through the crumbling foundations. He hitched his own horse to a small disfigured rowan tree and went in search of his friend.

He found Nikolaus crouching over something. This did not bode well. He had seen him in such a position too many times before, during the Peninsular Wars, when the thing he was bending over was usually the body of a dead enemy.

William caught sight of a twisted black boot and a blood-ied, stretched-out hand, with fingers fixed like a claw. The other hand was still hanging onto the bell rope. Unbidden thoughts shimmered across his mind. Angeline had been galloping away from this direction, as if the devil himself was chasing her.

'No it can't be!' William gasped when he saw the face.

'What sort of monster did this?' Nikolaus asked as William dropped down beside him.

'There are no monsters, Nikolaus,' he eventually replied, 'but some kind of beast has ripped the throat out. No human could have done this.' William stood up and looked around, searching for clues, but the long grass camouflaged any foot-prints. 'Could a dog or even a wolf have done this?' he asked.

'Possibly, but I should be able to smell it and I can't. All I can smell is something odious.'

William touched some broken blades of grass. 'Could that nose of yours be wrong?'

'It never has been before.'

The blood, thick and purple, was still bubbling and gurgling out of the hole where the voice box had been. The eyes were wide open and the imprint of the final horror they had witnessed could still be seen in them. William studied the body, soaked with the vital fluid. There was no gore; no torn clothing. Whatever it was had gone straight for the throat.

'Look at the size of the bite,' said Nikolaus. 'If it was a hound, it would have to be huge.'

'Odin?' William asked.

Nikolaus shook his head. 'I don't think even that dog is big enough. Wait, what's this?' He pointed to some blue marks on the clothing. William recognised the vivid colour. It was exactly the same blue as the painting on the wall in Angeline's house in the woods. He remembered that the mural was flaking and in need of repair.

'It looks like paint,' he answered.

Nikolaus screwed up his face. 'What is that vile smell?'

'Describe it to me,' William demanded.

'I can't,' said Nikolaus. 'It's like raw sewage. It's foul and I've never smelt anything like it.'

William rubbed his hand over his mouth. He could not begin to explain what had gone on here. All he could think of was Lady Angeline. What did she have to do with this?

'Nan!' The scream bounced off the walls of the courtyard when the two men rode through the gateway. Nikolaus had carried the body all the way back. He had covered the face with his jacket, but the body of Nan was instantly recognisable by her eccentric clothing.

The wind wailed around the walls in a prolonged mournful cry. A circling, violent rush knocked a milk pail off a tall wooden bench. As it clattered to the ground, the bluish-white liquid immediately sought refuge by secreting itself between the cobblestones. Another gush of wind caught beneath the jacket so that it peeled off as Nan was being lowered from the horse, revealing the appalling wound.

The men from the stables crossed themselves when they saw it and even Eric Sweyne flinched. Their unintelligible murmurings told William that the men feared something more than the dead.

'Nan!' cried Lady Angeline again, as she rushed towards the body.

The wind continued to whip around them like a dust devil, and grit lodged in William's eyes so he could hardly see.

The men kept muttering the same unfamiliar word which he tried to commit to memory before the sound of the impending storm drowned them out. Half blind, William reached for the sobbing Lady Angeline who was hanging onto Nan as if her life depended on it. Fighting against the tempest, he wrenched Angeline from the body of her loyal servant. Enveloping her in his arms, he pulled her to the safety of the castle.

'Mr Sweyne, take care of the body!' He screamed the order over the howling wind and thunder, just as Odin started to bark ominously, like a hound from hell.

'Nikolaus, deal with that damned dog.'

CHAPTER 11

He smelt male: spicy and musky. His scent was intoxicating and it made her heady. Tenderly he touched his mouth to her temple and immediately she felt her muscles relax slightly. She was shaking violently, but he held her so snugly and with such benign strength that it steadied her.

She felt him pull away and instinctively grabbed his lapel, not wanting to leave the safety of his arms. Gently he prised her away and led her into the library where he sat her down with a sip of brandy. The room was oppressively dark as the brooding storm hovered directly over the castle. He sat next to her, those kind eyes that Nan had once commented on, watching her with such concern. She wanted to languish in those peacock-blue pools forever.

'Angeline, you must tell me what happened today.'

Her heart leapt. He did not call her Lady Angeline, just Angeline. She could hardly believe that he felt so close to her, so intimate. A thrill of anticipation ran through her.

'What on earth were you doing galloping across the sands? Why was Nan ringing that bell?' She looked at him with a puzzled expression on her face. 'Nikolaus and I were there, on the cliff. We saw you. That's how we found her.' He moved nearer, 'Angeline, what are the men so afraid of?'

Angeline faltered. She was not trying to be evasive, but she genuinely did not know where to start.

Finally she dried her eyes, took in a deep breath, blew out a long stream of air and began to tell the story.

'I come from an ancient line of mystics. It is said we were here even before the Vikings arrived. Originally we protected the spirits who lived at the source of the river. You see, the people have always depended on our river for their livelihoods. Well, there are rituals that are still performed today. It's more tradition now, but people who live around here are very super-stitious – it comforts them. Last night was Imbolc.'

'What on earth is that?' William asked; a bewildered expression etched on his face.

'It means 'in milk'. It's the midpoint between the winter solstice and the spring equinox: it marks the turning of the season. On that night, I, like my mother before me, and her mother before her, must go to the source of the Rivendor with the Guardian, Nan, and light a sacred flame. The rites are spoken and milk is poured on the earth, nurturing it, making it fertile, marking the end of a long winter and the return of spring.'

Angeline looked up at William. She could tell he was trying to remain calm, but he was the type of man who railed against anything that was not logical or rational. The tension in his body and the deep furrow in the middle of his brow gave his feelings away.

'But where were you going this morning? And how did you disappear from the beach into thin air?' William pressed her, noting that she had been back at the castle long enough to change into decent clothes.

She gave a sad, dismissive laugh. 'There is a hidden path that brings you back here.'

'But I searched for you. I saw no path.'

'Along the coastline. You need to know it's there or you will never find it. It's a shortcut back to the castle.' She ignored the disbelieving look he gave her.

'I rode back home, as usual, while Nan completed the final act. I never go to the bell. I wasn't even there.'

'What's the final act?'

'To ring the bell, of course. Nan always rings the bell.' The mention of Nan's name caused a deep sense of loss to wash over her, turning it into an aching pain in the pit of her stomach.

'So Nan was alive when you left her?'

Angeline was shocked by the tone of his voice. No longer sympathetic, he was interrogating her. Suddenly, she understood she was a suspect.

'Yes, yes, she was alive,' Angeline replied anxiously.

'So tell me, Angeline,' he said with ill-disguised impatience, 'why was Nan ringing that damn bell? What does it signify?'

At that moment a bolt of lightning and a crack of thunder filled the room as the heavens opened. Torrents of rain fell from the sky. It made Angeline jump, but somehow she found the courage to continue. 'The ritual ends at sunrise, when the Guardian makes her way to the abbey to ring the bell. This keeps Fenrir away until the next sacred fire is lit. He is said to be frightened by the noise from a great bell.'

William had heard that name before: Fenrir. It was the word the men had been whispering when they saw Nan's death wound. 'Who is Fenrir?'

Tears welled up again in her eyes, 'A monstrous wolf who chases the sun and the moon to catch and eat them,' she said breathlessly.

William jumped out of his seat, clearly exasperated. 'So when the men saw how Nan had died, that bite to the throat, they thought it was Fenrir. They are frightened of a legend.'

Angeline nodded and glanced outside. The pitiless storm was pelting against the windowpanes, almost clawing to get inside, as if a beast itself.

'Sir, what *thing* did that to Nan?' She desperately wanted to call him by his given name, to call him William; to be that close to him in her grief, but she did not dare be so bold.

He inclined his head and observed her, as if he were a botanist studying a specimen. 'How very interesting. So you don't think it was Fenrir then?'

Angeline looked away sheepishly. 'I am aware that I perform traditional rituals, sir, so no, I don't believe that Fenrir really exists. Whatever did that to Nan is very real.'

William took her hand and gently squeezed it, relieved at her display of common sense.

'Indeed it is,' he replied. 'As soon as the weather improves, I will go with a posse of men to search the estate. I don't know what kind of beast did this terrible thing, but I will find it and destroy it. I give you my word.'

And she had no doubt that he would. 'So you believe me when I say I had nothing to do with this tragedy?' Angeline could see how, from his point of view, she might not be above suspicion. Her anxiety rose because he did not answer straight away.

'Yes, of course I believe you,' he finally declared. 'Nan obviously meant the world to you. What possible motive could you have?' Gently, he helped her to stand. 'You should rest now. You must be exhausted.'

A mixture of grief and relief finally overcame her. As she rose to her feet she wobbled. She had not slept all night and the brandy had furred her senses. William caught her in his arms, and delirious joy seeped through her veins, coupled with guilt and remorse at feeling such pleasure at a time like this.

A tremendous thunderclap rattled the windows and the lightning that accompanied it lit up the room like a beacon. A branch from the tree outside was thrust onto the window by the force of the squall. The black, curved, hook-like projection tore against the pane of glass. Angeline's nerves were so frayed, she shrieked in panic.

William's hold on her tightened and an immediate glittering sensation coursed through her body. She climbed deeper into the embrace, needing his strength. As she turned her head to look at him, her lips accidentally brushed against his. She heard him emit a soul-hungry groan and an overwhelming craving she did not understand threatened to consume her.

The assault on her senses was far too much to bear and she swooned. Moving in and out of consciousness, she felt him carry her up the stairs and sensed him lay her on the bed. Then she thought she felt him kiss her on the forehead. Or was she merely dreaming?

CHAPTER 12

She was so warm and swaddled in her bed that fleetingly she lost herself in his arms again. Angeline recalled his smell: woody and leathery. The thought of him made her stretch out like a cat, luxuriating in the heat as she felt the delicate flame of desire tickle her. She had swung from hating everything he stood for, to being grateful to him for saving her from Elewald. Now he had awakened something else within her and she could no longer fathom her feelings towards him. He was not the man she had thought he was. Not the trickster, nor the carousing rake she had expected. He was clever, noble and kind and he had completely ensnared her. What would her mother have made of him?

Deep heartache returned as she remembered that they had all gone. Her mother first: some malady she had seen before, but no one knew how to cure. Even the powerful remedies she had learnt to prepare by her mother's side could not halt it. She had just become weaker and weaker, then faded away. Afterwards, her father fell into such despair she no longer recognised him. No longer the man who had been her rock for so many years. When did love turn into a need so strong you could not bear to live with the loss, she wondered? Then today,

Nan had been taken from her, in the cruellest of ways. They were all gone and now she was totally alone. The loneliness made the tears fall. There was no sobbing, just an endless stream of wetness. She turned over and tried to focus on the deathly pale full moon as it beamed into the room. The storm had passed.

An owl hooted and she realised it must be very late. Angeline rose and walked up to the window to watch the clouds cover the moon, and noticed that the rest of the house was in darkness, except for candles burning down below, in the smoking room. Something drew Angeline to see who was there. She picked up the candlestick that was lighting the hallway, and padded down the stairs.

She stood behind the high wingback chair that was facing the fire. A small table to the side carried a decanter and a large glass of brandy, also a small medicine bottle. A hand inside a white frilled shirtsleeve fell across the arm of the wingback. She was thinking of moving closer when a silky voice wafted over the top of the chair.

'Are you feeling better, my dear?'

'How did you know I was here?' she asked.

'I can smell you. You always smell of heather. It is quite lovely.'

'Heather has no smell,' she said.

'It does if one has a heightened sense, as I have. It's a quirk of nature that I've inherited.'

Angeline suspected that Count Andrassy was a little drunk. She walked around to see nothing but a mop of long, raven-black hair. His head had fallen onto his chest. Suddenly he looked up at her, and it made her jump. The dancing light of the fire highlighted his exotic beauty and she caught the glimmer of his emerald eyes; wide open in the half light, unconsciously ferocious, they seemed to be asking some question of her.

'Are you a witch, too? Just like the old woman?' he finally asked.

'We have sometimes been called so in the past, and some of my ancestors have been burnt for it, but witches are merely women who do not comply with social expectations. The locals might call us white witches nowadays. There is no malice. It is our calling to help, so we provide folk magic; herbs for healing, midwifery, that sort of thing.' She noticed him relax a little. 'And what about you, Count Andrassy? They tell me you are a Hungarian.'

'That is true.'

'Where do you Hungarians live?'

'East of Austria.'

'Is there anything east of Austria?'

Nikolaus laughed softly. 'Oh yes, my dear, a mystical, magical land, full of forests and lakes and waterfalls. You would like it, I think. I come from the Carpathian Mountains, a place full of secrets and superstitions. Not so different from here,' he said with a tinge of irony. Nikolaus held his hand over his heart. 'I am truly, truly sorry for your loss. Nobody should die like that.' Then he leaned forward. 'Do you have the sight, too, just like the old woman?'

Angeline thought for a moment. 'I do not see things others cannot, but I sometimes see things others choose not to. When I look at you I see a man battered by the conflicting currents of the world.' She glanced at the bottle on the table. 'You should not take laudanum.'

Nikolaus gave a short laugh as he flung himself back into the chair.

'It will make you feel worse over time, and you will need to take more and more. I can give you something to help you, without making you morose.'

'Oh my dear, you have no idea how dreadful that would be; not to be dogged by my golden darkness. Misery can be such a pleasant drug,' he said. 'It has followed me around for years, like a faithful hound, and it will not so easily let me go.' He sighed deeply. 'Opium suppresses my cravings and extraordinary passions, but it also quells the numbness in my heart.'

Angeline pitied him. How awful to live with such a tormented soul. 'So Nan's vision was correct then. There is something chasing you in the dark.'

Nikolaus stared at her in silence for a few moments.

'I have never thought of it like that, but perhaps you are right,' he said.

'I shall prepare some medicine for you tomorrow; passion-flower and green oats.' She was just about to add something more when a voice from the other side of the room drifted over.

'I think you should go back to bed now, Angeline. You need to rest.' William was standing in the doorway. He must have heard everything.

'Did you find the monster?' she asked.

'No, I'm sorry. It's too wet. We will try again in the morning.'

'Where is Odin?' she asked, realising that he was nowhere to be seen.

'Ah,' said William.

'Where is he?' Angeline demanded.

'Nikolaus?' William asked in response to the question, for he did not know what had become of the dog.

Nikolaus stood cautiously and gripped the mantelpiece. 'That hound is very lucky. Sweyne convinced me not to shoot it but to lock it up instead.'

'Why?' she gasped. 'Why would you shoot him?'

'Because, Lady Angeline, he is the only suspect we have,' replied Nikolaus, indignant.

'Odin would never hurt anyone,' she declared. 'You can't keep him locked up.'

'Angeline,' William said soothingly, trying to calm her, 'it's for the dog's safety. People are so scared, they may confuse Odin with Fenrir.'

'People would never...'

'Angeline,' he said firmly, 'if you want to save that dog, you must do as I say. Odin stays locked up for the foreseeable future. Come now, I will walk you back to your room.'

She did not like his tone, as if he were talking to a child. Even her father would not have been so high-handed, but she was emotionally exhausted, so reluctantly she acquiesced.

He took the candlestick and walked her upstairs.

'Do you really think you can help him?' William asked her, changing the subject.

'Who?' she asked.

'Nikolaus, with your medicine.'

She shrugged. 'It depends how deep the melancholia goes, but I think I can alleviate some of the symptoms.' Angeline glanced over at him. 'You care for him very much, don't you?'

William's face softened. 'Well, you must admit, he has a certain medieval charm.'

Angeline stifled a grin. He could so easily make her smile.

'We have looked after each other for a long time, and we've had many adventures together. One day I will tell you all about them.' He sounded like an indulgent uncle, promising a child a fairy tale and it irritated her. Something within her snapped.

She stopped abruptly by the gothic arch of a window and glared at him.

'Please do not patronise me, my lord. You cannot protect me from the world, I have already seen too much.'

Shocked by her reaction to his concern for her, he bridled. 'Angeline, you are overwrought. I am merely thinking of your welfare.'

'Well, stop *merely* thinking of me at all. I can look after myself. I am not a child.'

William was just about to respond when he became trans- fixed. She had chosen to stop in front of a stained glass window, and at that very moment the moon decided to shine straight through and illuminate her like a Madonna. She radiated youth as the blue and red glass shimmered around her. It gave her a look of angelic innocence, except for a mouth that was too full, too tempting. For the first time in many years, William found himself struggling with his desires. He longed to take her in his arms and wrap her up in his burning heat. Standing there, without touching her, without a single gesture passing between them, made the physical all the more intense. He hungered, but it must never be.

'No, you're not a child, are you?' was all he could say in response. It was almost inaudible as he shrank away from her. Stunned by the strength of his feelings, he turned and fled, leaving Angeline alone, to wonder just what had happened between them.

CHAPTER 13

The funeral of Nan Absalom, the Guardian of the Source, took place at the local church. William might have been surprised to learn that Nan had been a regular churchgoer, but he had realised, some time ago, that nothing in this part of Northumberland should surprise him. It had its own social mores; its own way of doing things that had held the community together for hundreds of years. He was sure that most outsiders, throughout the ages, whatever their rank, would have found it all just a little too strange and hightailed it back to wherever they came from, as fast as they could.

One thing William was sure of was that he was made of sterner stuff than most people, and he was determined to stay, to tame this wild land and educate its people; for their own good. Times were changing and the outside world would soon come crashing in on them. They needed to be ready or they would not survive.

Nan's funeral was a remarkably spiritual occasion, filled with the rapture that came from believers who know with absolute certainty that they will be carried off to another sphere of existence after this life. A large crowd filled the church to pay their respects to a wise woman who had been treated with deference by the whole community.

After the ceremony, Nikolaus escorted the estate workers back to the castle. Everyone was fearful of walking out unprotected these days, but William took the opportunity to seek out the vicar and find out if he could shed any light on Nan's death. He stood in the churchyard alone, studying an ancient monument. Amongst the gravestones stood a cross that was tall and thin, made of yellow sandstone. It stood, perhaps, fourteen feet high and had complicated, interlocking rope patterns, winding their way up to the top of the cross. Underneath the patterns were crudely carved figures, locked in battle.

'Wonderful, isn't it?' said the vicar as he walked up behind William. 'It's unique among English Viking crosses for its size and the quality of carving.'

'I've never seen anything like it,' William replied.

'The interlacing roots depict the ash tree, 'Yggdrasil', which the Norsemen believed supported the universe. The figures at the bottom are the old gods, losing the battle for our souls to Christianity.'

'Extraordinary.' William moved closer to get a better look.

'That small one over there is even older. It's an Anglo-Saxon hammerhead cross.'

William had not noticed it until the vicar pointed out a red stone square cross with perfectly carved scrolls and four large holes dug out of the four corners of the head. The vicar, obviously keenly knowledgeable about ancient markers, spoke with the deep timbre of a man who was accustomed to being listened to. The Reverend Roberts was a striking figure, unusually tall and well-built, dressed head to foot in black, except for his white dog collar. William thought he looked more like an undertaker than a vicar. He had a long mane of pure white, wavy hair and a matching drooping moustache.

Ice-blue eyes made William recognise him immediately as a local man. William came straight to the point.

'Do you have any idea what could have killed Nan Absalom?' he asked.

The vicar did not seem surprised by the question but merely threw it back. 'I thought, perhaps, you could tell me?'

William was not used to people answering his question with a question and he found it mildly disturbing.

'It has to have been an animal of some sort. No human could have made such a wound. Unfortunately we could not find any tracks or any clues. They must have been washed away by the rain, so we have come to a dead end.'

'What, in your view, is the most likely animal?'

Another question. William searched his mind for the most obvious answer. 'A huge dog, perhaps. Even a wolf.'

'Ah, Fenrir,' stated the vicar.

'I doubt it,' William replied, unable to mask his irritation at such nonsense. He could see that the vicar had read his thoughts and was giving him one of those all-knowing, superior smiles that men of the cloth were so famous for.

'I doubt it, too,' the vicar replied silkily 'and wolves have not been seen in this part of the world for hundreds of years. So another dead end, I'm afraid, my lord.'

This circuitous conversation was going nowhere, William clenched his jaw.

'But,' the vicar boomed, 'I've never seen my flock so on edge. They do not like uncertainty. They are not used to it. Whatever type of beast it is, we must track it down and destroy it before it attacks again.'

'Be assured, Reverend Roberts, that is exactly what I intend to do. You have my oath on that.'

'Excellent. That is what I was hoping you would say.'

The two men walked towards the gate where Angeline and Mr Sweyne were waiting.

'Reverend Roberts, please explain to me how someone like Nan Absalom could be a member of your congregation whilst practising as a healer and partaking in what can only be described as pagan rituals.' William knew that, by inference, he was also accusing Angeline.

The Reverend Roberts smiled again, 'Yes, Lady Angeline told me she had explained Imbolc to you. Lord Lyndhurst, things are different up here in the north. People pay homage to the old ways, but they are still good Christians. The two faiths have lived side by side for centuries and in my opinion bring out the best in each other.'

William suspected that this was tantamount to sacrilege. 'Please explain yourself, sir,' he said.

The vicar stopped by an old tilted gravestone, yellow with lichen. 'Nan Absalom possessed intimate knowledge of herbal remedies that saved the lives of people who doctors had given up for dead. Luckily, Lady Angeline is blessed with the same gift. The gift of healing is a gift from God,' he said forcefully. 'The rituals are just tradition now. The old gods were fickle creatures; humans could be destroyed by them on a whim. Christianity gave the people security. They now have a pact with God. They know that he will treat them well if they live well. Their reward will be in Heaven.'

'But surely, your people have broken the first commandment, Mr Roberts. *Thou shalt have no other God but me.*' William's brow darkened.

'Lord Lyndhurst, they do not have any other God,' the vicar responded in a reassuring tone. 'It's just folklore and custom, nothing more. I give you my word on that.'

William wondered how he could be so certain. He turned to watch Angeline talking with the locals as they milled around the church. The affection they showed her was constant; the old feudal passions of service, respect and devotion were alive and well here. In return she obviously loved them unconditionally. A small girl, who was learning to walk, toddled over to Angeline and stretched her hand up high to give her a small bunch of wild flowers which she had just picked from the side of the path with her mother. Angeline bent down, took the flowers and gave the little girl a peck on the cheek. The mother, standing behind the youngster, had tears streaming down her face. Angeline took her own handkerchief and wiped away the tears as she spoke soothingly to try to give some comfort. Watching discreetly, William then understood how the vicar could have such spiritual certainty, in the same way Angeline always seemed so certain. There was a symbiosis between her and the people and the land; an almost magical communion. Even if he had thrown her out on that first night, as Nikolaus suggested he might, she would have been safe, protected and looked after by the community.

Although the people were superficially deferential to him, and undeniably grateful that he appeared to be a benevolent lord of the manor, he was an outsider and probably would always be so. It filled him with bitter sadness. He had been an outsider all his life and he so wanted to belong somewhere.

Because the weather had been unusually clement ever since the storm had passed, William and Angeline decided to walk to the town of Thornby, which was only a mile or so from the church. It was important to show the people that life should carry on as normal, despite their fears.

They were accompanied by Mr Sweyne carrying a gun for protection, and a housemaid who was trying her best to act as Angeline's lady's maid now that Nan was gone. William observed that Angeline was being very patient with her. The maid was beside herself for having forgotten Angeline's muff. He watched Angeline, once again, talking calmly and being inordinately kind at a time when it was she who needed all the kindness. It was a quality in her that he admired enormously.

The sun shone down on them benevolently as they walked through the lanes, passing wooden dwellings no more than shacks built on common land. William had observed many times how poor the people were in this part of the world, much poorer than in the south on the whole. People, dressed in nothing more than rags, stopped what they were doing; bare-footed children stopped playing and numerous pairs of eyes watched silently as they walked by. The quiet was only broken by the occasional babe in arms squealing for its mother's attention.

'How on earth do these poor creatures survive?' William asked Eric Sweyne as the two men walked a few paces behind the ladies.

'By foraging and poaching mainly. There's no work for them around about. We do what we can on the estate. We employ as many as possible, trying to spread the work across different families, but it's never enough. Of course, it became worse when the men started drifting back from the wars.'

They carried on walking and William marvelled that there was no anger in the eyes of the people watching them. No resentment of them, the landed gentry. In fact, a couple of the men doffed their caps in respect.

Eric Sweyne seemed obliged to continue. 'I must inform you, my lord, the Goldsboroughs have always turned a blind eye to the poaching.'

William now understood the attitude of the people towards them and gave a small nod, which was to be interpreted by Sweyne as acceptance.

William looked his companion squarely in the eye. 'The thing I will not tolerate, however, is smuggling. It's a barbaric activity, run by gangs who exploit the poor. Anyone caught smuggling on my land will feel the full force of the law. Do I make myself clear, Mr Sweyne?'

'Yes, sir,' replied Sweyne. 'I understand completely.'

They could see the town laid out before them, in the dip of a valley, as they continued on, following the muddy path that crossed a field. It was a mistake coming this way, William realised. The ground had not dried out enough from the rain. He heard the sound of a hunting horn to their right, behind the hedgerow. It was very close. The hounds were coming their way.

'Let's talk further tomorrow, Mr Sweyne. I have some ideas I would like to share with you about new crops and techniques that can improve our yields significantly. I've been to Norfolk to visit Thomas Coke's pioneering estate where he experiments with new methods of farming. I think we should try some of them. We could diversify and increase employment.'

'Very well, my lord, I would be interested to...'

Before Sweyne could finish, a fox popped its head up from under the hedge and scurried across their path, disappearing into a ditch that ran along the other side of the field. The hounds, baying and yelping, tore through the hedgerow in chase, but they were immediately distracted as soon as they discovered humans.

Spinning around, confused by different smells, the hounds lost the scent of the fox. They started to jump up at the two women, yelping, muddy paws smearing over their clothes. Angeline's maid screamed, a horrible, howling scream that tore from her throat and sent the hounds into a panic. Her high-pitched, piercing cry made them more and more agitated and they began to bark louder at her. Barking, barking, incessantly barking. Then the first horse jumped the fence.

Instinctively, William and Eric Sweyne pushed the women hard into the hedgerow and covered them with their bodies, pinning them down, and shielding them. William felt Angeline's body bracing itself for the worst as she sucked in a breath and squeezed her eyes shut. The sound of the hunting horn was deafening as horse after horse came hurtling over the six-foot hedge. William held her wrists pinioned and could feel the throbbing of her throat as his mouth breathed on it. The only thing he could see above them was smears of hunting pink, streaking across the sky. William knew if a horse stumbled it could come crashing down, killing them all. Angeline began to wrestle with him. He felt the movement of her struggle against his groin.

'Stop squirming,' he ordered through gritted teeth.

'You're hurting me. I can't breathe,' she gasped.

He swore harshly, but kept pushing down on her.

Thankfully, within minutes, the hounds were off, back to the chase, following the sound of the horn. In a moment a hush fell over the field, except for the distant sound of the hounds' baying and the horn, floating through the air. With a decisive move he freed himself from her and she caught her breath. William turned to watch the fleeing pack, his heart in his throat. It had been a close run thing. A couple of the riders had caught sight of them and came trotting back towards them.

As the riders came closer, one of them appeared so colourless, he seemed to disappear into the cloud behind. That was when William knew who it was, even before he could distinguish the features.

'Elewald, you madman, what do you think you are doing? You could have killed us!'

'Chance would be a fine thing, Lyndhurst,' Elewald scoffed. 'I've every right to hunt on this land. Besides, no one could see any of you behind that hedge. You shouldn't have walked this way during the hunting season.'

William turned away from him to attend to the women, their clothing disarrayed and mud-spattered, but Elewald lingered. Mr Sweyne was taking care of the severely shaken maid when William's eye caught sight of a river of blood running down Angeline's upheld hand. She had been snagged by the hedge. Roughly, he grabbed her hand and sucked it deeply.

She gasped, trying to pull away, but his sharp look challenged her, so she allowed herself to yield to him.

'Shame about the old woman. Terrible way to go,' shouted Elewald as William bound Angeline's hand with his handkerchief. 'The stench of death seems to follow you around, Lyndhurst.' William's companions froze on these words.

'Mind yourself, Elewald,' William threatened.

'Particularly when someone stands in the way of something you want,' Elewald hissed, leering at Angeline.

'Explain yourself, Lord Elewald,' Angeline demanded, impulsively rising to William's defence.

'Don't need to, my dear. Lyndhurst here comes from a long line of reprobates. Like father, like son, eh.'

'Elewald, I'm warning you!' William glared at him.

'I bet you couldn't believe your luck when that brother of yours died so conveniently,' goaded Elewald.

William launched himself at Elewald, but the viscount whipped his horse so hard that it reared up over him. William could see the whip being raised once again and managed to grab it, the force throwing William sideways just before the horse landed on him. Elewald was grunting and kicking out but William refused to let go of the whip. A boot flashed past William's face. As he swerved to avoid it, William twisted the whip around his wrist and pulled with all his strength. Elewald very nearly toppled from his horse, but the animal shouldered William and unbalanced him, so he had to release it. William fell back onto the mud and watched as Elewald pushed his horse on, heading straight for Angeline. The animal swerved just in time, but pinned Angeline against the hedgerow once more.

Elewald bent down from his horse and whispered to her viciously, 'Just ask Lyndhurst how his brother died. Like to hear him talk his way out of that one!' With that he tore off down the field in pursuit of the pack.

William stared after him, wrestling with his anger. When he finally turned around, he saw three pairs of eyes searching his face. He marched over to them and finished bandaging Angeline's hand.

'If a piece of thorn lodges itself in the cut it will become infected,' he explained.

'I will treat it when I get home,' she replied, her voice subdued.

'What did Elewald say to you?' William asked.

Angeline hesitated. 'He said, "Ask Lyndhurst how his brother died." '

William met her gaze and seconds passed before he finally said, 'It was a tragic accident.'

They soldiered on silently towards the town, where they walked straight into some sort of commotion in the town square. Men were standing around shouting at each other in accusatory tones. Most of them had tools or weapons in their hands, some swinging them menacingly.

'What is going on here?' demanded William, walking right into the middle of the crowd. All the men knew who he was and stepped back. William felt Eric Sweyne position himself reassuringly behind him to protect his back. 'I demand to know!' William said. 'You!' He pointed to the man facing him. 'Tell me what this is all about.'

Eric Sweyne whispered to William, 'That's John Smith. He's an Elewald farmer.'

'Speak up, man,' William insisted, keeping an eye on the branding iron that hung in Smith's hand.

'All my sheep have been butchered, every single one of them. Had their throats ripped out. Never seen anything like it. I'm ruined and he did it.' Smith pointed to a man in the crowd facing him. 'He's been after my land for years. His dog did it, I'll be bound.'

The accused man lunged forward. 'It weren't me. You did it yourself, trying to get me locked up. You've always coveted my land.'

'Alan Black. He's one of your farmers,' Eric Sweyne whispered again. 'They farm either side of the Rivendor. They've been feuding for years.'

'It's Fenrir, come to destroy us!' a voice shouted from the back. An uneasy murmur rippled through the crowd.

'Did you see the dog that did this to your sheep?' William asked John Smith.

'No, it happened in the dead of night. I found them this morning.'

'He didn't see anything because it was his own bloody dog,' came the angry reply from Alan Black. The two farmers edged closer to each other.

'Enough!' said William. 'Go back to your homes. Mr Smith, my men will come and help you salvage the wool and dispose of the carcasses. Mr Black, you will give Mr Smith half your flock of sheep.'

'What? I tell you, I had nothing to do with the slaughter of his sheep!'

'Nevertheless, Mr Black, you will give Mr Smith here half your flock. I promise, I will compensate you for the loss.'

Alan Black stroked his chin. The idea of some cash clearly appealed to him. Money was usually tied up in livestock.

'I will give you market price,' William said, reinforcing his position.

Alan Black thought for a second before agreeing. 'Very well, my lord, you have a deal, but I want it made clear – I'll not take any responsibility for what happened.'

'Agreed,' said William. 'Mr Smith, this is the best offer you will get. You will not be as well off as you were, but you will not be ruined either. What do you say?'

John Smith grumbled noisily, but the crowd finally persuaded him to accept.

As the men grudgingly shook hands, there were noises of approval for William's actions around the square.

'What about Fenrir?' shouted someone from the crowd. 'What are we to do? No one's safe. He'll attack again.'

William turned to the crowd. 'I, Earl of Lyndhurst, Lord of Goldsborough, give you my solemn promise that I will hunt down and destroy whatever killed Nan Absalom.' More murmurings could be heard, until gradually the men started to disperse, for these words, from the lord of the manor, were enough to appease the crowd.

Angeline watched from the sidelines. William was taller than average, but to her he appeared a giant amongst men. Posture like that could not be taught: a man was either born to stand like a leader or he could not do it. William had single-handedly brought the potential riot under control. A man like this wielded more force with his aura and the look in his eye than most other men with weapons.

But there was one question that had lodged itself firmly in the back of her mind. What had Lord Elewald meant when he'd said, 'Ask Lyndhurst how his brother died.' The insinuation was that it was more than a tragic accident.

CHAPTER 14

He was unnervingly calm, despite finding himself sitting amongst the ruins, staring up at the black tower that touched the heavens. A murder of crows, flying in continuous circles around the keep, cawed without mercy. The air, stale and putrid, stuck to his skin as he sat and waited, somehow knowing he had been waiting for a very long time. Something moved over his boot and he looked down to see his feet smothered with writhing white maggots but felt nothing; no revulsion, no dread. Mesmerized, he watched the maggots churning rubbish, turning it into something new, as if they were teasing out the threads of his future.

Then he looked up and saw her, standing before the tower, in nothing but the flowing chemise she had worn on the beach, her silhouette clearly visible, her expression impenetrable. Very, very slowly, a bead of sweat dripped down to rest in the hollow of her clavicle, and he marvelled at her beauty.

She beckoned to him, luring him in like a siren and unfettered desire overcame him. He yearned to go to her, for he knew he was unanchored and needing a harbour. An urge to escape washed over him: to run from convention and duty and responsibility. But he would never go to her. He could not, because he was infected; infected with guilt, tainted by death.

Sensation flooded his body as panic pierced his soul. He could feel a menacing presence behind him, smelled the carrion on its hot, damp breath, causing the hairs on his neck to rise. Whatever stood behind him was agitated, waiting to pounce and gnaw the flesh right off him. Impending doom had come calling.

When the lunge came, it was quick and sharp. The pain, sweetly unbearable, coursed through his veins. Spasms racked him, as he let out a primitive, guttural cry. His skin punctured and the pulsation burst forth, hot and sticky, trickling down his torso. An overwhelming impulse made him call out her name. Catching the look on her face, he could not decipher it. Was it rapture or anguish? He heard her scream for him, the first scream he had wrung out of her. Then the choking began and it blocked his airways. He tried to gasp, but could no longer breathe as the blackness descended upon him.

William sat bolt upright, shivering with the cold sweat that drenched him. He was adrift for some moments, like a drunkard, his mind addled, trying to recall what had just happened. He staggered out of bed to open the heavy curtains and daylight blinded him. He must have overslept. What time was it? He looked down at his wracked body. Gradually, he came to, he could never remember having had such a vivid dream.

Recalling the details of the dream, it disturbed him deeply. Where did these thoughts about Angeline spring from? Why did he not seem to be able to control them? He splashed cold water from the washbowl over his face. Holding his head in the towel, he managed to convince himself that the dream had been caused by his fervent desire to find and destroy the beast that had killed Nan. Nothing more.

Still dazed, he slowly remembered that Nikolaus had planned to leave early with a band of men to visit the Smith farm, to save the wool, destroy the carcasses and look for clues. They had to ensure John Smith did not try to salvage the meat and sell it, who knew what it was infected with. People around here were so hungry they would eat anything.

William needed air and physical exertion to exorcise his demons. Pulling on his shirt, he walked out onto the courtyard and watched two of his labourers chopping wood. They were splitting kindling for the estate workers.

Without a word, William picked up an axe and joined them. The men exchanged looks, but nothing more. He worked like the devil all day.

Angeline returned to her bedroom window many times that day to watch the lord of the manor labour like a peasant and wondered what had possessed him.

She watched the wind tousle his wayward hair affectionately. He looked free and had a glow of beauty about him, she thought. He stopped for a moment to take a drink of water and looked up. She knew that he had caught sight of her, but he just turned away and kept chopping.

By the time Nikolaus and the posse returned, as the sky began to turn red, William was finally spent. Men and horses milled around the courtyard. The men tried to carry on normally, stabling the horses for the night, but they looked at their exhausted lord strangely.

William knew that Nikolaus would be the last man left in the stables. He took such great care of his beloved horses that he had been known to sleep with them if he was concerned about one of them. Finally, William went in search of him and discovered a solitary figure, standing in a loose box stroking the forelock of the stallion, Cherub, who was nuzzling him affectionately.

'This really is a beautiful specimen,' Nikolaus declared. 'I would love to breed from him. I must talk to Lady Angeline about it. He could sire some marvellous racehorses.'

William walked over to Cherub's saddle, which had been thrown over his stable door and started to stroke it. It was made of the finest leather and felt like butter to touch, warm and silky. A vision of stroking Angeline in the same way jumped into his mind. Immediately William jerked his hand away. He wanted to touch her like that more than anything in the world, but she was his ward now and such thoughts of forbidden sensuality had to be dashed from his mind.

'William, what's wrong? You look like you've seen an apparition.'

William shook his head violently. Why could he not get that damn girl out of his mind?

'Did you find anything interesting at the Smith Farm?' he asked Nikolaus, concentrating on the present.

'It's definitely the same *thing* that attacked the old crone. The method of killing is identical and I could detect, very faintly, the same indescribable odour. But the ground is still sodden from all the rain we've had, so I couldn't make out the tracks.' Nikolaus inspected the flank of the horse. 'Some of the sheep had that strange blue dye on their wool. The exact same colour we found on the old lady's clothing.'

William frowned. 'How could that have got there?'

'I have no idea. I asked the farmer, but he has never seen it before. One thing I am certain of, though, Odin can't be the beast. He's still locked up. Poor animal, I will go and let him out.'

'Any sign of Elewald?' William asked as they walked together towards the kennel.

'No. Apparently he doesn't take much of an interest in his tenants as long as they are paying their rent.'

William kicked a stone away with his boot.

'William, what ails you?'

Before he could answer, a small commotion could be heard outside: galloping hooves, a snorting horse and a rider shouting:

'The Earl of Lyndhurst. I must see him immediately! I have urgent news. Where is the Earl of Lyndhurst?'

'I'm Lyndhurst,' William announced, striding up to the man.

The rider looked doubtfully at the dirty clothes, shirt billowing in the wind and the dishevelled hair.

'I have a letter for the Earl of Lyndhurst,' the man shouted over William's head.

Nikolaus stood beside William. 'Believe it or not, this peasant is who he says he is.' Having heard the shouting, people spilled out from the castle, including Mr Sweyne, who also vouched for him.

'An urgent letter for you, my lord,' the messenger said reluctantly. 'I'm ordered to wait for an answer.'

William snatched the letter. 'Go to the kitchens where you will find food and await my reply, should I choose to give one.'

Angeline had been standing behind Mr Sweyne in the courtyard, but quietly slipped back into the castle, wondering if the letter might affect her.

'What is it?' asked Nikolaus as William scanned the letter in the fading light of the day.

'My aunt. The storms that are sweeping the country. God no, the west wing of Lyndhurst Manor has collapsed. There have been fatalities.' William wiped his mouth with the back of his hand. 'It needs my urgent attention.'

'Then you must go immediately,' urged Nikolaus.

'But I can't abandon the people here. I've made a commitment to them. I've given my word, to destroy whatever killed Nan Absalom.'

'Then I will stay and act in your name,' Nikolaus replied.

William grasped Nikolaus's shoulder. 'I truly appreciate your offer, my friend, as I know you are not fond of the place, but I'm afraid that will not do either. My aunt also informs me that you have been summoned back to town by Princess Eszterházy for an urgent family conference.'

Nikolaus froze. 'This does not bode well. Believe me, truly, I would rather stay here. It is the lesser evil.'

William threw him a sympathetic look. 'You will be receiving a missive any day from your own aunt. Warning you that your inheritance depends on it.'

Nikolaus pushed his head down into his hands and groaned.

'I have to stay. I don't see how I can leave,' William continued. 'But deaths at Lyndhurst...'

Nikolaus quickly recovered his composure. 'William, you will not be abandoning the people here. Sweyne will take care of things. You can trust him, and the estate men are loyal. Recruit reinforcements if you have to, ones who are not spooked by the legend of a wolf. But you must return.' Nikolaus grabbed William by the arm. 'The gossips will already be saying that the new earl is as feckless as all those who went before him. I know there are dark secrets to uncover here, but you tarry too long. It's February. You must return to London to take up your seat in Parliament. I'm afraid, my friend, pressing things are calling you home.'

William ran his fingers through his hair, feeling the Northumbrian wood splinters lodged there. He knew Nikolaus spoke sense. One of the first steps to rebuilding the family reputation was to take up his responsibilities as a peer of the realm. Parliament began sitting in January. He was already late. Also, if it appeared that he was neglecting the family seat, society would so frown upon him, his reputation would never recover. The Lyndhurst Estate and his reputation meant everything to him. They were all he had. Goldsborough was meant to secure these things.

'Very well, Nikolaus, we will leave by the end of the week. I must take care of Lyndhurst and its people. I have faith in Mr Sweyne. He can manage things here until I return. So, Hampshire first, then London.'

CHAPTER 15

'I will be back as soon as I can.'

'You need not worry, my lord. I understand why you have to leave and I can take care of things whilst you're away.'

'Thank you, Mr Sweyne. I am most grateful.' William watched Nikolaus leave the castle and ride ahead of them to Hampshire. 'Keep the men armed. Call for reinforcements if you have to.'

Sweyne nodded.

Angeline stood in the courtyard, stroking Odin, listening to the conversation whilst biting her tongue. She was angry with William for making her leave at such short notice. It had not given her enough time to get used to the idea, and she did not like to admit to herself precisely how anxious she was about leaving home. Leaving everything she had ever known.

As she watched the interaction between the two men, she saw Eric Sweyne glance over to the entrance gate and rapidly take a second look. He stood, motionless, and stared. He only ever looked like that for one person.

Angeline followed his eyeline and her heart jumped. Standing there, in the dark blue velvet cloak that Angeline had given her, was a young woman with long, curly hair that shone like spun silk, and rosebud lips that were perfectly positioned on a milky-white complexion.

Sweyne walked over to her, as if in a trance. Bemused, William looked to Angeline for an explanation.

'Brigid Absalom has returned,' she said.

William searched Angeline's face, expecting more.

'Nan's daughter, the new Guardian of the Source.'

'Where has she been?' William asked, registering the travelling bag.

'Just away.'

Frustrated by Angeline's reticence, William looked over again and saw Mr Sweyne deep in conversation with the girl, who appeared to be about the same age as Angeline. 'I've never seen Mr Sweyne look so enamoured,' he remarked.

'He's been waiting for a very long time.' Angeline replied, smiling warmly.

'Waiting for what?'

'Waiting to be chosen.'

William knew exactly what that phrase meant, but did not know whether to be amazed or appalled. 'But he has to be at least ten years older than her.'

Angeline shrugged. 'As my father was with my mother. It makes no difference.' Suddenly emboldened, she gave him a look of such sensual challenge that William flushed and turned his back on her to hide his discomfort. Angeline smiled triumphantly. She enjoyed ruffling his feathers.

At that moment, Eric Sweyne brought Brigid over to be introduced to the new lord. William instantly recognised the large, saucer-like eyes but, unlike her mother's, these were encased in a face of exquisite youth. She curtsied deftly, much better than Nan, he recalled, before running into the arms of Angeline, sobbing and hugging the life out of her.

William felt for the young girl who was grieving for her mother. It was a terrible thing, not to be able to say goodbye to a loved one.

Minutes passed and, worried that the return of Brigid Absalom was going to delay them, William looked at his pocket watch. 'Angeline, regrettably, we must leave now or the light will not be with us.'

Reluctantly, with one last hug, she whispered to Brigid, 'I will not be here for the Ostara ceremony. You will have to perform the ritual without me.'

'Have no fear,' Brigid replied, wiping away her tears. 'Eric will help me.'

Angeline nodded approvingly. 'Look after Odin for me and keep Eric by your side. There is danger everywhere.'

Once inside the carriage, Angeline took stock of the man who was now officially her guardian. She had never met anyone like him before. A man whose sense of honour she greatly admired, but who could infuriate her with his arrogance and high-handedness. Then, suddenly, he could draw her to him by the raw power that seemed to emanate from him and something would flutter through her body like a delicate butterfly.

'What are you staring at?' he asked, without even looking at her.

'I'm surprised that it is considered appropriate for us to ride alone together in a carriage, my lord.' she said, trying to prick his pompous bubble.

'As you are now my ward, it is perfectly acceptable.'

Hiding behind civilities again, Angeline thought. William had become very formal, almost distant, ever since the incident on the stairs. He had changed towards her, she had no idea why, nor why it hurt her so deeply.

'There was no need for you to bring a maid,' he continued. 'We have plenty of servants. Ones who understand what is required during the season.'

Angeline registered the word 'we'. Indignant, she said, 'Do you realise, my lord, you have not told me where I am going, let alone who I will meet there?'

William looked down at his hands that were resting quietly in his lap and sighed. 'Forgive me, Angeline. I have been so preoccupied these past few days that I have not given enough consideration to your wellbeing. Something very important has called me away, otherwise I would never have left Goldsborough with so much unfinished business. I give you my word, Angeline, I will find what killed Nan, but I must return to Hampshire as soon as possible.'

'So, we are not going to London then?'

'No. I will deliver you to my cousin Simon, the Earl of Hurstbourne and his Countess, Lady Louisa. They are very excited about having you stay.' He tried to sound enthusiastic. 'Lady Vivian, Simon's mother, lives on the Hurstbourne Estate, in the Dower House. She and Louisa will prepare you for your debut. My aunt is beside herself at the prospect. She hasn't had a cause like you for years.'

'So, I'm a cause now?'

'You will like them,' he assured her warmly. 'They are all the family I have. Along with Nikolaus, they are my favourite people in the world.'

Angeline smiled nervously and bit her bottom lip. 'In that case, I'm sure I will like them very well. But what is so important in Hampshire that it calls you away at a time when the people of Goldsborough need you the most?' She saw him flinch at her words.

'A part of Lyndhurst Manor has collapsed. It has already taken a number of lives, but the building is still dangerous. It must be secured before anyone else gets hurt.'

'Oh, I'm so sorry,' she replied, feeling guilty. 'Who were the poor people?'

'Servants, mainly. We did not have many as my brother never lived there, preferring to stay in London. But they were people I have known all my life.' He closed his eyes and shook his head as if to remove an image from his mind.

Angeline felt the pain of empathy and sat silently, listening to the rhythmic clatter of hooves. Eventually, she tried changing the subject, hoping it would help him.

'Please tell me more about the people I will meet at Hurstbourne.'

William looked flummoxed. He had not anticipated the question.

'Where do I begin? Simon and I were the two younger brothers. We felt neglected, I suppose, because so much attention fell on the son and heir, so we stuck together. We have always been close since we were boys. We used to play at being soldiers, and eventually we joined the army together.'

'So you both had older brothers who died?'

'Yes, Simon's brother, Thomas, fell at Waterloo, and my brother, George, well you know about him.'

Angeline, recalling the words of Viscount Elewald, ventured, 'How exactly did George die? If you don't mind me asking.' She watched the pulse at William's temple start to flicker.

'I've told you, it was a tragic accident. Unfortunately, my mother died soon afterwards. From grief, I think. She adored George. He reminded her so much of my father, you see.'

Angeline was surprised by this remark. 'So your father was...'

'Yes, a rake and a scoundrel, too. I'm afraid I come from a long line of them. Some say, it's in the blood.'

'Well, you obviously broke the mould.' Angeline replied, trying to lighten the mood, but William glared at her.

'You know nothing about me, Angeline. You have no idea what I'm capable of.'

Angeline recoiled. He had never looked at her that way before. With so much bitterness in his eyes. She watched him struggling with his thoughts.

Holding onto a strap while the coach manoeuvred around a particularly rocky part of the road, William finally said, 'I suppose you'll hear it from the gossips in London soon enough, so I may as well tell you. My brother was practically bankrupt when he won Goldsborough.' She saw him search her face, trying to read her reactions. She gave none. 'The fact that George died so soon afterwards was, perhaps, providence. For, in truth, Goldsborough has saved my family from ruin.'

'Oh, I see.' Angeline coughed out the words as the coach jolted violently. 'Thank you for telling me.' She thought she knew William well enough by now to know how hard it must have been for him to inherit Goldsborough under such circumstances. She made a valiant effort to shift the mood, only too aware how painful such a confession must have been for him. 'You were telling me about the people I will meet in Hampshire.'

William seemed to understand what she was trying to do and gave her an appreciative smile.

'Angeline, I hold you in the highest regard, I hope you know that. Your composure and self- control in the face of adversity is exemplary. These are qualities I greatly admire in you.'

Angeline tried to look pleased, but somehow William's stilted attempt to praise her had fallen short of her hopes. She didn't feel composed at all; in fact, she wanted to cry.

'Where was I?' William continued, 'oh yes, well, Simon married Louisa about a year ago and they are expecting an heir any time now.'

Angeline put on the bravest of her brave faces. 'Oh, a baby. How lovely!'

CHAPTER 16

The journey south had been long, if uneventful. Bad weather had dogged them all the way. William seemed determined to keep the conversation superficial, almost banal, for the final leg of the journey, artfully sidestepping any further searching questions Angeline might have.

Looking out at the scenery, she marvelled at how dramatically it changed from one day to the next. She had never travelled so far before. Nothing was sharp and jagged any more, but seemed round and undulating. Angeline was used to the exposed and brutish rocks of Northumberland, but down south much of the countryside was covered in lush greenery, even in February, and the morning sunlight twinkled on the dew that covered the grass. The mixed palette of bilberry, bracken and sheep sorrel that she was so familiar with had been replaced by early blossom on trees and vibrant green shoots.

Angeline had become attuned to William's moods and sensed them change with the scenery. He became lighter, more animated, as they rode into Hampshire. Late one afternoon, the carriage turned into a sweeping drive and Hurstbourne House came into view for the first time.

The seat of the Earl of Hurstbourne, William's cousin, was magnificent, standing proudly within rolling lawns. It had been built to command attention, on classical lines, with huge fluted columns guarding the entrance. They reminded Angeline of home. Not the castle, of course, but her Bernician home with its living connection to the classical world, not to this neo-classical revival that had become so fashionable.

As the coach stopped at the entrance to the house, Nikolaus led out a party of aristocrats and servants to greet them. William surprised her by jumping from the carriage, almost before it stopped, and running to embrace his family. She had never seen him so delighted before, with such a broad smile on his face, and her heart melted, for he looked as excited as a young boy returning home from school.

He had not forgotten her, though, and quickly came to her aid. 'Lady Angeline, please may I introduce you to my family. My cousin, Simon Maitland, Earl of Hurstbourne.'

'Enchanted,' replied the earl.

Behind the terrible scar that slashed down his left cheek, a trophy from Waterloo she had been told, Angeline saw a striking-looking man. Nobody would have guessed, however, that he and William were related, except for the same penetrating blue eyes. He was built like a bear, whilst William was lean. The earl had wiry hair, the colour of corn just before harvest time, whereas William's was mahogany-brown and silky. The earl had hard, angular, uncompromising features, but there was a softness, even a kindness in William's face.

'My wife, Louisa, Countess of Hurstbourne,' said the earl.

Angeline turned towards a voluptuous, redheaded woman in the full bloom of pregnancy.

'Welcome to Hurstbourne House,' Louisa said, as if she did not really mean it, Angeline thought.

'And, this is my aunt, Lady Vivian,' William continued.

'*Elle est ravissante,*' Lady Vivian remarked, looking shocked.

'*Merci beaucoup, Madame,*' Angeline replied in a perfect French accent.

Lady Vivian's eyes lit up in surprise, 'Oh! *Vous parlez française.*'

'*Oui, parfaitement, madame. J'ai été instruit en beaucoup de choses.*'

'Excellent. Well, Lady Angeline, I do not think it is going to be as much of a challenge as I expected to have you accepted by society.'

Angeline understood that the comment was supposed to be a compliment, but it did not feel like it.

Lady Vivian had the same blue eyes and patrician features as her son. Sharp bones rode high above her cheeks, yet her frame was long and lean, like William's. She looked every inch the aristocratic matriarch.

'Come,' continued Lady Vivian, 'let's go inside. It has started to rain again. Will there be no end to this devilish weather?'

As they moved into the house, William slapped a servant hard on the back. 'Charlie, my cockney comrade, how the devil are you?'

'Very well, me lord, thank yer very much,' came the reply.

'And that charming wife of yours?'

'Oh we are expecting a little addition any time now,' Charlie replied proudly.

'Congratulations, old boy. I also hear you've been promoted to butler.'

'I 'ave indeed, me lord. Lord Hurstbourne came to 'is senses at long last!' Charlie winked at William, who laughed raucously, while Lord Hurstbourne raised his eyes to the ceiling.

Angeline was shocked by the familiarity. The butler had a strong accent, but it was one she had never heard before.

'Sirkett here was my sergeant major. He saved my life at Waterloo,' explained Lord Hurstbourne. 'As a consequence, I've never been able to get rid of him. So I have to keep promoting him out of harm's way.'

Everyone laughed as they walked through the marbled hallway into a room that took Angeline's breath away. It was the most splendid she had ever seen. The entire room was the colour of the golden sands at Blackrock Bay. Elegant tapestries lined the walls, with classical motifs woven into the centre like oil paintings. Intricate geometrical patterns on the ceiling, painted the same colour as the tapestries, were inlaid with classical circular paintings of the Roman gods at play. An exquisite carpet reflected the pattern on the ceiling, while golden-framed chairs and sofas blended into the background. The fireplace opposite the large windows drew Angeline in. She had never seen such a stylish but comfortable room in her life.

Sitting by the fire was a rather studious-looking young woman, wearing eyeglasses. She was introduced as Lady Annabel Hobart, a distant relation.

'Oh you were right, Nikolaus!' Lady Annabel exclaimed. 'She is a diamond of the first water. Lady Angeline, without doubt, you will be this season's incomparable.'

Angeline had no idea what Lady Annabel was talking about, but assumed by the way everyone was smiling and nodding that this was a good thing.

'Now,' said Lady Vivian, sitting beside Angeline, 'we do not have a lot of time to prepare you for your debut. A date has already been set for you to be presented to the Queen, at St James's Palace.'

Angeline was stunned, for in truth she had not thought much about what coming out into society entailed.

'We will be going up to London early. The season does not get into full swing until April, but the political families are usually there by March. Therefore,' continued Lady Vivian, 'we have arranged for the best modistes to visit us here over the next few days.'

William read Angeline's face. She was studying the way the other women in the room were dressed. He was inordinately proud of his female relatives for pretending not to notice how old-fashioned Angeline's styling was. For although her clothes were made from the finest silk, they were out of date, being very tight on the bodice with a full, hooped skirt.

Lord Hurstbourne looked at the black sash around Angeline's waist. 'Mama, how are we going to get around the fact that Lady Angeline is still officially in mourning? She should not be out in society.'

Lady Vivian waved her hand in the air as if she were literally batting away the problem. 'For goodness sake, Simon, there are significant exceptions to the rules for those firmly established within the *ton*. Let's not forget, I make up most of them.'

Again, everyone laughed, even the butler; all except Angeline. Tea was set out in front of them. 'But, it may be best to start with half-mourning: grey or lilac. Luckily, these colours will suit you perfectly.'

Angeline felt like she had been dealt a hammer blow. She had not considered for one moment the practicalities of a season in London. 'Lady Vivian, I'm afraid, I have not...' She looked at William and blushed scarlet before dropping her head down. 'I do not have the means to purchase a wardrobe,' she said quietly.

'My dear, there is no need to worry about a thing. William has been very generous. He has given instruction that there is to be no expense spared.'

'Oh,' was all Angeline could say in response, avoiding eye contact with William and wondering how he could afford it after the things he had told her about his brother. He must be using money from the Goldsborough Estate, she thought.

'After all, it will be a very wise economy on his part,' Lady Vivian continued. 'He needs to find you a husband this season and get you off his hands.' Lady Vivian threw her head back and laughed as she said it, but everyone else shuffled nervously.

'And all of us ladies are here to help you navigate your way around the fashion of the day,' Lady Annabel added, trying to cover up their embarrassment. 'It is imperative that you know the difference between a walking dress and a promenade dress.'

'And the difference between an evening dress and a ball gown,' said Lady Louisa, sounding thoroughly bored.

William gave his cousin a knowing look. 'Aunt Vivian, I think you are overwhelming Lady Angeline. She has had a very long journey and must be tired.'

His aunt looked horrified. 'Yes, yes, of course, William is right, you must rest before dinner. The servants will show you to your rooms immediately.'

It was the most opulent bedroom Angeline had ever seen. The aptly named red bedroom had walls covered with red silk. Matching curtains were ornately trimmed with large gold tassels. The dark oak four-poster bed was heavily draped with gold damask and a gold brocade settee had been placed at its foot, facing the fire.

Angeline lay on the bed, exhausted. Her senses had been bombarded from the moment she entered the house. She had never understood before how spartan life was in Northumberland, but she had a desperate urge to run back there as quickly as she could. It was not the welcome she had expected. This was a foreign world, one in which she felt she would never quite fit in. The people in this world were civil but not warm and she felt awkward and alone, like a problem child. Closing her eyes, her mind drifted and she dreamt of Blackrock Bay.

Dinner was a lavish affair and Angeline was almost over-whelmed by the vast array of food. Turtle soup, which she had never eaten before and decided she did not like because it tasted muddy, was followed by a series of fish entrées. A huge haunch of venison was the main course, accompanied by french beans, cauliflower and peas. Finally, the desserts consisted of an assortment of pastries, creams, jellies, nuts and fruit. A feast fit for a king, she thought. Or, at least, a few select members of the aristocracy.

The conversation over dinner was animated and erudite and Angeline realised with some embarrassment how dull life at Goldsborough must have been for William and Nikolaus.

Once the desserts had been laid out, Lady Vivian broached the delicate subject which everybody had been assiduously avoiding since William arrived.

'We are all so sorry about the tragedy at Lyndhurst. Those poor people. I went to the funerals, of course, to represent the family. I also made it clear that you would take care of the injured and the families of the bereaved. It is our duty, after all.'

'Thank you,' William replied. 'I knew I could rely on you, Aunt Vivian.'

'As you can imagine, the staff were all relieved when I told them. The Fitzalans have never been known for their sense of duty.'

'Do you have any idea how long it might take you to sort out the problems at the Manor?' Louisa asked.

'Not until I see the extent of the damage,' he replied, 'but I fear the worst. I'll be leaving first thing tomorrow. I'll write to inform you of the details as soon as I can.'

'Oh, you're leaving so soon.' Angeline said, finding it hard to hide her dismay as the familiar feeling of abandonment washed over her. 'Are you sure? It doesn't sound like this rain is going to let up any time soon.'

'You're in very safe hands.' He smiled gently, trying to reassure her. 'The next time we meet will be in London.'

'Ah, London!' Louisa exclaimed. 'Parliament awaits you, William. You and Simon shall be such a force for good,' she declared proudly, popping a small pastry into her mouth.

'Especially with you behind us, dearest, shaping policy in the background,' Lord Hurstbourne teased.

'Oh Simon, you said it yourself, with William as an ally, you'll be able to bring about the necessary changes so much faster.'

'I did indeed, dearest,' her husband replied indulgently.

'What kind of change is needed?' asked Angeline, genuinely curious.

'Lord Liverpool must gather around him open-minded men, like William and Simon, ready for economic reforms before there is widespread insurrection,' Louisa announced as if she was making a speech herself in Parliament.

Angeline had previously observed in Louisa a certain listlessness. She had seen it before in women who were about to give birth, but Louisa lit up with passionate intensity when she spoke about politics.

'As always, I agree with you wholeheartedly, Louisa,' William said. 'Poverty is a major recruiting agent for the radical cause.'

Angeline could not believe her ears. 'Are things as bad as that?' she asked, holding her hand around her neck. 'Could there be revolution, like in France?'

'I doubt it.' William sought to allay her fears. 'Revolution usually breaks out when governments lose control. British institutions are fundamentally sound, but there could be violence if we don't do something for the poor.'

'I would put a large wager on it,' Annabel cried, dabbing her mouth with a napkin, 'but you won't get any support from Castlereagh, you know. He's a terrible reactionary.'

'But isn't he...'

'My uncle? Yes, yes,' said Annabel, answering Angeline's question before she had even asked it, 'but it's still true.'

Angeline was shocked, not at women having such forthright views, but sharing them openly over the dinner table. Lady Vivian seemed to read her thoughts.

'I think we should take the time to explain to Angeline that within the family we have a frank exchange of views. It never does, however, for ladies to speak of such things in polite society.'

Angeline nodded curtly, indicating that she understood the rules.

'But why are people so poor?' she pressed.

'A very good question, Angeline,' Louisa said approvingly. 'War costs money. Paid for by increased taxes on essentials like salt, sugar, tea and candles. People can't afford things, so there is no demand, and as a result unemployment continues to rise.'

'Exacerbated by thousands of men being discharged from the army,' William interjected forcefully. 'So labour floods the market at a time when production is contracting.'

'It's a recipe for disaster, I fear,' chipped in Annabel.

'The poverty and misery is incalculable,' sighed Louisa.

Angeline stared at the food laid out on the table and wondered at the grotesque incongruity between words and action. At least they ate frugally at Goldsborough Castle.

Lord Hurstbourne lent over and touched his wife's hand. 'Now, now, Louisa. Don't go upsetting yourself. It's not good for the baby, you know.'

She inhaled deeply, heeding her husband's warning. 'You are quite right, my sweet.'

'I must say, I didn't expect you all to be so... well, liberal,' Angeline said. The others glanced at each other.

'Oh, don't be fooled,' quipped the earl, as he piled trifle onto his plate, 'there is self-interest at play here, too. The aristocracy must change with the times if we are to survive.'

His honesty satisfied Angeline. 'So, what is to be done?'

Annabel clapped her hands with delight. 'Oh Angeline, I cannot tell you how pleased I am that you are interested in politics.'

'I can't say that I am, in truth, but I am interested in the welfare of the people. There is terrible poverty back home. We do what we can on the estate, but it never seems to be enough.' From the corner of her eye, she caught an approving smile from William.

'There must be widespread reforms,' he answered.

'Such as?'

'The repeal of the Corn Laws, for a start, but I'm also determined to do something about import duties.'

'Really?' said Angeline, perturbed.

'Absolutely. They've been reduced to a mockery by the widespread smuggling that goes on. The regulations are impossible to enforce, so they're simply evaded.'

'And what do you intend to do about it?' Angeline asked him.

'I'm going to recommend a drastic reduction in duties and the formation of a coastguard. This will reduce smuggling, put money into the government's coffers and create jobs.'

'William, that is quite brilliant!' Louisa declared, looking at him in awe. Angeline detected that there was something between Louisa and William, a platonic meeting of intellects, and she felt a pang of what she had to admit was jealousy.

Instinctively, she turned to Nikolaus, who had remained silent throughout the discussion, mainly because he was ravenously eating his way through the various desserts laid out before him.

'And what of Hungary?' Angeline asked. 'Are there to be reforms there, too?'

'Goodness me, no!' he laughed. 'I'm pleased to say that in Hungary, feudalism is alive and well in all its barbaric splendour.'

Lady Vivian gently shook her head at him. 'Talking about feudalism,' she said, 'I hear you've been recalled by the family.'

Nikolaus nodded wearily.

'So, I assume you will be leaving for London as soon as possible?'

'You assume wrongly, Lady Vivian. I intend to linger in Hampshire for as long as I can and the terrible weather is a perfect excuse.'

'Do you have any idea what they want with you?' asked Annabel.

'Tragically, I do,' Nikolaus replied, placing a single nut in his mouth with great affectation.

Annabel scanned the room, frustration shining in her eyes. 'Well, do tell.'

Nikolaus shuffled in his seat. 'I'm afraid the time has come to return home and marry. I must wed the cousin to whom I have been betrothed since the age of seven.'

A rustle of surprise echoed around the table.

'Who is this cousin? Anyone we know?' asked Annabel.

'Luckily for you, no, you don't know her. Her name is Princess Darvulia.'

'Poor Nikolaus,' Annabel teased, trying not to laugh. 'Why lucky for us? Is she an ugly old witch?'

Angeline felt William's eyes fall on her when the word 'witch' was used.

'On the contrary,' replied Nikolaus, 'she is a rare beauty. But she is a harpy: a cold, calculating, shrieking woman.'

'Oh, she can't be that bad,' declared Lady Vivian.

'Trust me, she's worse,' he said mournfully.

'But what if you refuse to marry her?' asked Annabel, trying to be helpful.

'I'm afraid my inheritance depends upon it. I will be cut off without a penny if I don't.' Silence filled the room.

'Bad luck, old chap,' was the only commiseration Lord Hurstbourne could offer. William remained silent, for he had always known that one day this time would come for his friend.

Angeline bit her bottom lip and worried for Nikolaus. He had been doing so well since he had been taking her medicine and stopped using opium, but she could see him sliding back into melancholia right before her eyes.

'Oh, let's talk about something else,' Annabel cried, trying to change the mood. 'Nikolaus, did you ever tell Lady Angeline about how you and William met?'

'No, I'm afraid the opportunity never arose.'

'Oh Nikolaus, you must relay the story to her now. It's so funny.'

'Perhaps another time.'

'No, really, I'd like to hear it,' Angeline said, exchanging glances with Annabel as they both tried to cajole Nikolaus out of his sadness.

He looked at William, who said, 'Go ahead – why don't you? Amuse the ladies with the tale.'

Nikolaus cleared his throat. 'We met behind enemy lines, during the Peninsular War. We were both in the service of our royal masters. William was working for King George and I for the Emperor of Austria.'

Angeline blinked hard. She had not expected to hear that.

'William had entered the French general's house, disguised as a Portuguese servant. He intended to steal their battle plans, which were locked in the general's bedroom.'

'How did you manage that without being discovered?' Angeline asked, astonished.

Before William could reply, Lady Louisa whispered, 'He is a master of disguise and speaks many languages fluently.'

'Yes.' Lord Hurstbourne laughed. 'William here could pass for a peasant in almost any country in the world!'

Angeline recalled the disdain and uncertainty of the messenger that evening at Goldsborough, unwilling to deliver the letter to a woodcutter. William glanced at her, mildly embarrassed.

'Anyway,' continued Nikolaus. 'I had exactly the same intention. However, William and I always differed in our methods. You see, just as William was about to escape with said plans out of the window, I tumbled into the bedroom with the general's wife.'

Angeline gasped, an unwelcome blush rushing up her neck.

'Perhaps we shouldn't continue,' Lord Hurstbourne said, responding to Angeline's reaction.

'No, no, please go on. I'm fascinated. After all, this is part of my education.'

Annabel roared with laughter. 'Well said!'

Nikolaus continued. 'So, unbeknownst to me, poor William had to hide behind the curtain for an eternity, whilst I *persuaded* the general's wife to part with the plans.'

'Listening to sounds only animals make,' William interjected.

All the women howled with laughter, all except Angeline, whose eyes were wide with anticipation.

'Cutting a long, long story short,' Nikolaus said, 'the cuck-olded general, rather than surprise us with stealth, was so mad at what he suspected was going on that he could be heard shouting and swearing all the way up the stairs. By the time he burst into the bedroom, sword in hand, I was already smartly climbing out of the window.'

'But you…'

'Yes, I'm afraid, Lady Angeline, that I was stark naked.'

Angeline clasped both hands over her mouth, but could not stop a titter of laughter escaping.

'It was then, as I was hanging from the window sill, that I caught sight of William for the first time, standing behind the curtains, silently laughing at me with his eyes.'

'What happened next?' Angeline asked, enthralled.

Nikolaus lent forward. 'Luckily, the general's wife, very skilfully, kept her husband occupied long enough for both of us to make our escape. I suspected that this was not the first time she had been caught in such circumstances.'

Angeline giggled uncontrollably.

'I jumped from the window, quickly followed by William, and there I was, running through the village, in broad daylight, as naked as the day I was born.'

For the first time that evening, William's face cracked and he burst out laughing at the memory.

'We bonded instantly,' said William.

'No, not instantly,' Nikolaus rebuked him, 'but definitely after you liberated some clothing for me to wear.'

William nodded. 'We collaborated many times during that campaign.'

'Their partnership became famous, even reaching the ears of the King and the Emperor,' Lady Vivian said with pride and pleasure. 'I'm told they both loved to hear stories of this very unholy alliance.'

Angeline was seeing both men in a completely new light and noticed with relief that regaling the story had restored

Nikolaus' spirits, but she began to wonder when the ladies would retire, as she could feel that her cheeks were a little too flushed. She was just thinking about excusing herself when Sirkett entered the room.

'Me lords, ladies. I'm afraid I 'ave terrible news. The river is so swollen with all this rain that it's burst its banks. We must try to evacuate the families who live near, sir. I've been told some of the dwellings 'ave already been washed away.'

'Are there any fatalities?' Lord Hurstbourne jumped up from his seat.

'Can't say at the moment, me lord.'

'Right. William, Nikolaus, come with me. We must see what we can do.'

All three men stood to attention, military training kicking in immediately, and in an instant they had disappeared.

Louisa followed suit. Standing tall and taking command, she calmly declared, 'Ladies, we must find all the fresh linen and spare clothing that we can. I will tell Cook to prepare food. Many people will need our help tonight.'

CHAPTER 17

It was well after midnight when the women collapsed, bone weary, onto the sofas, waiting for news. The servants were packing the food and clothing into a cart to take to the church, where the destitute would congregate.

'Why don't you go to bed now, Angeline?' Lady Vivian said. 'You must be exhausted and we have done everything we can for tonight.'

'No, really, I should go to the church. I have knowledge of medicine and I may be able to help.'

'Oh don't be silly, girl! It will be no place for you on a night like this,' Lady Vivian proclaimed. Angeline was taken aback. Lady Vivian had a knack of undermining her self-confidence.

Louisa stood and began to pace up and down in front of the fire. 'Is the rain stopping?' she asked anxiously.

'I cannot hear any sign of it. Why?' asked Lady Vivian, concerned.

'Because I think this baby is coming.'

'Oh my goodness! I'll send Sirkett for the doctor at once!' Lady Vivian cried as she ran to the door.

'No, no, you must not.' Louisa called her back. 'He will be needed elsewhere tonight. No, we will have to manage somehow.'

But Angeline could see the fear in her eyes. 'I have helped my mother deliver many babies,' she said soothingly. 'I'm sure I can help you.'

'You can't be serious!' shouted Lady Vivian. 'This baby will be the next Earl of Hurstbourne if it's a boy. We must have a proper doctor.'

'Lady Vivian, let her help me if she can. We have no other option,' gasped Louisa, hanging onto the fire mantel. 'This baby won't wait a moment longer.'

When the new day finally dawned, William, Simon and Nikolaus wandered into the hallway, filthy and shattered but content. They had worked like Trojans throughout the night and although many houses lay in ruins, not a life had been lost.

Angeline walked down the stairs to meet them, sleeves rolled up, wiping her hands with a towel. Three pairs of eyes fell onto the bloodstains that were clearly visible on her pale silk dress. There was a moment's hesitation as the men tried to make sense of the scene, then she saw fear and panic in all of them. William's face had drained of colour.

'Good God, what has happened?' shouted Lord Hurstbourne, rushing forward. Angeline held up her hand to stop him.

'You have a son, my lord, a beautiful, healthy boy. I have delivered him,' Angeline announced, feeling rather pleased with herself.

Panic turned into astonishment. Lord Hurstbourne continued to stare at the blood as he ran up the stairs to meet her.

'And Louisa?'

Angeline realised then that she was so tired, she had been unnecessarily solemn with the news. So she smiled brightly.

'Mother and baby are both doing well,' she said. 'Lady Vivian and Annabel are with them now.'

'Oh, thank God!' he cried. He took Angeline's hand and kissed it fervently before dashing past her up the stairs.

'Lady Angeline, you are truly magnificent,' Nikolaus said, bowing respectfully. 'Champagne, Sirkett!' he hollered as he strolled into the library. 'A celebration is due.'

Angeline walked over to face William.

'Have you ever delivered a baby before?' he asked, sounding incredulous.

'I have assisted on a number of occasions. Luckily, this was an easy one. No complications.'

William pulled her towards him and kissed her lightly on the forehead.

'I can't thank you enough, Angeline. You really are a clever girl.'

There was a hint of unintended condescension in the voice, Angeline noted, but she mainly heard relief. Another pang of jealousy speared her heart.

'You care for Lady Louisa very much, don't you?' she questioned.

'Let's just say she reminds me of someone I used to know.'

Who could that be, Angeline wondered. A woman who occupied a special place with William. The thought made her body tense, but she kept her features rigidly under control. 'Oh, I see,' was all she could bring herself to say, before turning and walking away from him.

By the time she arose from much-needed slumber, he had left, without saying goodbye. Gone, with Nikolaus, to try to get to his beloved Lyndhurst, despite the flooding. A single tear of hurt and anger fell down her cheek as solitude enveloped her. Her feelings for William were creeping up on her like a predator in the dark. They frightened her and thrilled her at the same time. She seemed to know instinctively when he was near, so the pain of separation was almost too much to bear. But he was a man who took his role as her protector very seriously. A man whose sense of honour would never allow him to cross the line, even if he wanted to, and she thought that perhaps he had wanted to, once. That night on the stairs at Goldsborough, by the arched window. Something had made him act strangely, but she resigned herself to the fact that she would never ever know if he did feel something for her, and that knowledge was breaking her heart.

The following days that came and went were full to the brim with activity. The new baby, Thomas Simon William, Viscount Paulton, was a bustling bundle of joy who had the whole household running around after him without his even knowing it. Louisa and Lady Vivian were so grateful to Angeline for his safe delivery, they stopped treating her like a problem that had landed on their doorstep uninvited. It was almost as if she had earned her place in the family. And when the waters subsided, the modistes came from London.

'Wide petticoats have been abandoned for flimsier fabrics,' declared Lady Vivian as she sat amongst muslins, silks and crepe de chine. 'A lady's fashion was once determined by the circumference of her hoop, but now it is the length of her train.'

'But how do you dance with it?' asked Angeline.

'It has a small loop, *voila*, to raise the train whilst dancing.' Madame Dupré demonstrated as she finished Angeline's fitting.

Lady Vivian picked up a set of elbow length white gloves with buckles at the top. 'So much can be determined by a person's behaviour at a ball,' she commented as she passed them to Angeline. 'I can't tell you the trouble Annabel caused us when she was younger.'

Angeline's eyes widened with curiosity.

Lady Vivian chuckled. 'Well, she is rather headstrong. The poor girl was left such a vast fortune, being the only child of parents who died mysteriously in a coaching accident, that every cad and wastrel in the country was wanting to marry her. She was overwhelmed at every ball she went to, no matter how badly she behaved. In fact, George, William's brother, pursued her relentlessly. In the end, she was so convinced that nobody wanted to marry her for herself, she vowed never to marry anyone. I remember when she announced it, very loudly, one evening at Lady Castlereagh's ball. Alas, she has been a confirmed spinster ever since.'

'I rather admire her for being so single-minded,' Angeline said as Madame Dupré helped her to keep the gloves straight by fixing the buckles.

'I suppose so,' Lady Vivian replied wistfully. 'Louisa was a bit of a handful, too, but I'm sure we won't have the same problem with you, Angeline. Do you dance?'

'Indeed I do; the cotillion and the quadrille, but I enjoy the minuet the best.'

'Ah, that is not danced so often in London these days. What about the waltz?'

'No, I've never learnt to waltz. It's still considered risqué in Northumberland.'

'Oh, no matter. We can organise a dancing master for you. Yes, that would be best. Girls from the North usually dance far too energetically for London society. You have to learn to be demure.'

Madame Dupré stood back to admire her work. 'It is most important to dress well and to dance well,' she announced. 'Together, they display fine form, elegance and grace. You must display well, to marry well.'

'Is that so?' Angeline replied, smarting from Lady Vivian's cutting comments, even though she knew they were hurled at everybody. She slipped on a pair of satin slippers, decorated with delicate shoe roses.

'Indeed it is, Lady Angeline. You must not allow your head to be turned by a crimson coat,' chided Madame Dupré as she turned towards the window and ogled Nikolaus as he rode out. 'Good looks, tight trousers and a military bearing can derange the female mind,' she drooled. It took some moments for Madame Dupré to snap out of her enthralment. 'No, Lady Angeline, not an army officer for you,' she continued. 'You must hold out for an aristocrat.'

'Even royalty,' said Lady Vivian, eyes twinkling.

'Oh, I don't think so,' Angeline replied apologetically. 'I don't have the breeding.'

'My dear, a great deal is allowed to the girl of exquisite beauty with a small fortune. A younger royal son would be entirely possible.'

'Lady Vivian, I do not possess a fortune. Not even a small one.'

'Angeline, William has bestowed on you a dowry of £10,000. Which is extremely generous of him, considering how much it will cost him to restore Lyndhurst Manor. '

Angeline gasped and collapsed into a nearby chair. 'But why would he do such a thing?'

'So you can make the best match possible, of course. My dear, we all want the very best for you. This dowry will open doors that would otherwise be firmly shut.'

Angeline trembled with shock and outrage. How could he? How dare he, after he promised her that he would not interfere! Assuring her she could make her own choice. She clung onto the arm of the chair, trying to maintain her composure.

Both the other women misread her reaction as a sign of over-whelming gratitude.

'Oh, Angeline,' said Lady Vivian happily, 'we are going to find you the most perfect husband.'

CHAPTER 18

A few days before they were due to set off for London, Lady Vivian took Angeline for a carriage drive in order to show her some of the surrounding countryside.

Eventually Lady Vivian said, 'There is something specific I want you to see, but you must promise me that this will be our little secret.' Intrigued, Angeline looked out of the carriage window as they passed through an abandoned gatehouse.

The land was banked, as high as a man, on either side of the path they were following, producing near vertical slopes. Huge, ancient yew trees, gnarled and twisted by the landscape, loomed over the carriage, making the way dark and eerie. Some of the trees had split trunks, others had branches that were so long and heavy they dragged along the ground and spiralled out like long witches' fingers. Yellow mud clung precariously to their exposed roots. The soil had been eroded by the elements over many years, making the trees unstable and dangerous.

As the path meandered around a bend, an old house could be seen in the dip of a shallow valley. Lady Vivian told the driver to stop the carriage on a ridge so they could view the house from a distance.

'This is Lyndhurst Manor,' declared Lady Vivian as they alighted.

It was a modest building by the standards of the day, without any of the usual modish extensions. Constructed from red brick with stone dressings, it was symmetrical and well proportioned with three storeys and a shallow front piece, dominated by two projecting wings, one of which had collapsed completely, exposing jagged sections of the wood-panelled rooms that had once existed.

'The family were courtiers to the Stuarts and the house is exactly the same as when it was built in 1610. To tell you the truth, I'm surprised it has taken so long for it to collapse.' Lady Vivian sighed.

Angeline was speechless. It was in a worse state of repair than her beloved Goldsborough Castle. 'It must have been dangerous to live here for a very long time,' she finally managed to say, staring at the crumbling arched cloisters that flanked the entrance.

'I lived here when I was a child. It was a pretty place then, but when my brother, William's father, became duke, he began to stay away for long periods of time, and George, of course, always preferred London.' Lady Vivian gently shook her head. 'His mother, Katherine, absolutely idolised George, you see, to the point where she ruined him. I'm afraid Katherine has a great deal to answer for.'

Angeline watched a group of men clearing away the rubble, brick by brick, and wondered if William was amongst them, but they were too far away to see.

Lady Vivian continued, 'There is a wild streak that runs through the Fitzalans. The men have always had to marry for money because it falls through their fingers like water. My brother made a dynastic match. What he had not counted on was Katherine falling desperately in love with him.'

Angeline felt her heartache. Fitzalan men were easy to love, it would seem.

'She was a soppy little thing. Every time she saw my brother, she would say things like, *Oh, look how handsome he is. Look how he rides, there is none finer in all the county. Oh, don't you think he dances like an angel?*' Lady Vivian inhaled deeply. 'It wasn't supposed to happen like that, not in those days. I'm afraid William's father was a man of his time. Katherine embarrassed him so acutely that he just kept away. And the longer he stayed away, the more Katherine transferred her affections onto George. So when my brother died, in a hunting accident...'

'Despite being the best rider in the county,' Angeline said arching her brows.

'Exactly,' Lady Vivian replied. 'George became the 7th Duke of Lyndhurst but he already had such a terrible reputation for drinking and gambling that no family with any money would let their daughters anywhere near him.' Lady Vivian surveyed the scene below. 'I hate to say it, but William was neglected by his mother, and far better off for it.'

'William told me that his brother died in an accident.'

'He told you that!' said Lady Vivian.

'Well, yes.'

'Did he tell you anything else?' she asked.

'That George was a bankrupt and the Goldsborough Estate has saved the family from ruin.'

Lady Vivian shook her head in disbelief. 'Well, you are very privileged indeed to be told such private details. William usually keeps things very close to his chest.' Lady Vivian sighed. 'It really was the most dreadful state of affairs. I'm afraid George was the worst of them; a very devil. It might sound awful, but the whole of society was relieved when he died. He had been a scourge to so many families, not only his own.

Leading young men astray. Ruining their sisters. His death was a blessing.'

Angeline caught her breath and took stock, realising how lucky she had been that it was William who had inherited Goldsborough and not George. She shuddered at the thought of what might have been.

She scanned the old-fashioned garden, which although overgrown, still displayed its severely geometrical pattern, suspecting that even Goldsborough money would not be enough to stem the Lyndhurst decay.

'So, I suppose William will have to marry for money, too.'

'Almost certainly.' Lady Vivian gave Angeline a meaningful look, which she read as a warning. 'I know that the Fitzalans have turned your world upside down, but don't judge us too harshly, my dear. The ones who are still alive want to do right by you.' Lady Vivian looked down into the valley for the last time. 'William is better than the usual run. I know he can be a little high in the instep sometimes, but his heart and his head are in the right place. He will find you a good match.' They began walking back to the coach. 'He was England's most proficient spy, you know. Never to be mentioned in polite society, of course, as it is not considered an honourable activity. But they all know he did as much as Wellington to save England from that dreadful little Frenchman.'

Just before they were about to get back into the coach, Angeline said, 'By the way, what type of accident did George have?'

'Oh I told you, the Fitzalan's have a wild streak, always getting into danger,' Lady Vivian said dismissively. 'Now, come along, let's get inside before the weather turns again.'

By the time they arrived back at Hurstbourne House, a letter was waiting for Angeline, but her conversation with Lady

Vivian was playing on her mind. *'I suppose William will have to marry for money.'*

'Almost certainly.'

Angeline could not forget the warning look from Lady Vivian that went with those words and she was filled with despair.

She opened the letter and read.

Goldsborough Castle

Dear Lady Angeline,

Thank you for your letter. I am glad all is well with you.

I am writing to assure you that all is as it should be at Goldsborough Castle. Life has returned to normal as there have been no sightings of the beast, nor has any untoward event taken place. Of course, we remain vigilant.

The only unfortunate piece of news is that Viscount Elewald is taking every opportunity to insinuate that the attacks began when the Earl of Lyndhurst arrived and miraculously, now that he has returned south, they have stopped. Nobody is paying much heed to him at the moment, but he is intent on stirring up trouble.

Eric, as always, is a rock, and at your suggestion I have kept him close to me! As I write, Eric is preparing a full report for the earl, but there is nothing that cannot be managed by him until the earl returns.

Enjoy your time in London. Remember, it is your birthright.

Fondest Wishes

Brigid

p.s.   Things are underway for Ostara. Do not concern yourself with this matter, for all will go well.

Angeline stared at her reflection in the dressing table mirror and wondered what had become of the confident, assured young woman she had once been.

She was relieved that all was well at Goldsborough, but she felt as if she was in exile. She wanted to flee back there as fast as she could. Back to the world she knew so well, where she felt undaunted and in her rightful place. Her land lifted her spirits and steadied her, but Goldsborough was no longer hers. It belonged to the Fitzalans now.

William had told her that George had nearly ruined the family. She knew that her estate was wealthy because she had helped her father with the accounts. All the money William had was Goldsborough money. He had provided her with a dowry, which meant he was selling her off with her own money. It had probably been part of his plan all along. For him to truly feel like the Master of Goldsborough, he needed her out of the way, married off to someone who, ideally, lived a long way from Northumberland.

To be duped so badly was hurtful, but to be duped by William was almost too much to bear. She doubled over with a crippling pain that was lodged in the pit of her stomach and cried.

Very quietly, a little voice started to whisper to her and gradually it became clearer. It was the goddess Coventina, telling her that this life was her birthright and she should claim what was hers. Angeline took a good long look at herself and set her jaw as she crushed the letter that had been dangling from her fingers. She was the daughter of a marquis, but she was also a Bernician. She was no timid milksop, haunting the ballrooms, desperate to find a husband. She would stay in London for the season and be introduced to the Queen. She would go to the balls and the theatre and to the pleasure gardens, but she would do it *all* on her own terms.

PART 3

LONDON

CHAPTER 19

There was nothing elegant about this ball. It was a seething mass of bodies. Young ladies, up from the country for the season, waited eagerly to be paraded for the marriage mart.

They had arrived in London just in time for Angeline's first outing. William stood straight-backed and stoic, while Nikolaus lent against a wall, arms and legs crossed with his usual lassitude. 'Look at this,' Nikolaus cried, 'a sophisticated cattle market! If the girls are pretty, they will be hounded by the rich and the ugly. If they are rich they will be hounded by the poor and the beautiful.'

William raised an eyebrow. 'Choice, from the day we are born, is circumscribed.'

'How very true,' Nikolaus remarked coolly.

William looked over to see his aunt gossiping with the chaperones at the edge of the ballroom.

'She was a triumph,' Lady Vivian declared at the top of her voice. 'The Queen spoke to her. Her Majesty actually spoke to Lady Angeline.' Beyond, William caught sight of Annabel in a side room, playing cards, as usual. He watched and he waited. Lady Angeline's arrival was being anticipated by everyone.

They all knew that the Queen had spoken to her at her debut and she was already being hailed the season's incomparable, just as Annabel had predicted. So when Angeline finally arrived, with the Earl and Countess of Hurstbourne, the sea of bodies parted.

As he laid eyes on her, his heart stopped for a moment. She looked like a Grecian goddess, dressed in the current fashionable high-waisted gown in a lilac hue. Her hair, pulled back into a chignon, fell into soft curls that framed her face.

The dress had been cut away to reveal almost naked shoulders and William could not take his eyes off them. Her skin shimmered like pearl. He felt a familiar stirring in his loins and a roaring in his head as those glistening collarbones became imprinted on his brain. He tried to tear his gaze away, but could not resist the perverse pleasure of torturing himself with her beauty. There was cruel suspense in the air as an overwhelming desire for possession took hold of him.

The moment was broken by Lady Vivian gliding over to Angeline. 'Oh, my dear, you look ravishing. You will dance with William first, as he is your guardian. It will give you the ultimate opportunity for display.' By the time Angeline turned to him and flashed him a smile, he had managed to compose himself. What the devil had he been thinking?

'You look charming, Angeline,' he said stiffly. 'Come, let's get this over and done with,' he said and he escorted her to the dance floor.

'Do you not like to dance, my lord?' Angeline enquired.

'Like many things in this life, it is a necessary evil. But if I have to, I am delighted it is with you,' he said benignly, desperately trying not to ruin her enjoyment of the occasion.

As he expected, she danced divinely, with lightness and ease. All eyes were on her. Most young ladies would have buckled under the scrutiny, but she smiled all the while and acquitted herself beautifully. She displayed great poise in the excited atmosphere. Something William had come to expect from her.

'She is being looked at with admiration and interest,' Lady Vivian whispered to him as Lord Hurstbourne led Angeline away for the next dance.

'No she isn't, Aunt,' William protested. 'She is being leered at.' His aunt tutted at him before turning away to speak with the Duke of Lostwithiel.

'Oh she is a diamond of the first water, adorable, with a touch of naïveté and fire that intrigues. She offers promise and challenge, without even realising it.'

William and Nikolaus stared at each other as they overheard Lady Vivian talking to the duke.

'My aunt is in a class of her own when it comes to marriage brokering,' William admitted.

'So you are really going to put Angeline through this ordeal then?' Nikolaus asked in disbelief. 'Parade her in front of this circus?'

'I have no choice if she is to marry well. You know that.' He looked over at Angeline dancing. As he continued to watch, guilt welled up inside him, flooding his reservoir of emotions. 'Look how coltish she is,' William finally said, sounding full of remorse. 'She doesn't even know how to flirt.' He shook his head in horror. 'Good God, Nikolaus, what have I done? She isn't man-ready.'

'Why so righteous all of a sudden?' Nikolaus barked. 'Look around you, William. They are all innocents, shackled to society's rules. Every girl here will be bartered for.'

William took a deep breath. 'At least I have promised her she can choose her own husband. I will not force her into a marriage she does not want.'

'How very noble of you,' Nikolaus said as he walked away.

Lady Vivian was so excited she could hardly wait to blurt out the news as soon as Angeline found her way back.

'Oh, my dear! The Duke of Lostwithiel wishes to be introduced to you. This is marvellous! He is the most eligible bachelor in the country.'

'Really?' Angeline said. 'Tell me, where is Lostwithiel?'

'Why, it's in Cornwall,' declared Lady Vivian.

'Ah, Cornwall, how very convenient.'

CHAPTER 20

Nikolaus left William and walked straight into the diminutive figure of Princess Eszterházy.

'So, Nikolaus, you have finally made it to London then. What kept you?'

'Aunt Maria, how wonderful to see you.' Nikolaus glanced over his shoulder, hoping to be saved by someone. 'I did try to get here sooner, but you know how bad the weather has been.'

'Your uncle is not pleased with you.'

'My uncle is never pleased with me,' he replied. 'He's not here, is he?' Nikolaus asked, suddenly alarmed.

'Luckily for you, no. He is off clipping cigars and offending the French, or whatever it is ambassadors do. You know why we have recalled you, of course?'

'I do,' he said forlornly. 'Aunt Maria, I beseech you, is there nothing to be done?'

'Oh Nikolaus.' She stroked his cheek. 'You know you're my favourite, probably because we are so close in age. But you also know what must be. We are the largest landowners in the Habsburg Empire. Our income exceeds that of the Emperor. And how have we achieved this?'

'By keeping it in the family.'

'*Exactement*,' she replied. 'I need not remind you that we own four magnificent palaces, twelve castles...'

'Forty towns and one hundred and thirty villages,' Nikolaus parroted, 'which gives us unlimited power over our vassals to imprison, scourge and slay at our pleasure.'

Princess Eszterházy tapped his arm vigorously with her fan. 'Come now, Nikolaus, this is the nineteenth century. We don't go in for that sort of thing anymore.' Her eyes drifted away. 'Although Uncle Laszlo can still be a bit of a tyrant.' It took her a moment to snap back and focus on the issue at hand. 'Now, listen to me. You will marry cousin Darvulia. We cannot wait any longer. She isn't getting any younger and she needs to start producing children.'

Nikolaus' head drooped.

'I promise you, things won't be half as bad as you imagine. Look at us. Your uncle and I are very happy together.'

'But Aunt, that is because you are a kind and gentle woman,' Nikolaus cried.

'So kind, in fact, I have persuaded your uncle that you do not have to return home until the end of the season.'

Nikolaus bowed low. 'Please tell my uncle that his generosity overwhelms me.'

'Hmm, use your freedom wisely,' she said loudly over her shoulder as she walked away. 'Just make sure you are back home by the end of June. Without fail.'

Nikolaus wandered into the supper room alone. He found himself walking over to Annabel, who was tucking into poached salmon and prawns. She motioned for him to sit.

'What's the matter with you? Are you having a fit of the blue devils again?' she enquired.

'I will never be free of them,' he said, 'even when I descend into madness. They are my curse.'

Annabel winced at the melodrama. 'I suppose you're talking about that family of yours.'

'Who else?'

'Pass me the lobster, will you?' Annabel said. 'So, they're going to make you marry cousin Devil... What is her name again?'

'Darvulia,' he answered. 'And yes, they are. They are like a family of vampires, sucking the lifeblood out of me. They will not be happy until they have driven me into the bowels of hell.'

Annabel rolled her eyes. 'There is nothing wrong with you and your family that a good dose of out-breeding wouldn't cure. For people who are such experts on horseflesh, I am amazed they can't see that people are just like horses. You need to breed for spirit and intelligence.' She took a gulp of Madeira. 'All that inbreeding weakens the blood lines.' She began poking him with her fork. 'Develops a poor constitution and an inclination towards debauchery.'

'But my uncle is very set in his ways. He will never listen to such an argument. The purity of our noble line is paramount.'

'Is it true that the ambassador is the richest man in the world not seated on a throne?' Annabel asked.

'I believe so.' Nikolaus yawned. 'I remember once, Lord Leicester showing my uncle his two thousand sheep and asking if he had ever seen such a magnificent sight. My uncle replied that he had more shepherds than Lord Leicester had sheep.'

'How vulgar,' said Annabel, digging into the lobster. She watched Nikolaus' eyes follow one of his paramours across the room and tried to distract him. 'So explain to me how these felicitous family marriages work then.'

'Through various legal instruments and foundations, land and property are owned by the whole family, but governed by the head of the family.' Nikolaus picked at the tablecloth. 'This allows us to maintain all the palaces and castles. Family members are given substantial allowances in return for total obedience.'

'And this allowance will be cut off if you don't marry the bewitching Devilia?'

Nikolaus nodded. 'Darvulia. Will you stop making me say her name.'

'And without this allowance?'

'I am penniless.'

Annabel sighed deeply. 'Then, I'm afraid, Nikolaus, it really does look as if you have no choice.' She patted his arm sympathetically. As she pulled back, her elbow brushed against the glass of Madeira, making it tip over onto her plate, splashing her face with bits of lobster. Nikolaus laughed out loud at her mishap.

'I have always admired women who eat heartily and with real pleasure,' he said.

'Oh, stop laughing at me and clean my eyeglasses,' she said crossly, as she removed them to dab her face dry.

Wiping them with his handkerchief, he realised he had never seen her without eyeglasses before. 'You know, Annabel, you are passably pretty without these wretched things.' He looked through them to make sure they were clean, then he lowered them, before raising them again to take a second look through the lenses.

'What game are you playing, Annabel?' he asked.

'I have no idea what you mean,' she replied indignantly, tugging the glasses away from him.

'I think you do. There is plain glass in those things,' he said. 'You don't need to wear them at all.'

'You know perfectly well why I wear them,' she spat. 'They keep the fortune hunters away. Now, if you will excuse me, I have a card game to attend.'

PART 4

OSTARA

CHAPTER 21

'Oh do come along, my dears. We will be late for the Buckleys' musical soirée,' scolded Lady Vivian as she hurried Angeline and Annabel out of the front door of the Hurstbourne town house in Grosvenor Square.

It was a splendid spring evening, one that anticipated a beautiful summer, which was a great relief after the miserable winter that had just passed. Angeline was stunned at how London had managed to seduce her. She watched a juggler performing on a street corner as she drove past. He made her smile. She hated to admit it, but she was enjoying London more than she could ever have imagined. The city made her feel young and giddy. She had been to a number of balls already, even though it was still early in the season and everyone kept telling her that things did not really start to get underway until April. She could hardly imagine how exhausted she was going to be by the end of it all. No wonder most people headed off to the coast for the summer, in order to recuperate!

She had been to the theatre for the first time and had even seen a balloon ascension in the park, but Vauxhall Gardens were her favourite, with its many thousands of lamps hanging in festoons from the trees. All in all, London was the perfect tonic for an aching heart.

Angeline reflected for a moment as it was a very special evening. Tonight was Ostara, the spring equinox, and she felt a surge of guilt as she remembered Nan; she did not think about her enough, especially since she had been in London. Brigid would have to perform the Ostara ritual tonight alone. Anxiety welled up inside Angeline as she thought about the dangers, but she knew that Eric would not leave Brigid's side. There was no better man to keep her safe.

Angeline walked into the music room and curtsied to the Duke of Lostwithithiel, who noted her arrival immediately, but she was looking for William, who was not there.

'And where is that delightful husband of yours?' a lady asked Louisa. Angeline recognised the woman as someone who William had been dancing with frequently, despite his supposed dislike of the art form.

'Parliament is still sitting. He will be along later. With Lord Lyndhurst, I expect,' Louisa replied.

'I am so very impressed with their dedication,' the lady continued. 'Very few lords of the realm take their responsibilities so seriously. You must feel terribly neglected.'

Angeline watched Louisa bristle. 'Not at all, I approve wholeheartedly of my husband's vocation.'

The lady raised her eyebrows. 'Perhaps, but I would not tolerate a husband of mine being away from me for so long.'

'Who is that woman?' Angeline asked quietly as she watched the lady move on to another circle of people.

'Lady Caroline Shepherd, a very wealthy widow of impeccable lineage, who all too often gives the impression of being far above her company,' Louisa replied. 'I've always thought of her as a great intrigante. Not someone I choose to spend time with.'

'Angeline, Angeline! There is someone I want you to meet,' Lady Vivian called over. 'I would like to introduce you to Dr Ponsonby Tottenham, an old friend of the family.'

The corpulent doctor managed to get to his feet. 'Delighted to make your acquaintance, Lady Angeline. I knew your grandfather, the old marquis'

Angeline could tell that Ponsonby Tottenham was a great age because he still powdered his hair, just as her grandfather had done.

'He died when I was quite young. I did not think to find someone in London who knew him,' she replied enthusiastically.

'Yes, indeed. I knew him very well, in fact. He was a first-rate man, your grandfather. A cut above the rest. I'm sorry that I never met your father. He rarely came to London, but by all accounts he was cut from the same cloth.'

Angeline was gratified that there was still someone in London society who could vouch for her lineage.

'Oh, I would love to hear more about my grandfather, if you have the time?'

'I suspect he has all the time in the world, but you should ask *me*, Lady Angeline. I have lots of stories about those ancestors of yours.'

A cold chill crawled up Angeline's backbone as she registered the mellifluous voice behind her. Apprehensively she turned to see Viscount Elewald start to salivate as soon as his eyes rested on her décolletage.

'I don't think I would be interested in anything you have to say, my lord,' Angeline replied, holding her ground, despite the overwhelming urge to back away.

'Come now, Lady Angeline, that is no way to greet a neighbour.' Elewald was standing so close his saliva sprayed over her face. 'You need to be taught some manners, my girl,' he said, ogling her bosom as he wiped away some dribbling fluid from his chin.

Angeline felt nausea rise as she smelt his putrid breath and had to cover her nose with her handkerchief. She looked around for support, but everyone she knew had melted into the crowd. Then she felt Dr Tottenham tug at her arm, forcing her to stand closer beside him.

'I can tell her everything she needs to know, Elewald. I think my version of events would be more impartial.'

Elewald sneered, extended a grey, scaly hand and tweaked one of her curls. 'Well then, I'll leave you under the protection of the very peculiar doctor for now, my girl. Until we meet again.' With that he bowed, finally managing to drag his eyes away from her flesh.

'I knew his father, too,' the doctor whispered. 'A treacherous family. Now you must be vigilant, Lady Angeline. Things could become very dangerous for you.'

Angeline, physically shaken by the encounter, stared at him aghast. 'Really? How?'

Ponsonby Tottenham looked flabbergasted, as if she should have instantly known what he meant. He pointed to her dress. 'I blame all this light fabric and uncovered flesh for the rise of consumption, you know. You must be very careful indeed,' he said with utmost certainty.

'Well, fancy that!' Angeline replied, her comprehension strained.

'I see you met the old doctor,' Annabel said as they took their seats. 'He's harmless enough, but losing his marbles.'

Angeline was crestfallen. Perhaps Ponsonby's views on her pedigree would not hold much water with the rest of society. She surreptitiously watched Elewald sit on the other side of the room and say something to Lady Caroline.

'I see Lord Elewald has found Lady Caroline,' Louisa said, sitting on the left side of Angeline. 'What a pair they make!' She leaned into Angeline slightly. 'William told us about your family feud with the Elewalds. Over a plot of land, I believe.'

'Something like that,' Angeline replied.

'And Nikolaus spoke about the dreadful death of your maid,' Annabel whispered, looking suitably horrified. 'How terrible for you.'

Angeline felt the pangs of loss and guilt once more as Louisa patted her hand.

'You poor child, what terrible tragedy you have had to endure. But have faith, William will put things right. I have no doubt about that.'

Angeline did not doubt either as she glanced over at Elewald again. Thank goodness William had not arrived yet, she thought. It would be terrible to have him and Elewald in such close proximity.

It seemed that Elewald had possibly come to the same conclusion because, by the time William arrived, during the interval, he was nowhere to be seen.

Angeline, feeling a little more composed as a result, took some refreshment with William. Although they were often at the same functions, they rarely spent time alone.

'So, what is on the musical menu this evening?' William asked, feigning interest.

'Mr Cipriani Potter is playing some of his own compositions.'

'And?'

'Very continental, I like them.'

William studied her, attuned to the inflection in her voice. 'You sound forlorn, Angeline. Why is that? I have heard you are enjoying London, just as I said you would.'

She swallowed hard. 'Elewald's in town.' She watched the pulse pound at his temple, the only outward sign of his absorbing the news.

'Well, I suppose as long as he is here, he's not causing trouble back in Northumberland. I prefer him where I can see him.'

'Have you heard from home?' Angeline asked, desperate for news.

'Yes. Mr Sweyne tells me all is well. No further abominable crimes, thank goodness, but no further clues either as to what killed Nan. It is a complete mystery. We've sent out hunting parties to every corner of the land. We can find nothing.'

Angeline's head dropped.

'I will not rest until I find whatever it was that killed her, Angeline. I promise you that. But Parliament keeps me here for the present.'

'I understand. How are you finding Parliament?' Angeline asked.

'Fascinating, truly fascinating. I'm steering my bill through the various stages at present.'

'Ah yes.' Angeline recalled the dinner conversation on her first night at Hurstbourne House. 'The formation of a coastguard, if I recollect.'

'Exactly.' He was delighted she had taken enough interest in his scheme to remember. 'And the reduction of import duties to put a stop to smuggling. We must destroy the evil gangs who prey on the poor. I'm convinced this will make a huge difference to the economy, Angeline. It will improve the lives of so many people.'

She smiled at him hesitantly.

'Ah, there you are, Lyndhurst,' Lady Caroline cried plaintively, cutting across Angeline. 'I insist that you sit next to me.'

'Of course, I would be delighted,' William replied, with the upmost courtesy. 'Have you met Lady Angeline, my ward?'

'Enchanted,' Lady Caroline said.

Angeline observed that while the mouth smiled warmly, Lady Caroline Shepherd's eyes gleamed like daggers in the night. Angeline returned the look with her own icicle stare.

Brigid flexed her toes so that she could feel the texture of the ground beneath her bare feet and took a few deep breaths, drawing in energy and allowing it to flow through her. She moved her toes once more: the dewy, prickly grass made her skin tingle. The arches of her feet had begun to ache with the cold.

Holding the sacred goblet in one hand and the knife in the other, she opened her arms to invite the elementals into the circle.

'Air, Fire, Water, Earth,
I ask you to take your place.'
The bonfire burned brighter momentarily in response.

As the dawn approached, daffodils, replacing the snow-drops from Imbolc, appeared from the shadows.

Moving clockwise, she pointed the knife at each of the twelve people with vividly painted faces who were holding hands in a circle around her.

'Woman, man, woman, man,
All within the circle round,
Bear witness.'

She chanted as she symbolically closed the circle. Then, standing over the bubbling water from the source of the Rivendor, Brigid, dressed in white, a slight flush mounting under her skin, thrust the knife into the cup.

A few seconds later, she poured the contents of the goblet into the source. Seeds cascading from it were pushed along by the flow of the water.

'Tender Goddess, Coventina, provider of plenty,
Bring forth the time of harmony

When light and dark are equal
When female and male are in balance to bear fruit.'

Then, Eric Sweyne emerged from the darkness, holding a female hare under one arm, and a male under the other. The beating of their hearts made their bodies move in and out in syncopated rhythm. Brigid touched the top of the animals' heads with the tip of the knife.

'Gentle Mother, make all things fecund
So that new life can enter the world,
Bringing renewal and rebirth.'

Eric Sweyne bent down and let his arms slacken. The hares, momentarily stunned by their possible freedom, suddenly broke away and made their escape through the daffodils.

Brigid looked up towards the sky.

'Weaver of fates, and bringer of dreams,
Clear away all that is outgrown,
Sweep away and purify
Until we meet again, at Beltane.
When the horned one returns. Blessed Be.'

Leaving the circle of twelve, Brigid and Eric made their way towards the ancient bell for the final part of the ritual, to keep Fenrir, the great wolf, from catching the sun and the moon.

As the sun rose in the sky, they walked in silence, lips contracted, brows furrowed, each recalling the monstrous death of Nan, the last person to ring the bell. Eric carried a flintlock. Their clothing billowed as the chill breeze found its way through and touched their skin. Brigid shuddered, so Eric pulled her close to his body to protect her from the elements and keep her warm. They travelled along the coastal path to the ruined monastery, high on the cliff. From the single remaining arch of the chapel tower hung the great bell, looking as if it was glowing as shards of morning light bounced off it.

Brigid approached hesitantly. Eric stayed back, watching her every step. Grabbing the fraying rope, she pulled with the full force of her weight. It bounced back much faster than she expected and a rich, round sound peeled from the bell. Eric's fingers twitched on the trigger, but no thing, no person came across them. They were totally alone.

Angeline awoke when Eric and Brigid were safely back in Goldsborough Castle. She had seen everything and only Coventina could have put the scenes into her dreams. Angeline gasped for air as she heard a bell clanging outside her window, making her jump. Then she realised it was a familiar London sound, a journeyman selling his wares. The clatter of London life from the street outside settled her as she fell back onto her pillow and recounted the dream. Ostara had come and gone without incident. She thought of Nan again. She had gone over it in her mind a thousand times, but could never get any closer to working out what had butchered her. It was a complete mystery, especially as there had been only two attacks. One on Nan, the other on a flock of sheep. Perhaps they were not connected, although Nikolaus seemed to think they were.

It was curious that the attacks had stopped as quickly as they had started. Beginning when William and Nikolaus arrived at Goldsborough, but ceasing as soon as they left, surely this was a coincidence. The uncertainty frustrated her, but she had faith in William. He would discover the truth, just as he promised. He would not allow himself to be knocked off course. Not even by that dreadful woman who was distracting him, Lady Caroline Shepherd.

CHAPTER 22

A week later, Angeline found herself standing at the side of the ballroom, fanning herself madly as she watched William dance the waltz with Lady Caroline, yet again. He had never danced the waltz with her.

The woman was wearing an ivory dress, shot through with delicate silver thread which shimmered gloriously as she danced. But it was the Mamalouc cap of black velvet with a band of silver around it and a coquelicot feather that made Lady Caroline stand out from the crowd.

'I cannot believe that you have not been taught how to use a fan properly,' Nikolaus sighed with exasperation as he walked over to Angeline. 'Look at you, waving it around like a woman demented.'

'What are you talking about, Nikolaus?' she replied crossly as he whipped the fan out of her hand.

'Men are armed with swords, but women are armed with fans. Watch and learn,' he quipped. 'There is a whole language you need to understand.'

Angeline looked on bemused as, with his usual flamboyance, Nikolaus worked the fan.

'Fan resting on the left cheek means no. Fan resting on the right cheek means yes.'

A group of gentlemen, standing diametrically opposite suddenly seemed interested in what he was doing.

'Fan clasped tightly with both hands to the décolletage means, my love for you is breaking my heart.' Nikolaus caught sight of the gentlemen looking him up and down. The most foppish of them pursed his lips suggestively.

'Oh, don't be ridiculous,' Nikolaus shouted across the room. They all huffed indignantly and turned their backs on him, one by one.

Angeline, utterly confused, became distracted by William and Lady Caroline waltzing right past her.

'What does he see in her?' she sighed, letting her guard slip.

Nikolaus stopped in his tracks and followed her gaze. He turned to her, gave back the fan and gently stroked a curl that had escaped from her chignon.

'Oh Angeline, what have we done to you? It would have been kinder to leave you in that wild, godforsaken place you call home.'

Angeline tried to smile. 'You never liked Northumberland, did you?'

'It reminded me too much of Hungary.'

Angeline touched his arm. A rapprochement had been reached between the two of them ever since Angeline had prescribed the tonic that had kept him off the opium. On a number of occasions Nikolaus had publicly demonstrated respect for her, something she truly appreciated.

'You have not answered my question,' she said.

Nikolaus looked again at the dancing couple. 'She is wealthy, healthy and eminently suitable. He thinks he needs her to restore the family reputation in society.'

'But surely his position is secure. He is an earl, after all.'

'It hangs by a thread. His father and brother did a lot of damage. Reputation is a funny thing, Angeline. Everyone sees everything, but no one says anything. Certain things are just, well, understood.'

Angeline sighed deeply once more. She did not understand at all.

'Ah, Annabel, there you are. I have been teaching Angeline the language of the fan. I leave you to continue her education,' Nikolaus said.

'I hardly think so. I have never had any use for it.'

'Well, I must leave you both anyway. I am late for an assignation. If you will excuse me, ladies.' Nikolaus departed after a low and respectful bow.

'Where does he keep disappearing to?' asked Angeline. 'I saw him sneaking up Lady Culpepper's back stairs last week.'

Annabel gave Angeline one of her celebrated looks, which meant, I cannot believe you have not worked it out.

'Angeline, Nikolaus is extremely popular with the bored matrons of the *ton*. Let's just say, he provides a service. An excellent one, by all accounts.'

Angeline blushed wildly.

'Quite frankly, I would love to know what all the fuss is about,' declared Annabel.

Angeline's eyes became as large as moons. 'Annabel, you are incorrigible.'

Dabbing her tears of laughter with a handkerchief, Angeline was interrupted by a commotion at the foot of the stairs. She saw Nikolaus arguing loudly with a much older man whom she had never seen before. William stepped in between the two men.

'You have been warned!' the man shouted at Nikolaus, who went to walk away, but the older gentleman pulled at his jacket. 'Don't you dare turn your back on me!' he bellowed.

Nikolaus knocked his hand away, and with that, the man lunged at him.

William intervened, forcing himself between the two of them.

'You have taken too many liberties,' the older man roared over William's shoulder.

Nikolaus stormed off, cutting through the crowd that had gathered to watch the spectacle.

'You are a disgrace to your family,' the gentleman shouted after him.

'Is that the husband?' Angeline asked fearfully.

'Oh no,' replied Annabel, 'that is Prince Paul Anton. Ambassador of Emperor Franz of Austria; husband of Lady Esterhazy and Nikolaus' uncle.'

CHAPTER 23

'He has been missing for nearly a week. I've called at Half Moon Street a dozen times. His staff have not heard from him and are out of their minds with worry. Something is terribly wrong, I know it.' Annabel paced the room like a caged tiger. 'If you won't help me, I will have to go looking for him myself,' she shouted.

'Do not fear, Annabel. William is out looking for Nikolaus as we speak. My butler has gone with him,' Lord Hurstbourne replied calmly. 'There isn't a hell hole in London that Charlie isn't familiar with. I have every confidence they will track him down.'

Annabel slumped down into a chair. 'I pray they find him alive,' she said quietly.

Angeline paled. 'Oh surely things can't be that bad.'

'You've no idea the danger he is to himself when he starts dipping too deep into the alcohol and laudanum,' Annabel cried, holding her hand to her forehead. 'That family of his has a lot to answer for. I'm sure his uncle tried to force Nikolaus to return to Hungary immediately. That's why they argued on the stairs.'

'Now, now, let's not get ahead of ourselves,' Louisa said firmly as she handed over her son to a nursemaid. 'Come, let us have supper. No need to starve while we wait for news.'

The clock struck midnight as William and Charlie walked through the door. Lord Hurstbourne poured them both a brandy.

'Nuffink. Not a damn thing,' Charlie declared in disbelief.

'We've tried all the usual places,' William said. 'I wonder if he has skipped the country.'

'No, no. He's lying dead in a gutter somewhere. I can feel it.' Annabel was becoming quite hysterical. Angeline took hold of her hand, trying to calm her. She had never seen Annabel like this. Then a great thump echoed through the hallway, followed by another. They all ran to see the footman open the front door to a street urchin.

'I've found 'im, Charlie. The Hungarian, 'e's at number seventeen, Goodge Street. Mother Johnson's bagnio. He's in a bad way. You'd better come quick.'

Without a word, William and Charlie rushed out onto the street and followed the boy.

'I will be at his residence waiting for you,' Annabel called after them.

'I'll get my medicine bag and come with you, Annabel. We'll put him back together again,' Angeline said soothingly.

William found Nikolaus unconscious, lying on a pallet in a filthy, rat-infested room that stank of urine and vomit. He was surrounded by empty bottles of laudanum.

'Get him out of here. I don't want him dying on my premises. It's bad for business,' said Mother Johnson.

'Don't worry. We'll 'ave him away from this stinkin' hole in a jiffy.' Charlie said, throwing Mother Johnson a guinea. 'He wasn't 'ere and you've never set eyes on 'im. Do yer hear me, mother? Or we'll chase yer out of town.'

The old lady nodded briefly as Nikolaus was bundled into a waiting carriage.

William refused to let the women anywhere near Nikolaus until he had been cleaned by his valet and his clothes burnt. By the time Annabel and Angeline saw him, he was drenched with fever.

'The next twenty-four hours will be critical,' Angeline said, applying a damp cloth to his forehead.

Nikolaus lay in a heavy stupor for hours, then briefly opened his eyes. 'I entrust my soul to you,' he said to Annabel weakly before closing his eyes as if never to open them again.

'Nikolaus!' Annabel cried.

'He's still with us,' Angeline whispered.

'I must be allowed to go,' Nikolaus murmured. 'Too much pain.'

'No. I will never let you go, Nikolaus. Do you hear me? You must be greedy. Greedy for life. Oh dear God, save him,' Annabel pleaded as she threw herself onto his broken body.

'I hate God,' Nikolaus spat. 'I hate whatever made men like me possible.'

'Stop it, Nikolaus. It's your family that have done this to you. Not God.'

Nikolaus tossed his head. 'It's a family affair, you see. Our instincts are to possess,' he gasped.

Annabel looked at Angeline for an explanation, who shook her head in response. 'He's delirious.'

Annabel cradled his head as Angeline tried to administer a medicine.

'Essence of mountain avens,' she explained to Annabel. 'It should help with the fever.'

Annabel held him higher so Angeline could tip it into his mouth and Nikolaus opened his eyes again, but they instantly rolled back into his head. Angeline touched his cheek. 'He's burning up.'

They called for bowls of cold water and pulled back the bed covers. A sweet, decaying smell rose from his body, the opium excreting through his pores. They gazed upon him, naked except for a towel laid across his loins. Even with his muscles slack, his body was beautiful.

'He looks like one of those Roman statues you see in the museums,' Annabel said shyly.

They lifted his fevered body and began by washing his back, the cold water dripping a track that ran down the length of his spine. Then they laid him down and picked up his arms. Angeline took in every detail: the birthmark on his shoulder, the weight of his limb. She watched Annabel's tiny fingers working swiftly, cleansing his body; could see the toll it was taking on her to keep from crying. The two women glanced at each other, said nothing, just kept bathing his body in cooling water. Their hands worked in unison, pressing down and smoothing the skin with the cold cloths.

Eventually, the fever broke. Pale and still, he slept peacefully. This would be a waiting game, but Angeline felt it was safe enough to leave Nikolaus with Annabel, whose head was resting on his bed. 'I've done all I can. It's up to you now, Annabel. It's not his body that is broken but his soul. Only you can save that.'

William stood as she entered the drawing room. Angeline walked straight towards him and laid her head on his chest. She felt him bristle. She knew her action was improper, but she was too tired to care. He smelt reassuringly familiar. 'I think we have done enough to save him. The fever's broken.'

'Sit down,' William said, trying to detach her from his body.

'No, please let me stay here for a moment longer.' She could feel his hesitation, then the fragile tenderness with which his hands touched her arms.

She moved in closer, knowing it was wrong, and felt a bulge. She caught her breath and savoured the flutter of delight at his arousal. She looked up at him and instinctively let her lips brush against his. She could not help herself. His grip tightened, nails dug into her flesh and she yelped. He yanked her upper body away from him but she knowingly pushed her hipbone against his, sinking into him, feeling the magical, seductive energy. He was as solid as a rock, like the granite that had forged Northumberland.

Looking defiantly into his face, she could feel his harsh breath on her cheek. She knew she had awoken something in him, but the look in his eyes was so dangerous that she quickly lost her nerve. Trying to escape, he held her even tighter.

'Stop it. You're hurting me,' she protested.

'What did you expect, you little sorceress?' he hissed. 'A man could hurt you much more than this if he had a mind. Don't you realise how dangerous you are?'

'Let me go.'

'You're playing with fire, Angeline. Perhaps Elewald was right. Maybe you do need to be taught a lesson.'

She had never seen such burning heat in those eyes before and it terrified her. He had lost the ironclad control he was so proud of. She tried to disentangle herself from him, but he was too strong. She was saved only by a heavy knocking on the front door.

'Who is that?' Angeline gasped.

'Aunt Vivian,' he shot back. 'I sent for her. I must open the door. All the staff are asleep.' He released Angeline by almost throwing her away.

'But it's not even daybreak yet,' she said.

'It needs to look like she's been here all night, otherwise your reputation will be in tatters. Then we'll never find you a husband,' he said abruptly as he marched out of the room.

Standing there alone, she found herself staring at the Andrassy coat of arms on the wall. She focused on it intently, trying to compose herself. A few seconds later, she heard Lady Vivian behind her.

'Angeline.'

She did not respond.

'Angeline. Are you all right?'

'It's been a trying night for all of us,' William spoke for her. 'She's exhausted.'

'Have you taken a good look at the Andrassy coat of arms?' Angeline finally said. William and Lady Vivian moved closer to get a better look at the blood-red shield with a crowned black wolf, rampant on a green base. The wolf was carrying a lamb on its shoulders. A golden sun and moon hovered over the beast, cushioned in an array of gleaming stars.

'He has a wolf on his crest.'

'Many families have wolves on their shields,' William responded. 'They are courageous and noble animals.'

'They are also man-eating predators,' Angeline replied. 'That is Fenrir.'

William's head jerked back in surprise. 'Come now, Angeline. You are imagining things. We both agreed Fenrir does not exist.'

'Please, Angeline. Come with me,' said a bemused Lady Vivian. 'You need to rest.'

'Angeline. You must go with Lady Vivian now, before daybreak. We will talk about this another time.'

Her eyes fell onto the motto of the shield as she was led away.

Sic itar ad astra
Such is the pathway to the stars

CHAPTER 24

Nikolaus felt a merciful feminine presence beside him, a curl of silken hair brushing against his arm. He opened his eyes and watched her sleeping. She was not beautiful: chin too small, nose too long, but her skin was an unblemished ivory and he recalled vividly how she sparkled, just with the delight of living.

The rustle of his bedcovers jerked Annabel awake. 'Oh thank God,' she said, 'I thought you were going to die.'

'I wish I had,' he replied mournfully. 'Death holds no fear for me. There is no terror when one has managed to avoid attachments in life.'

'Please, Nikolaus. Please don't talk like that. All your friends want you to live.'

Nikolaus tried to inhale, which brought on a coughing fit. 'I have indulged to excess, Annabel. I have caressed the birds of paradise and tasted angels' tears in my delicious dreams, but each time it is harder to catch the divine, so then hope fades like the fading sun.'

Annabel bit her bottom lip to stop herself crying. 'Nikolaus, listen to me. I have been thinking and I have a question for you.'

He tried to raise an eyebrow in response.

'Will you marry me?'

He stared at her, seemingly not hearing what she had said.

'Nikolaus. Will you marry me?'

His eyebrows twitched as if he was trying to decipher what she was saying. 'But my family would disown me.'

'Hang your family.'

'Yes. That's a thought.'

Annabel smirked. 'No seriously. Let's run away together and get married. We don't need their money. I'm as rich as Croesus.'

'But, Annabel,' Nikolaus replied, reaching for her hand, 'we don't love each other.'

She blushed and looked away. 'Our kind don't marry for love, Nikolaus. But you cannot deny that we rub along together pretty well.'

He smiled sweetly. 'Annabel, we do more than that. You are the only woman I have ever met who brings out the best in me. You make me a better person. But I would not wish me on anyone.'

'No, Nikolaus. Don't you see? If I were married to you, I would not have to keep fighting off the gold-diggers. You would be my saviour in that regard.' She pressed home her argument. 'And I would not have to wear these dreadful eye glasses anymore.' She could see the clouds clearing from his mind as he started to ruminate over the possibility. After a few moments he spoke warmly to her.

'Annabel, I am honoured that you have asked me. You restore my badly battered chivalry; your trust and respect are more important to me than all the passion I have known with other women.'

Annabel tried not to blanch.

'A life of duty over self-indulgence has never seemed so appealing.'

'Well, I hope it would not be all duty. We could try to have a little fun,' she cajoled.

He wavered. 'I will give your proposal my full consideration. When I'm feeling stronger, I promise.'

Nikolaus watched the dappled sunbeams playing on the carpet. It had been a week since William found him in that godforsaken hellhole, and this was his first day out of bed.

His friends came in via the back entrance when visiting and the servants were under strict instructions to tell anyone calling that their master was not at home. He knew his family's demands on his soul would kill him and he had decided that he wanted to live. Mainly because it would vex his uncle, but also because it seemed to matter to his friends that he stay alive. For some inexplicable reason they thought their lives would be wanting without him, and that knowledge warmed him to the marrow.

'Why do you keep staring at my family coat of arms?' he finally asked Angeline. Although she had been providing various potions for his health and wellbeing, this was her first visit after the night they found him in Goodge Street.

'Why do you have Fenrir on your crest?' she responded.

Nikolaus looked at his emblem as if for the first time. 'Yes, I see. Your Northumberland superstition about a great wolf who chases the sun and the moon to devour them.'

'And in doing so, is responsible for the destruction of the world,' she added.

He turned and stared at her intently. 'Angeline, there are many myths about wolves. You know the legend about my ancestor.'

She looked puzzled.

Nikolaus glanced up to the ceiling as he recalled a memory. 'Perhaps you don't. I told the old lady the story.'

'What story?'

'The one about my ancestor being cursed by a gypsy and then mauled by a wolf. It is supposed to be what gave us our heightened sense of smell, but it's also what made half of us insane. Although Annabel puts that down to inbreeding.'

Angeline studied him as if searching for clues in the lines that etched his face. 'But it is too much of a coincidence. The wolf, the sun, the moon... and the lamb.' She trailed off.

'Angeline, my family's association with wolves goes back two thousand years. We believe we are descended from Julus, King of Alba Longa. The Romans are descended from the Albans and the Julians are the clan of Julius Caesar.' Nikolaus shifted in his chair. ' It is believed that the Albans lived with wolves and revered them. Which is why the tale of Romulus and Remus is plausible. Wolves were accustomed to people.'

Angeline gasped. 'This cannot be. I have heard of Julus. It is said Brutus of Britain was descended from him and I, in turn, am descended from Brutus, or so we believe.'

'How fascinating. We could actually be related, Angeline,' Nikolaus mooted. 'Local versions of the same myth grew as the great bardic tradition grew, so it does not surprise me that we have similar stories.' He closed his eyes with weariness.

'What does your motto mean, *sic itar ad astra* – Such is the pathway to the stars?'

'You will have to ask my father about that, if you ever meet him. I confess I have never fully understood it.' Nikolaus yawned. 'He calls it The Music of the Spheres. The stars and planets are supposed to make beautiful music together as they travel through the heavens. The cosmos sings, creating great harmonies that affect us on earth and our relationships.' He settled deeper into his seat. 'Apparently, only when the soul leaves the body can it hear the music. This is the pathway to the stars. Or so my father says.'

They were enveloped in peaceful silence for many minutes. When Nikolaus opened his eyes again he found Angeline looking at him in that slightly mysterious way that was hers alone.

'You never liked Nan, did you? You accused her of being a witch.'

Nikolaus shifted uneasily. 'Angeline, I was under the influence of the dreaded opium at the time and I deeply regret my accusation. I keep thinking about how I found her. I cannot imagine what kind of animal caused that wound.'

'A wolf, perhaps.'

'Yes, perhaps,' he answered, 'but unlikely.'

'Why?'

'Angeline, my family revere the wolf, just as the Albans did. We feel an affinity with them; they are intelligent, loyal and brave, but most importantly, the pack comes first. Family comes first.'

'So?' Angeline said, knowing she sounded frustrated.

Nikolaus held his eyes shut, trying to summon his strength. 'Wolves hunt in packs. They don't work alone. Besides, if it had been a wolf, I would have smelt it. But all I could smell was something vile, something putrid, something I have never smelt before in my life. Something I cannot describe.'

CHAPTER 25

Lady Caroline Shepherd's Grand Ball was considered to be one of the highlights of the season. Only those in the most rarefied circle of the *ton* were invited. Even so, it was a terrible crush, which, Angeline had learnt, was, every hostess' ambition.

Angeline was wearing a shimmering sheath of dark silver, trimmed with mother of pearl, one of Madame Dupré's most spectacular creations. Angeline knew she looked stunning, but she felt jaded tonight and she was missing Annabel, who had decided to stay behind to keep Nikolaus company. His friends had circulated the rumour that he had left the country after the very public argument with his uncle, but in reality Nikolaus was still hiding out in his London home. As a result, Angeline was having to listen to Dr Tottenham lecture her on the dangers of rhubarb.

'My dance, I believe,' declared the Duke of Lostwithiel. Angeline smiled gracefully and gave him her hand. They chatted amiably whilst waiting for the rest of the company to find their places in the sets. She scanned the crowd to find William watching her impassively. He had avoided her since that fateful night at Nikolaus' house.

'Finally,' said Angeline as the music for the cotillion began. She had danced countless cotillions since the season began. It was now April, so she went through the steps of this one mindlessly. She found herself relieved when it was over, so that the duke could return her to Lady Vivian, but she was dismayed when a gavotte with the Earl of Huntingdon followed immediately.

As she danced, she saw from the corner of her eye Dr Tottenham grab Lady Vivian's arm in an uneasy gesture. He was watching something distasteful by the entrance to the ballroom. Angeline twisted around and caught her breath as she saw Elewald standing in the doorway, observing the scene with an odious smirk on his face.

Her immediate reaction was to search for William. What would he do? This would be the first time that he and Elewald had come across each other in London. The gavotte was far too energetic, with too many turns for her to keep the two men in view, but they must have made eye contact because she saw William's impassive expression harden like granite as the chiselled jawbone clenched.

Angeline started to feel very warm and began to breathe faster as the dance took hold. She watched Elewald prowl around the room, weaving in and out of the bodies, never taking his beady eyes off his adversary. Angeline spun around, trying to find William amongst the bejewelled ladies who momentarily dazzled her. She watched him mirror Elewald's moves, stalking him and staring him down. Angeline could hear hundreds of voices chattering loudly in her ears. The various perfumes mingled and drifted into her nostrils, making her heady. She observed Elewald's mouth turn into a snarl as he came upon Dr Tottenham, when suddenly, out of the crowd, someone cut across Elewald's path and whispered something in his ear. Angeline knew the man, she had even danced with him. Indeed, he had marked her card for later that very evening. Lucien, the Comte de St Affrique, was a French émigré and a cousin of Lady Caroline. The dance stopped just as Elewald nodded and disappeared with the Frenchman. As she was being escorted back, she bumped into Lord Hurstbourne, who had just arrived with Louisa.

'Have we missed anything?' he asked jovially.

Angeline held her hand up to her neck anxiously and said, 'No, not a single thing.'

She did not feel like dancing anymore, but as usual, her card was full and she was loath to feign illness, so she soldiered on.

'Will you be visiting the Royal Academy's Annual Exhibition?' asked the Earl of Huntingdon, on his second dance of the evening with Angeline.

'I don't know.'

'Oh you really must. John Martin is a sensation. You will never have seen anything like *The Fall of Babylon*, I assure you.'

Angeline smiled thinly in response. She continued to smile at the disjointed conversations of her dance partners until she danced with the Comte de St Affrique.

'I believe,' said the Comte, 'that our hostess is searching for you.'

'Really?'

'Yes, there is a break in the dancing after this and I have been asked to escort you to her.'

Angeline lifted her eyebrows in surprise as he raised her from the final courtesy and guided her out of the room.

'Ah, Lady Angeline, how lovely to see you.' Lady Caroline waved her hand at the Comte, indicating that he should leave them. With the merest inclination of his head, St Affrique retreated.

'I have a note for you from Lord Lyndhurst,' said Lady Caroline.

'Why would William send me a note?'

'I haven't the faintest idea,' came the reply.

Angeline opened it. She realised that she had never seen his writing before. It was surprisingly elaborate. 'He wishes for me to meet him on the west terrace.'

Lady Caroline gave her an empty smile. 'This crowd is impossible, and you look a little wan. Some fresh air will do you good. Come, let me show you the way.'

'Where is Angeline?'

'I thought she was with you,' came the concerned reply from Lady Vivian.

'Have you seen her, Ponsonby?'

'No, William. Not since she was dancing with that Frenchie, St Affrique.'

Perhaps she was dancing with Lostwithiel, William thought, but he saw the duke dancing with his sister.

'The Earl of Huntington has been paying her a lot of attention this evening, perhaps...' but Lady Vivian trailed off when she saw the earl embroiled in a heated discussion with Viscount Castlereagh.

They all started to search the crowd anxiously.

'I don't like this,' said Lord Hurstbourne.

'No, nor do I, especially with Elewald around...' William replied.

'Is that her?' said Lady Vivian. They all turned to watch St Affrique disappear through the throng of people, but he was alone. 'Oh no, this is all my fault. I'm her chaperone, I should have been paying better attention.'

William ran an agitated hand through his hair, his instincts screaming out that something calamitous was about to happen. 'If she's not here, then where the devil is she?'

'I've just seen Elewald head for the terrace,' said Louisa as she was escorted back from the dance. 'I know he always looks like a weasel, but he was looking particularly furtive,' she said with rancour. 'He's definitely up to no good.'

Then William's heart seized as a grotesque thought took shape in his head. 'Oh God, he's going to compromise her.'

'What on earth...' But William cut Lady Vivian off in mid-sentence.

'Elewald, Angeline, terrace...' In the grip of terror he gave his orders. 'Quickly, we must split up and find her, before it's too late. If she is discovered alone with Elewald, it's all over.'

He was just in time to see Angeline disappear through some side doors into the garden. It was not the main exit onto the terrace, where many people would be milling about. This was secluded. Whatever could have convinced her to step out alone? William surreptitiously indicated to Dr Tottenham that he had located her, then walked through the crowd as fast as he could without rousing suspicion. When he reached the opening, he found himself peering down a long walkway that led out towards an arbour. He just managed to catch a glimpse of silk in the moonlight. She was standing at the end.

He turned his head to the left and saw a silhouette hiding in the shadows. William made a quick calculation. If that was Elewald then they were both quite a distance from her. The figure stepped out so that the lights of the ballroom fell on his face and William's stomach sank. It was Lucien de St Affrique. What was he doing here? Could it be as a look-out for Elewald, or worse still, as a witness to something that was about to happen? Lord Hurstbourne entered the garden and stood by William at the exact moment a scream went up from the end of the walkway.

St Affrique instantly made a squawking sound, like a bird, as soon as William ran towards the arbour, which William interpreted as a call sign for danger to Elewald. People began tumbling out onto the terrace to testify to the public disgrace that was about to unfold. He could not get to her in time. All was lost.

'Don't worry everyone. All is well,' shouted a voice from the arbour. William stopped dead in his tracks. Elewald would be triumphant, for they had played right into his hands. He had more than enough witnesses now. Elewald just needed to reveal to the world that Angeline was with him, underneath the arbour, and she would be destroyed.

William would challenge him to a duel, of course, for his dishonourable conduct, but it would make no difference to her. She was done for. People would say she had chosen her path by coming out into the garden with him. He may have become a little too ardent, which was why she screamed, but the fault would be laid squarely at her door.

William held his breath and seconds ticked by as three people emerged from the recess.

'I'm sorry to have caused such a fuss, but I had a bad turn, and it scared poor Lady Angeline here.'

William blinked hard as Lady Angeline and Lady Vivian helped a poorly Dr Tottenham walk up the pathway.

'Do not fear,' said the doctor loudly. 'It was too hot for me in the ballroom, so my two companions here helped me get some fresh air. But it's chilly tonight and the contrast must have been too much for my poor constitution.'

William rushed up to take Dr Tottenham's weight from the two ladies.

'Thank you, William. I will be corky, just as soon as I sit down with a glass of brandy,' said Dr Tottenham breathlessly.

'Where's Elewald?' William hissed.

'Ran off and jumped over the garden wall, but not before I managed to whack him with a garden shovel,' the doctor whispered. 'Overdid it a bit, I think.'

William instinctively looked behind him to see Angeline and Lady Vivian following.

'Oh, don't think about giving chase,' continued Dr Tottenham. ' He will be far gone by now.'

As William turned his head back, he caught a movement from the corner of his eye and saw the silhouette of St Affrique slither into the darkness. William would deal with him later. He could not afford to make a scene now. 'I can't thank you enough, Ponsonby,' William said.

'Think nothing of it, my boy. Rather exciting actually.' Playing to his audience, the doctor pleaded with them, 'Ladies and gentlemen, please go back inside and carry on enjoying yourselves. I am fine and dandy now.'

Lady Vivian and her son, Lord Hurstbourne, escorted Doctor Tottenham inside. Louisa followed, commenting admiringly on the kindness of the Ladies Vivian and Angeline towards the ageing doctor. Everyone agreed wholeheartedly.

'Oh dear. What a terrible turn of events for poor Ponsonby,' said Lady Caroline, running up to William and Angeline, who had stopped by the entrance to the ballroom. 'Thank goodness you were there to help, Angeline.'

Angeline ignored her. 'William, why did you put me in that position?' she demanded, blinking back the tears.

'What do you mean?' he answered.

Angeline was trying so hard to hold back the tears that she could no longer speak. Instead she thrust the note into his hand.

'I never sent this. This is not my writing. Where did you get it?'

Angeline glared at Lady Caroline.

'One of my footmen gave it to me,' Lady Caroline answered calmly. 'He said he had been given strict instructions by you, William, that I should give the note to Angeline.'

William eyed her suspiciously. 'Why would I do such a thing, Caroline?'

'Well, I don't know, do I? I thought, perhaps, you were trying to make me jealous.'

His face darkened and he shook with incandescence. 'I do not play such games, Caroline.'

She sighed heavily, looking him up and down. 'No, tragically you don't, do you, William?' Surveying the room lazily, Lady Caroline continued, 'I will question the footman to see if I can get to the bottom of this. But it doesn't really matter, does it? There's no harm done. Probably someone playing a practical joke, that's all.'

Lady Vivian returned to Angeline's side and took hold of her trembling hand just as Lady Caroline walked away.

'Well, that was a close run thing.' Relief rang out in Lady Vivian's voice. 'I have never avoided a scandal so narrowly in my entire life.'

'How did you manage it?' asked an astounded William.

'Ponsonby and I found a side door that was open, so we scooted around to the back of the garden. Thank goodness we came across Elewald just as he was about to pounce on poor Angeline here. Ponsonby gave him a good thwack with a spade before that rascal ran off.' She touched Angeline's cheek. 'You poor girl, you've had a shocking fright. You look so terribly pale.'

'I don't understand what has just happened,' Angeline mumbled.

'My dear,' said Lady Vivian, 'Lord Elewald has just tried to compromise you. If you had been found on your own with him, your reputation would have been ruined.'

Angeline stared at her in a daze.

'In the eyes of society, you would have had no option but to marry him.'

Angeline's lips twisted into a pained grimace. 'I would kill myself before I let that happen,' she said defiantly, 'No matter what society thought.'

Lady Vivian glanced at her nephew. 'Well, thankfully, it won't come to that. Angeline, this was all my fault. It's a chaperone's duty to keep an eye on her charge at all times. I'm so terribly sorry. Please forgive me.'

'Of course I will. I don't blame you at all.'

'Elewald is a monstrosity.' Fury boiled over in William's intonation. 'I will deal with him, Angeline, once and for all. He will never threaten you again.'

'What do you intend to do?' she asked urgently.

'It need not concern you,' he replied.

'Of course it concerns me. You won't do anything foolish, will you?'

'Angeline,' he said, trying to soothe her, 'have you ever known me to do anything foolish?'

'No,' she replied quietly, embarrassed that she felt a twang of disappointment at the thought. She stared at the floor. 'I want to go home.'

'Indeed. I think it best we both go now,' Lady Vivian agreed.

'No,' replied Angeline sorrowfully, 'I want to go home, home.'

CHAPTER 26

William stayed at the ball after the others had gone, but he was battling with himself to contain his anger. Few things could have stirred his nature so deeply. How dare Elewald try to destroy she who was under his protection; this insult was too much to bear. William would hunt him down, like the dog that he was, following him to the gates of hell if he had to. Elewald needed to be taken care of. William would call him out: a duel was the only way honour could be satisfied now. To that end, he would make contact with his old network, the people William had worked with whilst England was at war. Elewald would not escape. They would track him down, wherever he was.

William focused. He could not allow his anger to cloud his vision, and action was needed. He had already interviewed the footman who supposedly gave the letter to Lady Caroline, but much to William's chagrin, the servant could only repeat that the man who gave the letter to him, if it was not William, looked exactly like him. He had interrogated enough men in the past to know the servant was lying, but whoever had got to him had terrorised the poor man, probably by threatening his family, into sticking to his story. So William let him off the hook, for the time being.

He searched for St Affrique, who had conveniently disappeared. William would attend to him, too, in the fullness of time.

Lostwithiel was next on the list. William was becoming increasingly impatient. It was already April and the duke had not yet declared his hand. What was keeping him? It was obvious to all he had an interest in Angeline, a great interest even. William's mind flitted back to that night at Nikolaus' house, when he had experienced Angeline's restlessness firsthand. Marriage had to come quickly now.

As soon as Lostwithiel read William's face he left his card game to join him.

'Do we have something to discuss?' asked the duke.

'Someone,' William answered.

'Ah yes, the lovely Lady Angeline.'

William nodded. 'Where exactly do we stand regarding the lady? If you don't mind me asking.'

Lostwithiel sighed deeply. 'Lyndhurst, I find her utterly beguiling and she would suit my needs perfectly, I'm sure of that. However, and I have to say this has never happened to me before, I clearly do not spark her tinder.'

William had not expected such an answer.

'At first I found this a great challenge, and it increased my ardour, but finally I had to admit it. Her eyes are dead when she looks at me.'

William opened his mouth, then shut it. He was lost for words.

Lostwithiel went to walk away, then turned his head back towards William. 'She always seems preoccupied somehow. As if someone else fills her thoughts, but I could not say who.' Lostwithiel shrugged. 'Sorry, Lyndhurst, but I've thrown in my hand.'

The next day William was still in a rage. He had not slept a wink, his mind turning over the previous evening's events. He had begun to suspect that things were slipping out of his control and he hated feeling this way; it was not something he was accustomed to. Instinct demanded that he act decisively, to keep circumstances and feelings firmly where he could manage them. So, after orders to find Elewald had been put into motion, the next step was to give Angeline a stern reprimand. She would get severely burnt if she contrived to play with fire. Going out into the garden alone had been reckless, rebuffing Lostwithiel had been plain stupid. What was she playing at? She was no dullard, but she was becoming a problem. The sooner she was safely married off the better.

He found himself pacing the floor of the library at the Hurstbourne town house. Simon was at his club, so he waited impatiently for the ladies to return from Somerset House. A clever tactic, William thought, taking Angeline to an exclusive preview of the annual exhibition; only Lady Vivian would have the social clout to arrange such a thing, but it would distract Angeline's thoughts from the frightening events of the previous night.

He was standing in the middle of the room when the door opened.

'I can see why John Martin is the big draw of the year,' said Louisa. 'He paints sensational visual drama.'

'But you cannot call him a great artist,' replied Lady Vivian. 'He's a populist.'

'He is adamant that *The Fall of Babylon* is historically accurate,' Angeline declared.

'Yes, but how... Oh William, I thought you might be here when we returned.' Lady Vivian greeted him with a peck on the cheek.

'Really. Am I that predictable?'

'Usually,' she bantered. 'Well I suppose you are here to discuss the news,' she continued.

'What news?'

All three ladies stared at him with startled surprise etched on their faces.

'The unbelievably wonderful news that arrived this morning,' Louisa said. 'You must have received a letter, just as we have.'

William shook his head. 'Probably, but I do not open my correspondence until the evening.' He watched Angeline sit as a whimsical smile played about her mouth.

'Nikolaus and Annabel have run away to Gretna Green, to be married,' she announced.

'What?'

'Isn't it wonderful news?' Louisa said, clapping her hands with delight.

William felt the ground beneath his feet move like shifting sand and he had to grasp onto the back of a chair to steady himself. 'Are you insane?' he barked.

'Not in the slightest,' replied Louisa, going off into a peel of laughter as Lady Vivian went to fetch the letter.

'This is preposterous,' he burst out. 'It's a joke. It has to be.'

'No joke,' replied Angeline. 'They are a perfect match, don't you think?'

William did not answer. Everything in his world was sliding away. 'He'll be cut off by his family, without a penny.'

'I suspect Nikolaus finds that prospect something of a relief,' said Lady Vivian, handing him the letter. 'Besides, Annabel has enough money, even for his lifestyle.'

William read. 'Did you know they were planning this?' he asked his aunt in an accusing tone.

Lady Vivian held up her hands. 'We are all as surprised as you are.'

He turned and stared out of the window. 'This can't end well,' he said eventually.

'Why not?' asked Angeline.

'Because they are marrying for the wrong reasons. They are both running away from something.'

Louisa looked at him aghast. 'Well, we all know what Nikolaus is running away from, but what is Annabel running from?'

'Loneliness,' he said.

There was a long moment of hesitation as the word resonated with the ladies.

'Well, let's just wait and see, shall we?' said Lady Vivian. 'So, if you are not here about the letter, then why are you here, William?'

'I wish to speak to Angeline.'

Louisa took her cue. 'I must see how my darling little boy is doing. He has a spring chill, you know. If you'll excuse me.'

Lady Vivian went to leave with her.

'I think you should stay, Aunt,' William said.

'As you wish,' she replied cautiously, sitting next to Angeline.

After a second or two, William cleared his throat. 'I'm pleased to see you looking so well today, Angeline. I was worried for you after the events of last night.'

'I'm so truly happy for Nikolaus and Annabel,' she replied.

Lady Vivian smiled warmly at her. 'I also explained that it was imperative for us to be seen out and about, as usual, today. To make it absolutely clear that nothing untoward, whatsoever, happened last night.'

William nodded. 'I spoke with Lostwithiel last night,' he said stiffly.

'And?' asked Lady Vivian expectantly.

William composed himself. 'And nothing, I'm afraid.' He studied his ward, whose eyes had dropped to the floor. 'But this doesn't surprise you, does it, Angeline?'

'No,' she murmured, flushing deeply.

Lady Vivian shot her a glance. 'What does he mean, Angeline?'

She did not reply.

'Apparently,' William continued, 'Angeline has made it quite obvious to the duke that she has no interest in him.'

'Oh Angeline,' Lady Vivian chided.

Defiance reared within Angeline and she looked steadily across at her guardian. 'You promised me I could choose my own husband,' she said, 'and the duke does not suit me.'

William bridled. 'The duke does not suit me,' he echoed. 'So, pray tell, is there anyone who does?'

'No. Not really,' she stammered.

'What does *not really* mean? Is there someone, or not?' he demanded.

'I cannot say.' Her soft bottom lip trembled.

William gasped and held his hands up in the air. 'I don't understand you, Angeline. I never have.' He turned his back on her and stared out of the window again.

Hearing those words, Angeline gave a tiny sob and the tears brimmed over. Lady Vivian saw the pain that encased Angeline's face and jumped to her feet, hands pressing to her breast.

'Oh Angeline,' she cried, 'I've been such a fool.' She shook her head with pity. 'You poor child, I'm so terribly sorry for you. I know how you truly feel. I have known for some time.'

Lady Vivian's sympathy was far too much to bear. All vestiges of control left her and Angeline fled the room.

'Come back here!' William shouted sternly, but she had already disappeared.

'Aunt, explain yourself. I am not in the mood for histrionics.'

'Oh William, I am a fool, but you are an idiot.'

William stared, speechless.

'Can't you see? It's you. She's in love with you.'

William stood, rooted to the spot, a strange sensation thrilling through him. How could he have been so wrong-footed?

'It's blindingly obvious,' she said, holding a hand to her forehead. 'I've been trying to ignore it. Hoping that Lostwithiel would charm her.'

'But I'm ten years older than Angeline.' Her name seemed to escape his lips like a butterfly on a whisper.

'So?'

'Aunt Vivian, stop this immediately. She is my ward.'

'That is inconsequential,' replied his aunt. 'Tell me, William, how do you feel about her?'

'I... I... she is my ward,' he spluttered. 'What would society think?'

'William, the matrons of the *ton* spend most of their time facilitating good marriages to ensure land and lineage are kept intact. A match between the Fitzalans and Goldsboroughs would enable a smooth transition of the estates. Society would come to see that.'

William grasped the back of the chair again. 'Aunt, you have no idea what you are suggesting. She is wild beyond excuse.' A vision of Angeline galloping across the sands jumped into his head.

'I hardly think so. You told me yourself you admired her composure. She has enjoyed London and behaved impeccably ever since she arrived. The only improper thing she has ever done was to walk into the garden alone, but I understand why, because she thought she was meeting you.'

'Aunt, you don't have any idea about the sort of life she leads in Northumberland. Yes, she enjoys London, purely because it's a novelty. She behaves well enough, but if you look deep into her eyes, she's like a caged animal, desperate to escape. You heard her last night. She just wants to go home.'

A flicker of remorse passed over his face. 'Back to where she can be her true self.'

Lady Vivian squared up to him. 'Do you love her?'

William hesitated. 'I don't know.'

Lady Vivian placed her hands on her hips. 'William, what you say about Angeline may be true, she may have a wild streak, but you are the only man who can rein her in, I'm sure of that. You cannot pretend you don't find women like that attractive. Why, the marqueza, by all accounts was strong-willed…' She stopped mid-flow. 'That's it, isn't it? You're still in love with Theresa. You would rather marry someone you do not love in order to protect her memory.'

William slammed his fist down hard onto the back of the leather chair. 'I don't understand why you are taking this position all of a sudden. You approved of me courting Lady Caroline at the beginning of the season.'

'Because I have become incredibly fond of Angeline and I have always been fond of you. And, well, you were right about Annabel,' she said. ' Loneliness is a terrible thing, but you can be just as lonely inside a marriage. Believe me, I know.' She walked over and touched his hand lightly. 'I want you to be happy. Just like Simon and Louisa.'

He took her wizened hands in his. 'I need funds to restore Lyndhurst.' His voice cracked with emotion.

She pulled away. 'You're making excuses now. You're good with land, William. The money will come. It may take a little longer, that's all. Anyway, Simon will loan you what you need, he's told you that.'

'I will not be beholden to my cousin.' The seconds moved slowly. 'I need time to think,' he said, rubbing the frown between his eyebrows with his index finger. 'I'm sorry, Aunt, I need time,' he repeated as he sped from the room.

He sat at his bureau, rereading the letter that Nikolaus had sent. It did not say much: it just described a plan to make a dash to Gretna Green, with no explanation of why. William did not know what to make of it. He did not know what he thought about anything anymore. He had been asked if he loved Angeline, but he could not answer, for he truly did not know. He had fought his innermost feelings ever since meeting her. She haunted his dreams, but she was not Theresa. A smile of secret delight warmed his face as he imagined Theresa licking her lips and stretching her limbs in anticipation of some delectable treat that he would bring for her. His soul had been a bonfire of heat and passion for the marqueza. He was riddled with guilt whenever he thought of his departed lover and he felt wretched at the possibility she might fade from his memory. He owed her so much, but he craved for the void she had left to be filled.

Theresa had been at ease, both within the inner circle of the royal court, or sleeping rough in a cave, just as he was. They had been equals. Quite different from his northern sorceress. It had been a mistake to bring Angeline to London. She would never bend her nature to society's will. Angeline's affinity with the wilderness was too strong. It gave her a sensual mystique. She was a beautiful woman whose ancient power enthralled him. Was that witchcraft? Or was that love?

His anxious contemplation was violently interrupted by the library door swinging open and his aunt rushing in.

'She's gone!' she cried.

PART 5

BELTANE

CHAPTER 27

He left at around eight o'clock in the evening, riding through the night and all the next day. Everywhere he could find an opportunity he asked after her: innkeepers, fellow travellers, but no one had seen a lone female on horse-back. He did not know whether to be thankful or not. She was in such danger alone. The agony was burning a hole in his heart. She had taken one of his cousin's horses most suitable for endurance riding, so where else but to Goldsborough? Where she belonged.

'You must bring her back quickly, or all is lost,' his aunt had shouted from the front doorstep as William mounted his horse. 'I can make excuses for her absence, blaming it on the spring chill that is going around, but after seven days the gossipmongers will be baying.'

William understood only too well the necessity of getting her back as soon as possible. He had been such a fool, bringing her to London in the first place. What had possessed him of such folly? Bewitchment, perhaps?

Elewald's warning rang in his ears: *'You'll regret this, Lyndhurst. The women from that clan are pure trouble.'* Damn girl, she was like a wild horse that would not be broken.

He hoped to catch up with her quickly, but she could be as much as four hours ahead of him. Desperation mounted as he drove his horse on, further and further northwards, dragging innkeepers from their beds in the dead of night to provide him with a change of mount, paying over the odds to stop them palming him off with less than reliable stock. He felt sick, sick with fear for her.

He finally arrived at the castle in the darkest hour before the dawn, just as the purple sky began to bleed with pale lavender light out of the east. He had been travelling for over thirty hours. He repeatedly banged on the great door until someone answered. Exhausted by the journey, he collapsed onto Eric Sweyne's body.

'Is she here?' William rasped.

'Is who here?'

'Lady Angeline.'

'No, my lord,' said Mr Sweyne, leading him to a chair in the hallway. 'Why would she be?'

'Ran away,' William choked out as Sweyne tried to pull off his mud-soaked boots. 'Ran from London. If not here, where?' He did not hear the answer. He slipped into unconsciousness, the dark enveloping him like a cloak.

Angeline cried and cried like a helpless child. She had never felt so wretched, not even when her parents had died. Then, she knew why she was crying, but today her emotions were in such turmoil, it felt like she was crying for a million different reasons. She felt humiliated that her secret had been discovered. She felt the pain of unrequited love and the hurt at what she saw as William's rejection of her. She just wanted to run, run as far away as possible and hide inside a hole somewhere.

Then a thought struck her: home. She needed to go home. She would be safe there. She could heal there. Once the thought took hold she could not shake it off. Half crazed, she fled from her room and began to search for a means to escape. She deftly manoeuvred past the kitchens without being detected, saw some bread and cheese in the pantry, which she grabbed, before finding the laundry room. Hanging up were the day clothes of one of the valets, the clothes he wore when he was off-duty. They fitted her perfectly. She could make do with the walking boots she was wearing. Her hair tucked snuggly under his cap. Now for the horse. She had to wait in the shadows until the stable boy went for his tea, then she made a dash for it. She had studied the horses long enough to decide which one she would take. Swiftly, she rode down the mews, past the back of the house and was quickly out of sight.

Her tears were still streaming, but a blast of air slapped her in the face as she approached the crossroad and for the first time in hours she began to think clearly. London was a maze. How was she going to get home? Panic welled up inside her, she could not possibly go back to Grosvenor Square. She could not suffer the humiliation.

Noise from the house on her left caught her attention. There was an entourage circling around a carriage, which was sitting outside the front door. She heard the lady in the carriage shouting.

'Quickly, we must make a dash for Stanwick. My beloved Hugh is sickly.'

Stanwick was only a few miles away from Thornby. Once there, Angeline would be able to make her way home. She could not believe her luck. Then she heard a voice in her head. It was Coventina.

'Listen to your inner voice. I will guide you home.'

Angeline followed the coach. She managed to keep it well within view as the coach made its way out of London, although it was not so easy to be inconspicuous once they hit the country roads. Most of the time it was just the coach party and Angeline, trying to keep her distance, on the dirt track. Eventually, as night fell, the coach pulled up at an inn. Angeline managed to sneak her mount into the stables, finding a small empty stall at the side of the entrance. No one who worked there took any notice of her, assuming she was a member of the lady's staff. She planned to sleep in the stable with her horse. Silently, Angeline removed the saddle and lifted it onto the stable door, when the lady from the coach stepped into view.

'Who are you and why are you following me?' she demanded.

Angeline swallowed hard and decided to take off her cap. Her hair tumbled down.

'You're a girl!' exclaimed the lady.

'Yes, I must get home to Northumberland, but I did not know the way. My only hope was to follow you."

The lady raised her eyebrows and looked Angeline up and down.

'Well, you must be desperate. Just as desperate as I am to get there. Come inside and tell me your story, but put your hat back on first. It will be too difficult to explain why a woman is dressed like that.'

The lady was very beautiful and very finely dressed. The voice in Angeline's head told her she could be trusted. So Angeline, although fatigued, told the story of why she was running away from London. The lady, whose name was Venetia Pembroke, listened sympathetically.

'Ah, men,' she finally said, shaking her head. 'What can we do? They burden our souls and break our hearts, but we love them just the same.'

Angeline learnt that Venetia was the long-time mistress of a Northumberland aristocrat who she loved very much.

He had been suddenly taken ill. He was on his deathbed by all accounts, calling for her. Venetia needed to get to Northumberland just as quickly as Angeline.

It was decided that Angeline would ride the rest of the way in the coach with Venetia, as her companion. Venetia, very kindly, provided more suitable clothing and a comfortable bed for a few hours sleep. Angeline felt she had met a guardian angel.

The room seemed familiar to him. He recognised the heavy damask wall lining: it was his bedroom at Goldsborough. William awoke gradually, but had to battle his fatigue to keep his eyes open. Pulling himself up, he dragged his body across the room to look at the clock. It said five o'clock. He deduced that meant five o'clock in the afternoon. He needed more sleep, but willed himself not to succumb. Walking through the castle corridors, he was aware of a strange silence, as if a blanket had fallen over the place. He looked out of a lancet window. The courtyard was empty. Where was everyone? His lone footsteps echoed through the hallway until he entered the room where he had first laid eyes on the beauty that was Angeline – The Lady of the Source.

He spied a letter, addressed to him, placed conspicuously on the table.

My Lord,

Lady Angeline has arrived safely, thank heavens. She arrived many hours after you. She travelled by coach with a lady companion who is a friend of Viscount Stanwick.

All is well, but she refuses to reside at the castle and refuses to say who or what has caused her distress. She wishes to be left alone, preferring to stay in hiding at a secret location.

I must abide by her decision.

She will be looked after and will be safe. I give you my word.

Eric Sweyne

William had never experienced such relief. How on earth had he missed her on the road? But his relief quickly turned into torment. He knew exactly what Mr Sweyne meant in the letter: she wished to be left alone by him, William, the man who had sworn to be her protector. But she was very much mistaken if she thought he would accept that. He knew where the secret location was and he intended to teach this impossible woman a lesson.

He was interrupted by a young maid, who squealed when she came across him.

'Girl, where is everyone?' he barked.

She looked around fearfully.

'Spit it out, girl,' he demanded.

'They are all in the woods, my lord. Preparing for the celebration,' she replied, unable to control the wobble in her voice.

'What celebration?'

'It's a very important day, today, my lord,' she answered as if she could not believe he did not know. He looked up into the corner of the room, trying to work it out in his head.

'Tomorrow is May Day,' he said.

'Yes sir, which means at sunset, Beltane begins.'

'What the devil is that?'

The maid smiled brightly, rather proud that she knew something the lord of the manor did not.

'Why sir, it's the celebration of the sacred union. When the great mother goddess walks through the land with the horned one of the forest.'

William could not believe his good fortune to find, in the stable, the same mare that had taken him into the forest all those months ago. She would remember the way. He raced towards the wooded copse that was protected by the ancient stone markers, but once there, he held back. Watching from some distance away, by the glow of eventide, William witnessed a strange ritual unfold. A tall, grey-haired man, so distinguishable a figure it could only be the Reverend Roberts, led a group of young men around the boundary markers that protected the land beyond. Angeline's land.

In the soft, diffused light, William saw Roberts whip the boys with a willow wand and push them hard, almost violently, onto the stone monuments. He caught snippets of what he was reciting.

'Thou has set a bound that they may not pass over…
He sendeth the springs into the valley…
They give drink to every beast…

William recalled it as Psalm 104.

The boys' raucous laughter raced away through the air over the exhortation, and William nearly smiled. He recognised this ancient custom of 'Beating the Bounds', which had been handed down from the laws of Alfred the Great. Knowledge of boundaries needed to pass down the generations to stop markers being moved and disputes flaring up. So the whipping and shoving were ways of getting the young men from the district to remember where the boundaries were.

The sunlight shifted and darkening shadows fell. At that moment, the vicar took one boy by the hair and knocked his head on top of the long thin marker, the one with the Viking runes. The other boys yelled with delight as they danced around the stones in unrestrained enjoyment before making their way into the forest. William followed, moving through the woods slowly, keeping a safe distance. His horse skittered sideways, remembering it had been this way before, and fearing what lay ahead. This time the path was lit by torches, inviting them in, but the skulls and amulets were still hanging from the trees. Now they looked almost benign to William, but he remembered the fear he felt the first time he came across them and wondered at the power of the imagination to produce such wild foreboding. He continued to coax his horse along the path.

Night had overtaken him by the time he arrived at the open field that housed the Roman ruins and the source of the river. William decided to stay hidden in the bushes and observe the scene in front of him. Perhaps as many as one hundred people had gathered there. Men wearing leafy green masks made from the forest, and girls with wreaths of spring flowers in their hair were ebbing and flowing with the music. Three bonfires placed in the shape of a triangle burned brightly. In the middle, a wooden fire arch blazed over the bubbling water of the source. The burning stopped quite quickly and left the twisted wires of wood glowing vivid orange in the dark. The heat from the bonfires distorted the air, making it difficult for William to see, and woodsmoke filled his lungs, so he crept around the perimeter of the field and tethered his horse to the same post as the last time he was here, outside the house with the mural of the Lady of the Source on the wall. He hid his jacket in the saddle bag, pulled his shirt out from his trousers and ruffled his hair, knowing he could easily mingle with the crowd undetected. He walked past a kissing couple and spied a mask perched precariously on top of the man's head. As the maid's hand came up to stroke her lover's hair, she knocked the mask and William swiped it away unnoticed, pleased with himself that he had not lost his touch from his days spying for king and country.

A horn sounded as he placed the disguise over his face. The fresh, green smell tickled his senses. Suddenly, the music became wilder as men started to leap over the flames of the bonfires, urged on by the cheering crowd. In the darkness it appeared as if they were jumping out of the mouths of dragons. The men tumbled headlong into the unruly crowd and there was some pushing and shoving before the horn sounded a second time and the music stopped. A hush fell over the field and people stood in silence, anticipation seeming to crackle in the air.

From out of the night, Reverend Roberts emerged, leading Lady Angeline. He beckoned her to stand with him underneath the burning glow of the arch. She was wearing a long, white diaphanous gown and hawthorn blossoms in her hair. Her lush primitivism cried out to William and he yearned for her with ravenous desire.

'This place has been sanctified by centuries of observance,' bellowed the reverend. 'It is a sacred place. The land is ripe and fertile and we express our love for it.' Flamboyantly, he scattered seeds onto the ground. 'Let us together honour the greenwood marriage that will take place here tonight.'

William's heart stopped. What was she about to do? Give herself to someone else, just so she could be rid of him?

As the crowd shifted to let someone through, William's life, ever since he met Angeline, flashed before his eyes. He felt every tangled emotion, from the surprise of discovering that she even existed, to quashed attraction. Then paternal duty, mixed with irritation at this wayward child. Eventually, immense pride grew as he observed her intelligence, composure and kindness, but these feelings were always mingled with flashes of suppressed lust that made him ashamed of his desires.

All these feelings came crashing down on him in that very moment. To his intense shock, he wanted to scream out, '*No! She's mine!*' out of pure sexual jealousy and a haunting, ancient need for possession.

Brigid Absalom and Eric Sweyne stepped forward, to William's amazement, and the horn blew again. Tonight was their marriage.

'Both parties approach this union as equals,' said the reverend. 'Neither is given away.' There was a murmur of approval from the crowd. 'Is this union for a year and a day, a lifetime, or for all time?' he asked.

'For all time,' Brigid and Eric chimed in harmony. Holding hands, they held them up as Reverend Roberts carefully tied the hands together with silken ribbons.

'With this hand-binding you are forever bound to each other,' proclaimed the reverend. Angeline began to walk around the couple sun-wise, east to west, chanting an incantation.

'With feminine cup and masculine blade,
Unite now the two and a blessing be made.'

William instantly recognised what she was holding. The gloriously decorated goblet and knife, the treasure he had discovered in the house the last time he had come calling, glittered spectacularly in the firelight that snapped and cracked.

'With feminine cup and masculine blade
Unite now the two and a blessing be made.'

Angeline repeated it again as she stopped in front of the newly-bound couple. 'Take the lunar cup,' she said to Brigid. 'Take the ritual athame,' she instructed Eric. 'Now bond forever.'

With her free hand, Brigid held up the cup and Eric, very slowly, plunged the knife into it. Brigid then pulled the vessel, still containing the knife, towards her and drank. William could see she held some of the liquid in her mouth as she raised the goblet for Eric to sup, but he did not. Instead he drew Brigid to him and kissed her greedily, taking the liquid from her mouth.

The reverend coughed. 'I see appetites are keen tonight,' he said, removing the goblet and ceremonial knife from Brigid. 'Go now. The Great Mother summons The Horned One with his verdant strength. Celebrate this union.'

Brigid and Eric smiled at each other knowingly, and took their leave.

'But,' protested the reverend, 'I expect you two to be married in church within the month.' They both nodded shyly before slipping away.

The Reverend Roberts placed the lunar cup and athame on the pedestal of the statue of Bacchus, standing next to the arch, and lifted an elaborate crown of green leaves which had small antlers placed proudly within it. Then he spoke,

'My Lady Coventina. Weaver of fates, bringer of dreams, Choose your consort.'

The reverend looked up to the stars.

'Summon your vessel, Coventina.'

The horn sounded once more as a warm breeze stirred and stroked Angeline's skin.

He is here.

Angeline heard the whisper on the wind. She looked up, could sense his presence. She scanned the crowd and her breath caught at the back of her throat when she laid eyes on him. No one but she could have known it was Lord Lyndhurst behind the mask. Only she knew the set of his shoulders, the breadth of his thighs. She wanted to flee, but did not dare look away, for he made no attempt to disguise the predatory look in his eyes. He enthralled her and it broke her will. She pointed to him, signalling that he had been chosen.

'I will choose for Coventina tonight,' she said.

There was a ripple of a murmur from the crowd, as if this move was unexpected.

William looked like a man possessed as he approached her with long, prowling strides. They stood facing each other, waiting for the other to make the first move. Her breathing became fast and shallow.

'Do you want me?' she asked, her voice shaking with emotion.

'More than anything else on earth.'

'Then break the chains that fetter you,' she pleaded.

The look in his eyes was as raw as anything she had ever seen and fear fused with longing for him. She removed his mask and the crowd jostled, whispering loudly when they realised it was the lord of the manor. The reverend leapt in between them.

'My lady, are you sure? It is common practice for a married couple to step forward. The ritual is symbolic, you know that.'

Taking the crown from the reverend, Angeline placed it on William's head, and the reverend sighed heavily, resigning himself to this outcome.

'We celebrate the union of the Great Mother and the Horned One,' he announced. 'The sacred union of the Lord and the Lady.'

William pulled Angeline towards him roughly. The rush of seductive delight thrilled through her as she yielded to him, like a creature giving itself up as prey. The Lord of the Forest picked her up and caged her in his arms and she sank into them willingly. The revellers parted as he spirited her away with haste.

Odin, lying in front of the hearth, started to bark viciously as they entered the house.

'Quiet, Odin,' Angeline commanded and the dog obeyed immediately as William kicked the door shut.

Once inside the inner sanctum of the bedroom, dimly lit by burnt-down candles, he trapped her in his arms and kissed her. A long, bruising kiss that ravaged her lips. Eventually she tore herself away from him, so she might breathe. She threw off his crown and brushed the leaves out of his hair.

'Passion. You have suppressed it for too long, my lord,' she whispered, then returned his kiss with her own fiery kisses. Although innocent, she followed her instincts blindly.

He slowly unpeeled her clothing, feeling jealous of the gown brushing against her body as he anticipated what lay below the collarbone that had tantalised him for so long. He shrugged off the material from her shoulders and it slipped to the ground, pooling around her feet. Staring at her nakedness, William swallowed hard and skimmed his finger along her collarbone, making her quiver with delight.

'You are so beautiful, just like an angel,' he rasped. 'Looking at you could make a grown man cry with need.' He did not take his eyes off her body for a single moment whilst discarding his own clothing. She grew hot and hungry under his relentless gaze.

William laid her on the bed and slipped down beside her. His hands roved all over her body. He kissed her everywhere as if stamping her with his mark, to ensure every part of her body belonged to him. Then he took her, almost cruelly, such was his desire, and she revelled in it, knowing it would tie him to her. She cried out as he entered, feeling him high inside her, almost touching her heart. There was a moment of panic when she felt he might tear her apart. She nearly begged him to stop, but after the pain, came a searing heat, like molten lava coursing through her veins, which soothed her. She gasped with the wonder of it.

The relentless pace of his lovemaking was frenzied and unrestrained and she was glad of it. Glad he had no control; in that moment he belonged to her. With such little light in the room he was a dark presence, a phantom lover. Listening to his deep, low groans as he satisfied himself with her body, she became filled with the supreme power of the goddess.

Despite the tight, throbbing sensation, her joy bloomed. She sank her fingers deep into his hard muscles, which were taut and tense with exertion. She implored him for more, much more, without understanding what it was she was demanding from him. Her body yearned desperately for some kind of resolution. It needed to reach an unknown destination. Her body understood it, but her mind did not. This craving had to be fulfilled. There was the tiniest moment of complete stillness when she felt totally alive; every fibre of her being sang. Then the pleasure hit her and she was gone. It ran up and down her body, inside and out, like an invisible aura. It hit with such force she almost could not bear it and screamed with intense delight as the rapture rolled over and over her, like the waves of an ocean.

The waves continued to roll and roll, their rhythm lulling her until eventually they slowed and she felt wrung like a cloth dolly. Her lover continued to strive for his reward in a violent, physical effort, pushing and thrusting onwards. Finally he cried her name and the wildness was over. He was sated.

He stayed quite still inside her for several precious seconds, while Angeline returned to an earthly existence. She listened to his soft panting and felt his body sticking damply to hers as he slid out of her. She reached for him in the dark. His hard muscles were now warmed and loosened. He was replete and she was proud she could do that for him. Finally, she had found a man worthy of her.

CHAPTER 28

William awoke to find the dawn peeping through the window shutters, and the Lady of the Source studying him. She lay naked on the pillow beside him, hawthorn flowers tangled in her hair, others crushed among the linen. Her eyes sparkled with the look he had seen so many times before, but had never recognised it for what it was. Love.

'I'm sorry I hurt you,' he said.

She smiled contently. 'You could never hurt me.'

He knew that was not true, but hoped it would never be put to the test. He bent his head down and kissed her breast. Her breath hitched with surprise and pleasure. He caressed the full length of her back and sensed her delight. He would make sure this time would be sweeter for her. He touched her all over, like a rare exotic flower, before stealing into her body.

He watched his pagan goddess intently, her face beautified by the flame of passion. Listening to her exquisite whispers, his vanity was truly gratified. She had chosen him.

His tongue slid along her lower lip and he felt her hunger rise. She urged him on, but was too eager, too innocent, so he loved her slowly in order to teach her. She began to tremble with lust. Her eyes opened and they pleaded with his.

'Please,' she sighed, stroking his face, 'take me to heaven again.'

Her silken plea set him on fire. His lips traced a line down her throat to where her pulse throbbed, just above the collarbone that enthralled him so. He had wanted this magical woman with a need that had shocked him to the core and now, here she was, lying in his arms demanding pleasure from him. He could feel her breasts rise and fall, could hear the rapid rhythm of her breath that came from a heart beating too fast. He kept his lovemaking unhurried and luxurious until she arched her back and he sensed the wave was about to sweep her away. His eyes feasted upon her as his pace became more urgent. She clung to him, then gave a fractured cry, like a goddess being sacrificed. Only when he was sure her surrender was complete did he allow his own release. Holding her tightly, his head buried in her hair, he shuddered and convulsed in spasms, which set him adrift from the world. No thought, just feeling. His weight relaxed down on her for a while before he summoned the strength to separate and lie beside her, drifting in a sea of tranquillity.

Wrapped up in the sensual spell that fate had woven around them, Angeline turned over and laid her head on his shoulder, her hand touched his chest and she tantalised him with feather-like strokes.

'I had no idea that coupling could be so beautiful,' she said. 'With animals it's so brutish.' As she looked up at him, a single tear dropped from her eye.

She filled him with such tenderness that he knew, then and there, that she had stolen his heart and he was lost to her. Brimming with emotion, he knew this was love. It was a frightening realisation, but some things were not to be questioned, just accepted. He felt an overwhelming sense of destiny.

His hand moved down over her breasts, sweeping around to her buttocks. He had an elemental need to know every part of her body. He rested there and stroked her satin skin. The caress evolved into more explicit touching as his hand moved over her mound of curls. He stroked the inside of her thigh and felt wetness. Withdrawing his hand, it was stained with reddish moisture and he winced. He had bedded many women before, but never an innocent. He had not been considerate enough to her.

'Are you sore?' he asked.

'A little,' she replied, embarrassed.

Turning away from her, he sat up and pulled on his clothes roughly.

'What's the matter?' Angeline asked.

'I will only be a moment.'

He went into the kitchen to find a bowl. Odin was still lying by the hearth. The dog's head came up and its flame-coloured eyes followed William around the room. William knew he was being watched, so turned and stared at the dog, who growled in response. William growled back and Odin quickly sank into a submissive position, and did not raise his head again.

William went outside to collect water from the spring. He walked through the debris from the night before, tripping over a drinking vessel. The place smelt damp and smoky from the burned-out wood of the bonfires. He needed to relieve himself in the bushes and almost urinated on a dishevelled sleeping couple. He shook his head in disbelief at the madness that had taken place here, last night. William had been completely caught up in the maelstrom and it had changed his life forever. He knew he should start thinking about the consequences but did not want to, not yet. He just wanted to be.

Back inside the bedroom William found a cloth, dampened it in the water, gently parted her legs and began to wash away the reddish, sticky substance from Angeline's body. She blushed and recoiled slightly at the intimacy of what he was doing, but the coolness of the water against her inflamed skin was a welcome relief. She watched him shyly, all that self-possessed maleness, felt the water trickle down into the creases of her skin and became emboldened enough to lie back and enjoy the ritual cleansing without reserve. Every stroke was reverent, every nerve in her body was alive to him and she would never tire of him touching her.

Absorbed in the sensual aura, Angeline heard a familiar sound drift into the house, but it took her a while to realise what it was. She looked up and saw William staring at the window. He had recognised it, too.

'It's the bell ringing. I can't believe I forgot about it,' she said, scrambling for her chemise. 'Brigid is too late!' she gasped as she ran to open the wooden slats. William followed her to see, standing outside the window, a few feet away, Reverend Roberts looking towards the sound of the tolling bell.

'I had to wake them,' he said. 'Brigid and Eric.'

'Will she be all right?' Angeline asked him.

'I think so. Eric is with her.'

'But will everyone be safe, even though the bell is late?' she asked.

The vicar turned and narrowed his eyes when he saw William come into view.

'I hope so,' he replied as he came towards her and thrust the lunar cup and athame into her hands, 'I hope so.' Then he gave them one of his superior smiles. 'Good May Day,' he said and walked off.

William left Angeline to run outside and catch up with the Man of God. He pulled at the reverend's sleeve. 'Can you explain to me, Reverend, what sort of witchcraft was going on here last night?'

Ice-blue eyes glared at William. 'There was no witchcraft here, my lord. What you witnessed was priestcraft.'

'Explain yourself, sir.'

'I certainly shall. If you knew your religious history, you would know that in this land, Christianity overlaid itself on existing beliefs hundreds of years ago. People were not forced to convert. It happened naturally.'

'So?'

'So, these old rituals have always lived alongside Christian teachings.'

'Excuse me, Reverend, but I cannot believe the Church would be happy with what I saw last night.'

The vicar spluttered with outrage.

'No more than it would be happy with your actions last night.'

William balked at the reprimand.

'Every man and woman here last night is a God-fearing person,' bellowed the reverend. 'They will all be in church on Sunday, I can assure you of that.' He moved in closer to William. 'For your information, my lord, Beltane has always been observed by the Christians of England. It was only the Puritans who banned it, and they banned Christmas, too.'

'Come now, Reverend. The Puritans banned Christmas because they saw it as an unwanted remnant of Roman Catholicism, encouraging dissent,' William replied, showing off his knowledge of religious history. 'It's hardly the same thing.'

'Well, my lord, you seemed happy enough to partake in the events of last night,' the reverend threw back.

'Perhaps I was bewitched.'

The reverend stared at William for some time, as if sizing him up.

'You do not believe that, my lord. You strike me as a thoroughly modern man. A nineteenth-century man.'

William, struggling with his inner turmoil, failed to answer. The reverend composed himself as if realising that he had overstepped the mark.

'My lord, in truth, there is a sort of magic at work here. The history of our ancestors is written in the soil. The echo of past lives can be heard on the wind. But I give you my word as a man of the cloth, this place is a source of good, in more ways than you will ever know.'

William wanted to believe him. His judgement told him that although this was a wild place, there was no evil at work here. The reverend took William's silence as tacit understanding, so doffed his hat and took his leave. Then he turned back.

'One last thing, my lord: you will do right by the Lady Angeline?'

William nodded. 'I give you my word as lord of this realm.'

The reverend did not appear satisfied with that response. 'The Lord, our father, is mightier than any worldly lord,' he preached. 'He watches over us and he judges us.'

With that warning, the reverend disappeared into the forest.

William found Angeline still looking out of the window. The ringing had stopped and she was waiting for the return of Brigid and Eric. He placed his arms around her waist possessively.

'Angeline, whatever did you mean when you asked the reverend, *'Will everyone be safe?'* You told me you do not believe in the legend of Fenrir.'

'I don't,' she said dismissively, 'but we've never found the monster that killed Nan, have we?'

'No, but I will find it, and destroy it. I have given you my promise on that.' William watched her expression change; she looked disappointed. He was sure he knew what she was thinking. *What is taking you so long?* He had been making the same promise for months and was no further forward. He had no new clues, no new ideas.

Then they saw Brigid and Eric walk up the path, returning home to their cottage at the other end of the field and Angeline's relief was plain to see. Brigid caught sight of Angeline and ran up to her. They embraced each other through the window, whispering to each other like excited schoolgirls whose dreams had just come true. The two men acknowledged each other from a distance with an embarrassed nod, knowing things would never be the same again.

'Let's eat,' Angeline said, watching Brigid return to Eric, 'I'm starving.' She stretched up to kiss William on the cheek before running into the other room. Why did he always feel she was holding something back, keeping secrets from him?

Angeline prepared the food: cold meat, cheese, bread, while William stood in the living area, studying the mural on the wall. The chalice and knife had been placed back on the wooden altar under the painting.

'Is that you?' he asked.

'No, it's one of my ancestors. We all look remarkably alike, the women in my family. The painting is very old, hundreds of years, I think.'

William took a closer look. He remembered the blue paint on Nan's clothes when he found her body. He was sure it was the same blue as that on the wall. William had assumed she had been working on the mural, but it looked in the same sorry state of repair as the last time he saw it. The painting had not been touched at all.

'When I found Nan's body, she had patches of blue dye on her clothes. It was the same colour as the paint on the wall. Do you have any idea how it could have got there?'

Angeline shook her head. 'None whatsoever. It could be the dye from a plant, I suppose, for a remedy: woad perhaps. It cleans wounds and stops bleeding.'

William thought that sounded plausible. It was probably woad that was painted on the wall. 'What does the wheel symbolise?' he asked as he studied the golden strands of hair that divided the wheel into eight parts.

'It's the wheel of life. We celebrate the seasons, the turning of the year and the vital elements we need to survive.'

William looked at the symbols: water, earth, air, fire. They intertwined with golden depictions of the sun, moon and stars. There was something else. He remembered identifying it the last time he was here: a spirit figure. He nearly forgot himself and almost mentioned his first visit. He had to remember that Angeline had no idea he had ever been here before.

'What is that symbol?' he asked.

Angeline looked up from slicing a hock of ham. 'She is called Coventina. Often we find ourselves lost, either physically or spiritually, and we need the help of Coventina to find our way home.' She laid out two platters for the food. 'We are often lost because we keep secrets, even from ourselves. We need to be honest in order to find true happiness; inner peace.'

'Are you keeping secrets, Angeline?' he asked.

She threw a piece of meat to Odin. 'Not too many, are you?'

'Hardly any,' he replied, as a fleeting image of Theresa came into his head, vivid as life itself, appraising him, mocking him.

Angeline ripped a piece of bread away from the loaf. 'We need to feed our soul as much as we nourish our body. But right now, I'm famished, so my soul can wait.'

His lips curved in a spontaneous smile. He, too, was starving. He had not lived like this, so simply, since fighting the French in Portugal, and he had missed it. Angeline fed him a piece of meat and the gesture reminded him of Theresa, but he banished all thoughts of her from his mind. It was not fair to either woman.

'After we've eaten, let's go swimming in the sea,' Angeline said brightly. 'I haven't done that for such a long time.'

'It will be freezing,' he protested, but within the hour they were walking down a shelving beach into a deepening North Sea and there they swam naked, their skins stinging, turning blue with the cold. He knew he should be worried: worried they would be seen, worried they would catch pneumonia, worried about the beast that had killed Nan, worried about the future, but he could not bring himself to feel that emotion because a wonderful serenity had taken hold of him. He watched her dance between the shimmering drifts of white crested waves that sat on top of an agitated slate-blue sea. He had never seen Angeline so light and carefree, like a water nymph, and it warmed his soul, unlike the sea that numbed his skin. He trod water, letting the silky fronds of seaweed ensnare his limbs, welcoming their frosty embrace. He listened to Angeline's gurgles of laughter, mixing with the many different voices of the ocean, then pulled her to him with one fluid, easy motion and she sighed in anticipation.

CHAPTER 29

He held her so closely as he lay sleeping that she was cocooned by his body. It almost hurt to feel such joy. Angeline felt as if she had been allowed to run free in paradise and silently thanked Coventina, the benevolent caretaker, for bringing William to her. Angeline was in love, and in return had been loved passionately and beautifully. She wondered what she needed to do to keep him in her thrall forever. Coventina would guide her, she realised, as she always had.

Angeline felt William's warm, regular breath on the back of her neck. He was so still she had to stretch out and touch him with a velvet caress, just to make sure he was really there. Her beloved stirred.

She turned to face him and studied the network of lines on his face. She pressed her mouth against his, using her tongue to prise it open and explore, just as he had taught her. She boldly touched him and felt his delight. He was roused. She was fascinated by how quickly she could do this to him. She explored his body, her palms gliding over his contours, savouring all the various textures: the rippling smoothness of the skin covering the muscles on his back, the silky hair on his chest which was quite different from the coarser hair on his legs that tickled her. She wanted to learn everything about him, all through a lover's touch.

'I burn for your luscious body,' he said as he lifted her, adroitly, onto his torso. She inwardly smiled, glorying in the power she held. She drew in a long, deep breath and exhaled on a groan as she wrapped herself around him, locking him inside her body.

His large hands curved over the swell of her hips, anchoring her there, then he rocked her gently. Their dance began – slow, steady undulations.

'*I love you!*' she wanted to shout at the top of her voice. The words welled up inside her chest but she caught the breath on a sob, too frightened to reveal herself.

As the dance intensified, she felt a surging sensation stir up the blood in her veins. She saw the sustained concentration on his face as he buried himself deep within her, so deep she felt they were one being. Their soft moans and murmurs mingled together, producing a haunting harmony. There was no him and her, no lord and lady, just oneness. A true communion.

Searing heat thrilled through her as he moved his hands up to her breasts. They moulded into his palms.

'You are so soft,' he whispered hoarsely.

She shivered with desire and pushed against his hands. He uttered an urgent groan in response. She was consumed with passion for him and could scarcely breathe as his hips changed rhythm and moved in quick, tight strokes.

His eyes opened, glistening brilliantly in the shadows. One of his hands released her breast and moved down her body to thread his fingers through her soft curls at the apex of her thighs. Seeking the sensitive bud, he stroked her. She bucked wildly, beyond restraint. Her head fell back and she called his name. Her nails dug into his chest and ripped at his flesh. He responded with a low, savage roar.

Within seconds, Angeline felt the explosion of a million glittering fragments shudder through her body, over and over again. Then William's final euphoric cry bounced off the walls as he thrust home and filled her with his seed.

Her essence dropped delicately back to earth, like falling snowflakes, and she almost cried with sheer joy. She prayed that she was with child, his child, a daughter. The next in line to the Bernician legacy.

She could see the shadows had fallen away from his face and all his features were softened with sensual relaxation.

'You belong to me,' he rasped. She stroked his fine patrician jaw.

'And you to me.'

Their limbs entwined as they fell asleep.

CHAPTER 30

'Oh no, it can't be. We are so late.'

He heard mild panic in Angeline's voice.

'What is it?' he asked, propping himself up on one elbow.

'Listen to the bells,' she said as she ran around the room. 'Quickly, we must get dressed.'

He could hear bells ringing and rubbed his eyes. This was not the bell from the old abbey, Fenrir's bell. This was a different sound.

'Quick, quick,' she said, 'we can still make it.'

'Make what?' he asked, exasperated.

'Church!' she cried. 'It's Sunday, and we are late for church.'

Angeline and William crept into the building as the reverend was in full flight with his sermon. They had to sit in the front pew, as was their station, so walked the length of the aisle in full view of everyone. There was not a murmur, nor a look. All eyes were averted, fixed on the vicar.

William glanced at the faces. He recognised many from Goldsborough; some he thought he had seen at the Beltane festival. Brigid and Eric were there, seated in the second pew.

They sat and listened to the address. The reverend never wavered.

'My beloved spake, and said unto me,
'Rise up, my love, my fair one, and come away.'

William screwed up his face, covered his eyes with his hand and almost laughed out loud. *The Song of Solomon.* What else? Nothing more appropriate after Beltane, he thought.

'For lo, the winter is past,
the rain is over and gone;
The flowers appear on the earth;
the time of the singing of birds is come,
and the voice of the turtle is heard in our land.'

William paid close attention to the sermon, a newfound admiration growing within him for the clergyman who seemed to marry his two worlds effortlessly and without a shred of doubt. William envied him his certainty.

'I charge you, O daughters of Jerusalem,
by the roes and the hinds of the field,
that ye stir not up, nor awake my love,
till he please.'

The reverend said the last line forcefully, then paused, looking straight at William, who smiled graciously, pretending that he did not understand the unspoken castigation for being late.

William was surprised at the joyous atmosphere that surrounded the congregation after the service. People were almost elated, as if they believed that things were now how they should be and all was right with the world. They talked and laughed with the lord and lady, as if they were a married couple already and Angeline responded in kind. Everyone seemed convinced that providence had intervened, directing the affairs of humans with divine care.

But leaving the enchanted forest had broken the spell for William. It was like a bucket of cold water being poured over his head. He knew he needed to get back to the castle, to think about reality and its consequences. Angeline did not protest.

They collected Odin from the house in the woods and rode back to the castle. William picked his moment. 'You know we must marry, and soon.'

'I know nothing of the sort,' came the reply.

William bristled. 'Angeline, your pagan customs have no place in the modern world. You may be with child.'

'So?'

William spoke through clenched teeth. 'If it is a boy, he will be heir to Lyndhurst.'

She shrugged. 'If it's a girl, she will be heir to the Bernician dynasty, far older than that of the Fitzalans'.

'Damn it, Angeline, I am asking you to marry me! What more do you want from me?'

She turned and locked eyes with him. 'If you do not know, I am not going to tell you. You need to discover it for yourself.'

They rode on in brooding silence. He knew what she wanted from him: a declaration of love, but he had never said the words before, not even to Theresa. He had known with her there was no need. The thought of saying the words terrified him. Even though he was sure he did love Angeline, the vulnerability terrified him. It was about the only thing on this earth that did frighten him. *Why are you hanging back?* he said to himself. It would make everything so simple if you would just say, *I love you.* What was this fear of the emotion that binds one person to another? The emotion he had fled from ever since childhood. He suspected his family had something to do with it. He had not even liked his father or brother, let alone loved them. And as for his mother, she had been a pathetic figure, someone to pity, not love. He had been so different from all of them: he had always felt alone, like an outsider. It had made him totally self-sufficient from a very early age, never needing anybody. The perfect breeding for someone who would, one day, become the pre-eminent spy for the king of England. He knew deep in his soul that things would not end well with Angeline unless he wrestled and conquered this irrational dread.

William and Angeline had just dismounted and given their reins to the stable boy in the castle courtyard when an unmarked carriage sped across the bridge and stopped abruptly at the front entrance to the castle.

The lord and lady shared a troubled look.

'Well, what a surprise!' declared Nikolaus loudly as he jumped from the carriage with his arms wide open in greeting. 'What are you two doing here?'

'I should be asking you that question,' William replied, watching Nikolaus help Annabel out of the coach.

After a long display of congratulatory hugs and kisses from Angeline to Annabel, William said, 'Well, it is always delightful to see you both, but why are you here?'

'We are on our way back from Gretna Green to Annabel's estate in Somerset,' Nikolaus explained, 'but we thought we might hide out here for a while, if that is agreeable with you?'

Annabel touched her husband's arm affectionately. 'Yes, we still need the dust to settle a little bit before we are officially seen in public. Do you mind the intrusion?' she asked.

'Of course not,' declared Angeline.

'I fully expected to be asking Mr Sweyne if we could stay,' Nikolaus said, sounding confused. 'You should both still be in London. What has happened?'

William glanced at Angeline. 'It's a long story. Let's go inside.'

'Come, let's get you settled,' Angeline said to Annabel as soon as they entered the hallway. 'I'm so excited about showing you my castle.'

Both ladies ran up the stairs, talking non-stop, followed by Odin. Nikolaus raised an eyebrow.

'Her castle?' he said to William.

'It is complex.' William pointed to the room he wanted them to go to. 'Library,' he said. Once there, he offered Nikolaus a brandy. 'You tell me your story first.'

Nikolaus carefully stuck to the details of their dash to Gretna Green, studiously avoiding the reasons why. William flicked through the correspondence on his bureau as Nikolaus talked. He picked out a particular letter he had been waiting for.

My Lord,

As per your request, we have been tracking Viscount Elewald. He left London on the 28th April, travelling North, and has taken up residence on his estate.

We await further instructions.

Trebyan

So, Elewald was back in Northumberland. This time scores would be settled, once and for all. William vowed this to himself.

'Have you listened to a word I've said, William? I'm not used to being ignored,' Nikolaus berated his friend.

William turned to gaze on him. 'Have you lost your mind?'

'Whatever do you mean?'

'Heavens, man, what possessed you to marry Annabel?'

Nikolaus shrugged. 'She asked me.'

William held his hands up to the sky. 'Why doesn't that surprise me?'

'It's one of the things I like most about her,' Nikolaus said. 'She behaves as she sees fit, regardless of prevailing attitudes.'

'But why did you agree to marriage?'

Nikolaus halted, finding the words difficult. 'Because I was so exquisitely bored with my old life. I used to think every day about opening a vein. Annabel is my only hope of salvation.'

William crossed his arms. 'Do you love her?'

'She fills me with contentment.'

'Do you love her?'

'She promises domestic bliss.'

'So you don't love her?'

Nikolaus considered his answer. 'William, I have often wondered whether I am human or not.'

William shook his head. 'What are you talking about now?'

'Tragically, I do not believe I am capable of romantic love. I say tragically because I believe it is that ability alone which distinguishes us from the beasts.'

William stared at him, expressionless. 'You know she loves you, don't you?'

'Of course I do. I have seduced too many women not to know the signs for what they are.' Nikolaus stepped forward. 'I feel such compassion for her,' he said in earnest.

'Compassion. That is a strange word to use.'

Nikolaus began to fiddle nervously with an ornament sitting on a side table. 'I have such deep sympathy and sorrow for her, William, to be stricken by the misfortune of loving me.'

'Nikolaus, stop it.'

'No, really. I have a strong desire to alleviate her suffering.'

Suddenly, William could not disguise the horror on his face. 'Nikolaus, be kind to her, please.'

'Yes, yes, of course.' Nikolaus waved his hand floridly in the air, 'I mean to be kindness personified. It's the least I can do for the poor woman.'

'Nikolaus, stop your maudlin indulgences for once, will you!' William said crossly. 'I doubt she sees herself in that way. Just try to make her happy.'

'William, I will do my level best, I promise. It's a novel experience, putting somebody else's feelings before your own.' Nikolaus flicked some dust from his cuff. 'I quite like it.'

He peered over. 'What are you reading?'

William passed him the letter.

Nikolaus scanned it, then looked up. 'But why the need to track him and why have you and Angeline left London mid-season?'

William took back the letter. 'I'll give you the abridged version of the story. Elewald tried to compromise Angeline by being discovered alone with her in Lady Caroline's garden. Luckily, Ponsonby Tottenham gallantly saved us from catastrophe, but Elewald escaped before I had the chance to challenge him. His accomplice was St Affrique.'

At the mention of the Frenchman's name, Nikolaus grimaced, as if he had just tasted something toxic.

'On that same night, I discovered from Lostwithiel that Angeline had spurned his advances.'

Nikolaus raised his eyes in mock amazement.

'The next day, I visited Angeline to give her a piece of my mind, for she had been foolish on both counts.' Recalling the events made William sigh heavily. ' She took it rather badly. That evening Aunt Vivian came to me in a panic to tell me Angeline had run away.'

Nikolaus' eyebrows rose of their own accord on hearing that piece of news.

'I chased her back here to Goldsborough, and well...' William studied his shuffling feet, 'well, let's just say a marriage must take place soon.'

'Ah, ha. At last!' Nikolaus shouted, as he ran to embrace his friend warmly. 'Congratulations, William. Thank goodness you have come to your senses and escaped the clutches of the venomous Lady Caroline.' He clapped his hands. 'Oh, Annabel will be overjoyed.'

'Ah well, we must not get ahead of ourselves,' William retorted. 'She hasn't accepted yet.'

Stunned, it was Nikolaus' turn to cross his arms. 'And you have the audacity to lecture me.'

'What are you on about?' William asked.

'You haven't told her, have you?'

'Told her what?'

Nikolaus slapped William hard across the top of his arm. 'A woman like that is not going to marry without a proclamation of love.'

'I know that,' William protested. 'I just haven't found the right moment.'

'Well, you had better find it soon, before she bolts again.'

William knew his friend was right. He had learnt that much from bitter experience, so he would have to plan his next move carefully. 'If you will excuse me, Nikolaus, I have some letters to write as a result of the unfolding circumstances. I will see you at dinner.'

Firstly, William wrote to his Aunt Vivian, who would be jubilant at the news, but she had work to do. He had resigned himself to the fact that it would be impossible to get back to London in time to save his and Angeline's reputations, although he felt they might be salvaged eventually. He would marry Angeline, even if he had to drag her to the church. They would live quietly until Aunt Vivian had worked her magic and they were accepted back into society. It would take some time but Lord and Lady Lyndhurst would even receive admiration from the younger generation for being wild romantics.

Secondly, he wrote a letter to Simon, Lord Hurstbourne, explaining the situation and giving his instructions. He could not begin to guess what his cousin would think, but he was confident that Louisa would smooth things over. Simon needed to push, on William's behalf, for the reforms to the law on excise duties that were so close to his heart. Smuggling needed to be stamped out. William was convinced more than ever that this would be a major building block to economic recovery and helping the poor, which, in turn, would ensure political stability.

William knew it would be much harder to regain favour with his fellow members of parliament. They would assume it was typical Fitzalan behaviour: abandoning a cause at the crucial moment. Like father, like son, they would say, and this was something that pained him greatly, but not something he could put right in the immediate future, and he only had himself to blame. If he had hauled Angeline back to London as soon as he found her, he believed he could have been back early enough to save the day, but he had chosen his path when he stayed the night with her and he must suffer the consequences.

Finally, he wrote to Lady Caroline. Luckily no promises had been made, although there may have been an unspoken understanding. He would try to let her down gently, allowing her the right to cry off, but she would feel like a woman scorned, especially once the gossips went in for the kill. As such, she would be bent on revenge, and a dangerous enemy in the future.

CHAPTER 31

In later years, William would come to reflect on his time at the house in the forest and those following few days at Goldsborough as some of the most delightful he had ever known. The four friends revelled in each other's company whilst wrapped up in the mysteries of romantic love. Even Nikolaus managed to display uncharacteristic happiness. So much so, Angeline decided to change his medication and prescribe a tonic of spring gentian to drop into his wine. It would help the patient maintain a positive attitude to life, she assured them all.

The days that followed at Goldsborough were filled with fun and laughter. The nights were fuelled with unbridled passion as William harnessed all his skills in the bedroom to seduce Angeline into marrying him, without having to say the words she needed to hear. Little did he know then, that these halcyon days were to be the lull before the storm.

William awoke one night to discover that Angeline was not where she belonged, in bed with him. He listened in the darkness. Strange noises were being carried on the air, heavy grating and rolling sounds that he could not decipher. He was mildly amused to note the flash of irritation with her: she would always do that, slightly aggravate him. It was what made their relationship challenging. Another pagan ritual that Angeline was performing in the middle of the night, no doubt, he said to himself as he dressed. These things really had to stop, he thought, as he bumped into Nikolaus half way down the corridor.

'That is the very same noise I heard on the first night we were here,' Nikolaus whispered. 'Listen.' A deep hauling and scraping sound was coming from the bowels of the earth. 'I told you it was like dead bodies being dragged along the floor.'

'Well, let's find out what it is, shall we?' William replied.

'Not without me.' They turned to see Annabel scurrying down the hallway to meet them.

'Annabel, my sweet, please go back to bed,' Nikolaus pleaded.

'Not likely. I'm coming with you.'

Nikolaus looked at William and shrugged. 'She does as she sees fit.'

William tutted with resignation. 'Be quiet, the pair of you.'

They wandered down rambling passageways that led nowhere. William knew his way around the castle well enough by day, but in the darkness he easily lost his bearings. They seemed to be walking in circles, through large and dreary chambers, when suddenly Nikolaus stuck his nose up in the air and sniffed.

'Well, that's peculiar. I can smell oak and brandy. We must be near the cellar.'

'No, I don't think we are,' whispered William as he tripped on the lip of a wooden floor, the light from the candelabra ballooning as it bounced off tall open walls. William had fallen into a cavernous room, the wind whistled menacingly through the eaves. He orientated himself and discovered he was standing in the Great Tudor Hall.

'The smell is coming from that direction,' Nikolaus said, pointing to the corner of the room. In the shadows they could see an opening in the wall and William recognised it as the secret entrance to the hidden altar and confessional box.

They all tiptoed forward, the thuds and thumps becoming louder as they approached.

Suddenly, the noises stopped. All was quiet as the three friends held their breath and listened through the doorway.

'What was the cargo this time?' asked a voice.

'Brandy, lace and silk, my lady.'

William could not believe what he had just heard. He lurched into the room and the light he was holding fell on two startled faces, those of Lady Angeline and the Reverend Roberts.

'What in the name of God is going on here?' William demanded.

The faces stared, dumbstruck, as William, Nikolaus and Annabel proceeded to inspect the wooden boxes and barrels that were piled up around the tiny room. William walked to the far side and saw a hole in the floor. It held a wooden ramp, which led down to the courtyard. Kegs could be rolled up and down; boxes could be hauled. These were the sounds William had heard. He held the light down, and saw the familiar face of Mr Sweyne peering up at him from the courtyard below. He was surrounded by burly men who William did not recognise, but by their ragged clothing he deduced they were men from the camp they had passed when walking into Thornby on the day of Nan's funeral.

William turned back and fixed his gaze on Angeline. 'You're the leader of a smuggling gang?' he asked incredulously.

'I can explain.'

'Oh, I don't think you can. Tell me, are we expediting or receiving tonight?'

'Receiving,' Angeline replied sheepishly.

William looked down the hole again to see no contraband remained in the courtyard. Mr Sweyne and his men had finished the task.

'My lord, let the men go please. It's dangerous for them. There are naval officers patrolling,' said Reverend Roberts, who was hovering protectively over Angeline.

'You have the gall to ask me that!' William spat, shaking with unabated fury, for he did not know if he should let them go or call the officers himself. It took long seconds for him to decide.

'Get out of here, Sweyne,' he finally shouted down to him from the hole in the floor. Then he swung back to look around the room, 'and you, sir, get out. All of this booty will be destroyed. None of you will see a penny.'

Reverend Roberts tried to protest, but Angeline persuaded him to leave by sliding down the ramp to join the men in the courtyard. The ramp was pulled up after him by William and Nikolaus, who then secured the floor hatch. William lit the candles in the room, then forcefully gave his candelabra to Nikolaus who understood the signal to retreat with his wife, leaving William and Angeline alone.

'Courage,' Annabel whispered to Angeline as she was dragged away by her husband.

'Do you hate me so much that you would do this to me?' William finally asked.

'No, I...'

He paced the room slowly. 'I know my brother destroyed your world, but your father had a hand in his own downfall. He was not totally innocent, Angeline.'

'William, it's not like that. Let me explain.'

'Explain what exactly? That you cursed me with your beauty from the very first moment I laid eyes on you? That you vowed revenge and would not stop until you had ruined me?'

'No, no, William. Please listen.'

'Well, you have ruined me, just as you intended. When you ran away from London, you knew I would come after you.'

Angeline shook her head in protest.

'You tricked me into your bed, knowing then we would never get back to London in time to save my reputation.'

'You don't believe that, William,' she gasped.

He collapsed down and sat on one of the boxes. 'I don't know what to believe any more. You know how important it is to me to stop smuggling. To do this under my very nose, when I have been working like a dog in Parliament to put an end to it.' His head sank. 'I will be a laughing stock.'

Angeline ran to him and fell to her knees in front of him. 'We'll destroy everything, we'll destroy it all, I promise. No one will betray us. This is a closed community.'

He took hold of her shoulders and shook her. 'Everything has been a lie from the day I met you.'

She touched her trembling fingers to his lips, trying to placate him. 'William, you know none of what you say is true.'

He turned his face away. 'Elewald tried to warn me. *Born and bred for scandal*, that's what he said about you.'

'Please let me explain,' she begged.

'Explain,' he repeated, then he suddenly grabbed hold of her arm and dragged her along the floor towards the altar. He forced her face against the crucifix that rested there. 'Swear to me in front of God that what you are about to tell me is nothing but the truth.'

'I swear,' she choked out, 'as God is my witness.'

'How can I believe you, a pagan sorceress? You only pretend to believe in God.'

'May I be struck down dead if I'm not telling you the truth,' she pleaded.

He pressed his face against hers and whispered harshly into her ear, 'Are you a wrecker, Angeline? Do you lure men to their deaths?'

''No,' she whispered.

'Club them over the head so their brains spill out onto the sand if they're unlucky enough to make it to shore?'

'No, no, I swear. It's all arranged from France. No one is in danger as long as we all follow the rituals. It was planned that way.'

'Planned by whom?'

'My father, years ago.'

William heaved her up onto her feet and they faced each other. 'Tell me everything.'

Angeline swallowed hard. 'One night, years ago, two men fell to their deaths from the top of the cliff. We knew smuggling was going on but, like the poaching, we turned a blind eye, what with the poor being so desperate. We could not stop it, but we could organise it to make it safer.' Angeline wiped tears away with her palm. 'Ships unload at Blackrock Bay. The goods pass through my land in the woods, then finally they come here before being distributed throughout the country. Although some are suspicious, they are too scared of the magic and the folklore to come out at night.' She passed the back of her hand under her nose to catch the drips, 'Even Elewald is wary. He believes in the supernatural. It is said the Elewalds are descended from elves.'

'Oh God, give me strength!' William cried, disgusted at the medieval beliefs. 'Go on.'

Angeline heaved loudly to catch enough breath to

continue. 'The venerations, the stories about Fenrir, people truly believe in them. The rituals have been performed for a thousand years or more, but they have been embroidered in recent times to keep prying eyes away. The boats come in during the solar festivals and the fire festivals. They make up the wheel of the year.'

William pictured the wall painting of the wheel in his mind's eye.

'We light ritual bonfires along the coast for the boats to see.'

'You know such signalling is a crime?' William said.

Angeline's breath quivered as she nodded. 'The boats are unloaded and the goods hidden in Brandy Cave. That is the cave I disappeared into when you saw me riding along the beach, when the bell was ringing, just before poor Nan's death.'

William let go of her body as if he had been holding onto a leper, finding it hard to conceal his revulsion. 'So the ringing of the bell is all part of this ruse?'

'Yes,' Angeline rasped, 'the bell signals to the men inside the cave that dawn is breaking and they must hide any incriminating evidence and disappear.'

William's face contorted as he tried to unravel in his head the depth of the intrigue. 'Which is why you were so anxious on May Day, when Brigid was late ringing the bell. You weren't worried about Brigid, you were worried that the men in the cave might be discovered.'

She bowed her head. 'Yes.'

William stared at her with horror in his eyes, 'So, Angeline, Nan was butchered because you are a smuggler?'

She could no longer contain herself as he accused her, and collapsed, sobbing uncontrollably onto the altar. William held his face in his hands. 'You have known all along why Nan was murdered.' Then he threw back his head as if he had seen a revelation. 'It's all about the smuggling. Everything has been about the smuggling.'

'No, William,' she gulped, 'Nan's death was so unnatural, only a monster could have done that. I can't believe it had anything to do with the smuggling.' Angeline shook her head slowly. 'We still don't know what it was that killed her. We have all been praying that you will bring us justice.'

'A smuggler praying for justice – how ludicrous.' He laughed contemptuously, then glanced down at her face, half hidden by tangled hair, and was, for a moment, caught up in the torment that hovered in the space between them. He felt something inside himself being squeezed with huge physical intensity until it seemed to snap. William spread out his arms and dropped to the floor in front of the altar. 'I hope you are happy, Angeline. You have brought this lord of the realm to his knees, just as you desired.'

'No'

'My reputation in London is in tatters; everyone assumes that I have run off with my ward. I have deserted my post in Parliament and abandoned a cause I am committed to, which will brand me a contemptible. Only to find that I could be accused of smuggling myself if any of this is uncovered.' He laughed out loud. 'Is revenge sweet, my dear?'

'I never intended any of this, William, please believe me.'

'I asked you to marry me: a godless pagan with no pedigree to speak of. Do you have any idea what I was prepared to give up for you?' William closed his eyes, finding it hard to believe that he had allowed himself to be duped like this. 'You have broken my heart, Angeline, and broken the man. Are you satisfied now? Is that enough for you?'

She crawled towards him on her knees. Tears streaming, she took his face in her hands and kissed his lips over and over, trying to reignite his passion for her. 'I didn't mean to hurt you, my love. Please forgive me.' She kissed him again, desperately. 'I never truly understood before now what you were sacrificing for me. I love you, William. We can make this all go away. Of course I'll marry you. It's all I've ever wanted.'

He pulled her hands away. 'It's too late, my dear,' he said as he wearily got to his feet. 'It's far too late. Come, I will walk you back to your room and I shall retreat to mine. Tomorrow you will show me everything. The cave, the route. All will be destroyed. It's all over.'

CHAPTER 32

'Everything must be destroyed before I return. Not a trace of that despicable trade must be left.' William shouted his instructions to Mr Sweyne so all could hear as he left the castle with Angeline. She looked a pale and pathetic figure: face puffed, eyes sunken – the light in them clouded. She appeared shamefaced and exhausted, as if she had cried all night long. Those full lips were cracked and wan, but William's heart was hardened to her anguish.

They rode down to Blackrock Bay and along the sands. William could not imagine where the cave would be. He had ridden this way before, when he searched for Angeline as she galloped away from the sound of the bell on the day of Nan's death. Today they rode right up to the grey rock stretching out into the North Sea, so impenetrable, it had forced William to retreat previously. A cloud of salt sprayed onto his face, when suddenly Angeline turned sharply to the left and rode towards the cliff. It was only when they were really close that William spied a gap in between the rocks. It could not be detected unless you were right on top of it. It was an optical illusion. A perfect cave for smuggling. The entrance was only just big enough for a horse to pass through, and many would refuse.

The passage was narrow and pitch black. 'I can't go on,' Angeline cried. 'There are usually torches burning. I can't see where I'm going.'

William was prepared. He had a lantern tied to his saddlebag.

'Follow me,' he commanded. He sounded confident, but at heart he felt anxious, not because of the eerie shadows that were thrown against the damp walls by the lantern, but because he knew they would be in grave danger if the horses panicked.

'How do you get the cargo through here?' he enquired of Angeline, who was following behind on the surefooted Cherub.

'On donkeys.'

'Clever,' he said grudgingly. 'What percentage of the profits do you take?'

'Not a penny,' she declared. 'The Reverend handles that side of things, but it all goes to the poor.'

'How can you be so sure?' William asked.

'Because I trust Reverend Roberts completely,' she replied.

A few minutes later, William heaved a sigh of relief as the cave opened up into a shimmering dome.

'This is where we sort and store the goods before moving them onto my land,' Angeline said. 'The exit is over there.'

They moved forward carefully because the floor was becoming dangerously uneven as they started the sharp ascent. None of this would be feasible without donkeys moving the contraband, he realised. As they turned, a shaft of light glinting through the rock became visible. William was curious about the light, which did not stream in. It was dappled and constantly changing. He understood why once they emerged. The exit to the cave was in dense woodland, the canopy of the trees waving back and forward in front of the sun.

'If you go that way you get back to the castle,' Angeline said as she pointed to a path leading off to the left, 'but this way leads to my house.'

'Is this your land?' he asked.

'No, this is still your land. It's farmed by Alan Black.'

William remembered him as one of the protagonists in the argument he had put a stop to in town some time ago.

'Is he involved?'

'Not directly, but he is paid to keep quiet. His family have farmed this land for generations. He is one of us. He will never betray Goldsborough.'

'But would he betray the new lord of the manor?' William challenged.

Angeline stammered, the thought never having occurred to her.

'The man whose sheep were slaughtered, what was his name?'

'John Smith.'

'Yes, that's it. Doesn't he farm near here, too?' William pressed her.

'Yes, on the other side of the river.'

'So, the sheep were savaged close to here?'

'Yes, not too far away.'

'Don't you think that odd?'

Angeline shook her head. 'Forgive me, I do not understand.' She felt so tired.

'Well, two brutal attacks by some sort of beast that stopped as quickly as they began.' William paused for thought. 'Because we knew the attacks were not by a human, we have not been looking for a motive, but what if the beast is being controlled by a human?'

'For what reason?' she asked.

'It's likely to be something to do with the smuggling,' he said. 'Alan Black is starting to look like a suspect.'

'What would he have to gain?'

'Much more money than he was receiving from you, if he could take over the operation.' William was finding it hard to believe that he had to spell it out to her, but when he looked at her face he realised she was suffering from fatigue. She needed to rest.

Angeline bit her bottom lip as she contemplated the possibility that Alan Black was the murderer. 'I don't believe he is capable of such a grand design,' she said.

'I'm never surprised at what men are capable of when money is involved,' William replied. 'But it could just as easily be John Smith.' He thought for a moment. 'Perhaps they're in it together. Working with someone powerful.'

Ten minutes later they came to a clearing. William recognised it as the place where Angeline's house stood, but they had arrived at the opposite end of the field where Nan's cottage was positioned. They rode past a paddock, in which he counted ten donkeys. Then he spied a large barn at the back of the cottage.

'We usually move the goods and then store them in that barn until we can put the boxes on a wagon and transport them to the castle,' explained Angeline.

William dismounted and walked towards the barn. As he did so, he saw from the corner of his eye someone step out of the cottage. It was Brigid, drying her hands on a towel. He knew she was now living here with Eric Sweyne. Their eyes met and it stopped her in her tracks. He went into the barn and had a good look around. It was totally empty. Everything must have been moved up to the castle last night.

'You're not hiding anything from me, are you Brigid?' he shouted as he walked back outside.

'No sir, on my honour.'

'Why store the contraband here? Why not take it straight to the castle?' he asked her.

Brigid looked at Angeline slumped on her horse, 'Everything depends on the moon. We have to wait for a clear night when the moon is full before we can move it on to the castle, otherwise the way is too dangerous.'

As he went to get back on his horse, Brigid ran up and whispered to him, out of earshot of her mistress.

'Sir, I know what we have done is wrong, but it was done with the best of intentions. To help the people who live around about.'

William did not respond.

'Sir,' Brigid pleaded, 'Lady Angeline loves you with all her heart. She would not do anything to put you in jeopardy. None of us would, but we were all caught up in something we could not easily get out of.'

William grabbed hold of his reins. 'You do realise that I should turn you all in to the authorities?'

Brigid gave a slight nod.

'Most men in my position would do just that. I'm putting my reputation on the line for you people. People who do not seem to appreciate it.'

'We do, sir, I promise we do.'

CHAPTER 33

They arrived at Angeline's house, where she immediately went inside to rest. William walked to the water source to drink. After he had quenched his thirst, he poured the water over his head and face. It felt refreshing and purifying. He lay down on the grass beside the bubbling water and closed his eyes for a moment, listening to the sound the water made as it gurgled into the stream. He could not explain the sense of calm and contentment he always experienced when he was here, as if nothing else in the world mattered.

A shadow fell across his face and his heart leapt. When he opened his eyes, he saw, in front of him, a tall lady with long, white-blonde flowing hair, but he could not make out her features. He blinked wildly. 'Angeline,' he said, knowing it was not her, yet there was something so familiar about this woman.

'No, not Angeline,' she said silkily. 'I am the weaver of fates and the bringer of dreams.'

William had heard those words before: the Reverend had used them at Beltane. He sat up. 'Coventina!' he cried in disbelief.

She bowed serenely in acknowledgement. 'I am here to warn you there is great danger ahead. You must tread carefully. Your future depends on it.'

'What kind of danger?'

The spectre looked around slowly. 'I cannot say, but something in the dark chases you.'

William started. That was exactly what Nan had told them on the day he and Nikolaus had arrived at the castle.

'It is written in the stars that Goldsborough should be yours. The sun and the moon are aligned. It is foretold that you will father a great dynasty from here, but there is a terrible evil walking the world of men that is bent on denying you what is rightfully yours. You must be on your guard,' the lady said. 'Angeline is with child. You must protect both mother and babe. Otherwise all is lost, and the lives of the people I have watched over for centuries will become unbearable.' The lady sighed wistfully. 'Lord Lyndhurst, we are all depending on you. Angeline is depending on you.'

William blinked; the glare from the sun blinded him momentarily. The lady had vanished.

He ran towards the house and into the bedroom to watch Angeline as she lay sleeping. She looked ghostly. A maelstrom of emotions whirled around him. Could that be why she looked so tired? Was she carrying his child? A strange frisson ran through him. He let her sleep as he thought about the warning of danger the spirit had brought to him. A flame flickered in the half-light of his mind. He would not lose Angeline, he vowed this to himself. He had to do as his nature commanded and protect at all cost. Whatever evil was out there, blackening everything it touched, he would destroy it. He knew there could be no peace for him until he had slain this unknown enemy. He felt like a man branded by fate.

Eventually, William woke Angeline as softly as he could. The sun was fading and they needed to get back to Goldsborough. He felt awkward with her. Everything had changed once more. He did not know how to rebuild a bridge to this woman to whom he felt eternally bound.

As they prepared to leave, they heard the sound of galloping hooves outside which halted abruptly. A fist pounded on the door.

'Thank goodness we found you,' said Reverend Roberts as he burst in. 'You are in grave danger, my lord.' Nikolaus was with him.

'What has happened?' William asked Nikolaus.

'I only know what the reverend here has told me. He came to the castle to warn you.'

'There has been another savage attack by the beast,' said the reverend, trying to catch his breath. 'John Smith and Alan Black, the farmers. They are both dead.'

William and Angeline glanced at each other.

'My lord, there is a mob descending on the castle,' said the reverend. 'People have heard you had the cargo from the ships destroyed and they are angry. They depend on smuggling to survive. So now they choose to believe what Elewald has been saying for months, that you and Count Andrassy are responsible for the brutal killings.'

Angeline gasped.

'Because they only happen when you are in residence,' he continued.

'We must return to the castle at once,' William said, but as he tried to step towards the door the reverend held his hand up to William's chest.

'I don't know if that is a good idea, my lord. It may be safer to remain here. The mob are baying for blood, but people are afraid to step onto this land uninvited. This land is magical to them.'

'No, the castle offers more protection.' William looked at Angeline as he said it. 'I will speak to the mob, reason with them.'

'William, I'm not sure,' said Nikolaus worriedly.

William shook his head. 'I've made up my mind.'

Looking up at the sky upon leaving the house, it seemed to William to be filled with portentous omens. Both the sun and the moon could be seen clearly through a burning red haze that made the dark clouds look demonic. A murmuration of starlings swooped and soared like a satanic black mass as they swirled around and around over their heads. Then they heard it: a long thunderous, heart-severing howl that curdled the blood. Instantly, the birds dived into the trees and disappeared.

'Is that a wolf?' asked Angeline.

'That is not a wolf,' said Nikolaus. 'That sounds like a thousand wolves.'

Total silence followed except for the trickling of the stream. They waited. A screech owl made them jump. Nikolaus lifted his nose into the air. 'It's in the woods, that direction.' He pointed right. 'And it's coming this way.'

'How can you be so sure?' asked a fearful reverend.

Nikolaus pulled out his officer's pistol from his inside coat pocket and tapped his nose with it, 'Because this is the organ of the night. And that foul smell I have detected before, which hovers over the dead like rotten flesh, that's coming this way.'

'He has a heightened sense of smell,' Angeline whispered to the reverend, 'like an animal.'

'We need fire torches,' William said. 'It will be dark soon.'

'There are some around the back of the house,' replied Angeline, 'left over from Beltane.'

'I'll get them,' volunteered the reverend.

'Angeline, go inside,' William insisted as he rushed to his saddlebag in search of his pistol. 'Lock all the windows and doors.'

She began to protest.

'Whatever happens, don't come out.'

She stood fast.

'Do as I say,' he commanded, just as the sun disappeared and the darkness loomed. The reverend returned from the house with two flaming torches. He handed one to Nikolaus. Then they heard it again, much nearer this time, a haunting howl that sounded like it was calling to the souls of the dead.

'The hell hound hunts with the devil tonight,' Nikolaus said ominously.

William grabbed hold of Angeline's arm and started dragging her back towards the house when suddenly Nikolaus announced, 'It's here.'

They turned to face the darkness. Nikolaus raised his torch and they were all seized with total dread at what prowled towards them. It was the most colossal hound they had ever seen: taller and heavier than any wolfhound. Its huge face, square and solid, was covered with blood. The monster stared at them with a wild, insane glare, teeth gnashing with potent rage, but perhaps the most deranged thing of all was that the beast was blue. Its fur had been dyed blue. It stood and watched them as if awaiting a command.

'What the...?'

'It's an ancient breed of mastiff,' cut in the reverend. 'The Britons used them to fight the Romans.'

'*Pugnaces Britanniae,*' said a disbelieving William. 'The war dog of the Britons.'

'But they are extinct!' exclaimed the reverend.

'Not so.' They all recognised that menacing voice. 'My family have bred them for generations.'

'Elewald, you depraved, villainous aberration,' spat the reverend, 'you bred that foul obscene beast?' The reverend moved forward with his torch and Elewald came into view. The infuriated animal growled, baring its teeth, froth dripping from its jowls.

'The devil is mocking me,' gasped the reverend when his

eyes fell upon Elewald. William felt a cold convulsion run through his body as Elewald laughed maniacally.

Whip in hand, Elewald was completely naked, except for a loin cloth. His entire body was painted woad-blue, just like the dog, but more bizarrely, every bit of his body that would normally be covered by clothes was tattooed with intricately interwoven patterns. The meaning of the symbols could only be guessed at. His white hair hung in a matted mess around his face, making him look fierce and warlike, just like the ancient Britons who struck fear into the hearts of the invading Romans hundreds of years ago.

William felt Angeline at his back. He locked eyes with Nikolaus and they read each other's thoughts. *Both man and beast are mad; only one outcome.*

The reverend rushed forward, roaring oaths. 'Elewald, you vile fiend, you have always preyed on death. Haunting wherever a carcass of a poor soul is to be found.'

'Reverend!' William hissed, trying to call him back.

The hound crouched, claws fixed, eyes full of fury.

'Down, devil, in God's name,' commanded the reverend. Elewald gave a signal and the monster rushed past Nikolaus, knocking him off-balance, and sprang upon the reverend. Instinctively, Nikolaus fired, but missed as he toppled and fell to the ground, hitting his head on a rock. He did not get up again.

The creature pounced upon the reverend, who was screaming curses and execrations. William wanted to fire, but could not get a line of sight, while Reverend Roberts was trying to throttle the monster with every ounce of strength he had in him. William witnessed the hooked fangs seize the reverend by the throat, then he fired. By sheer luck William found his target, but the creature did not let go of its prey. A piercing, cold shiver ran through William as he realised he had not delivered a mortal wound.

The contorted face of the reverend convulsed and William made a desperate lunge to draw off the beast, attempting to tear the creature from the body. William heard Angeline behind him scream his name, again and again.

Jumping onto the hound's back, William sank his fingers into the monster's eyes. It yelped in pain, let go of the vicar's throat and threw back its head, trying to bite William, who managed to pull the hulking mass of the creature off the bloodied body of Reverend Roberts. William knew death, felt it in his marrow, and realised that the reverend would not last more than a minute.

'Great God, can there be such evil in the creatures thou hast made?' the reverend gasped as the last spark of life left him.

The beast escaped William's clutches. It rolled onto its back in the dirt, then righted itself, its grotesque features glimmering with rabid fury. William tried to scramble to his feet. He stretched for the flaming torch that was lying on the ground, next to the dead body of Reverend Roberts. He heard Angeline scream his name once more as the blue monster moved in on him. Then it pounced. The shadow of death followed.

CHAPTER 34

The stench made her retch. The putrefied air was suffocating. Angeline did not know how she had arrived at this godforsaken place. All she could remember was being captured from behind by Elewald and screaming at William for help. Terrorised, she had witnessed the beast's savage attack on the reverend, before it turned on her beloved William. Then she must have passed out. Oh dear God, was William dead? Were they all dead?

Angeline tried to move, but chains pinned her wrists to damp, dripping walls, cutting into her flesh as she struggled. She could feel her heart pounding so hard she thought it might explode.

Flaming stakes protruded from the flagstones and afforded her some light. The room that held her prisoner looked like a medieval torture chamber. In the corner, a rectangular wooden frame resembled a rack. On it rested a whip with barbs on the end. It had a silver handle. Angeline knew it to be the one that belonged to Elewald. Next to the whip sat a set of keys. They would set her free, she was sure of it. An old, discarded pillory had been knocked sideways, but most chillingly of all, some branding irons were sitting, nonchalantly, in a flaming brazier. Angeline's eyes bulged at the sight. She looked up. Swollen animal carcasses hung from the ceiling. They were slowly being devoured by maggots. The rancid smell was overwhelming. It stuck in her nostrils. A small, iron grille in the roof displayed a few stars sprinkled across the sky. She tugged again at the chains that bound her.

'Coventina, please help me,' she whispered. A long silence followed before she heard the tiniest voice in her head.

'I cannot. My power is weak in that evil place.'

Angeline closed her eyes and saw eternity behind her lids. She had never known such hopelessness. When she opened them she saw something in the far corner of the dungeon glint in the darkness. Then another glint, followed by a third. Her vision became accustomed to the shadows and she began to make out the hideous forms. Three pairs of eyes stared at her.

A bubble of recognition came shooting up: three maleficent hounds were studying her intently. They all looked exactly like the one who attacked the reverend and William, but as far as she could make out, these were rock-like in colour. Not painted blue with woad.

They were enclosed within a huge iron cage, not making a sound, as if they had been trained to keep deadly quiet. Was one of these beasts the one who had savaged Nan, she wondered.

They seemed to be considering her intelligently. Angeline could not fathom the depth of longing in their eyes. She shook her head and moaned; her dread of the unknown could not be exorcised.

Angeline had no idea how long she had been there. She felt faint, her stomach hollow. She could not remember the last time she had eaten, but she was beyond hunger. Then the door, half hidden by a pillar, creaked open and soft, padded steps crossed the room. She waited, then jumped when his face appeared from nowhere.

Elewald was standing close, gloating, stony eyes blazing with raving insanity. 'Welcome to my temple,' he said.

Looking up and down Elewald's tattooed, woad-blue, naked body, Angeline could not disguise the panic in her eyes. He seemed to revel in her fear.

'I see the delectable Lady Angeline is fascinated by my body.' He turned full circle for her, to show off the tattoos, which were detailed and exquisite, intricate scrollwork entwined with depictions of fearful warriors and ancient symbols. Some symbols she recognised as Celtic, but the majority she could not understand. His body was covered with them.

'Homage to my dear, departed ancestors. I am King of the Elves, did you know that?'

'You murdered Nan, didn't you?' Angeline cried. 'You and those beasts of yours.'

'Of course.'

'You're a monster!' she said, suddenly defiant.

Elewald laughed and walked over to the cage to study his dogs. 'We are all monsters, my dear, even that lover of yours, Lyndhurst, who is well and truly dead by now, I can assure you. My darling hound will have seen to that.' Angeline gasped.

Elewald turned his head towards the door. 'My lovely boy should be back any time now. I left him to complete his work, whilst I carried you back. He is so clever, my hound, so easy to train.' He then looked at Angeline, his eyes slowly working down her body. He gave a vile grin. 'Did you know your lover murdered his own brother so he could inherit Goldsborough?'

'I don't believe you.'

'Well, you should. I'm surprised you didn't hear the whispers in London. Shot him stone dead.'

'You liar!' she shouted.

Elewald jerked forward and grabbed hold of her neck with a grubby hand. Angeline yelped in pain and he sniggered at her distress. 'You and your land should have been mine. I offered to pay handsomely for you. If Lyndhurst had agreed, I would never have had to kill that silly old woman.' Elewald sniffed Angeline's delicate skin, as if he were a dog himself. 'But as it was, you both defied me, so someone had to be punished.' He stroked her arm; took hold of a tiny piece of skin from the inside, placed it between his finger and thumb and pinched hard. Angeline screamed like she had never screamed before and the tears rolled.

He roared with delight, eyes bright with madness.

'You will discover, my child, there is no end to my depravity. I will enjoy teaching you everything I know.'

Angeline shook her head in fearful apprehension.

'You belong to me now, you know.'

'People will come looking for me...' She choked on her tears.

'They won't find you. Not before I marry you. A priest is on his way as I speak,' Elewald gloated, 'then everything you own will be mine. The source of the river will be mine.'

Angeline shuddered. 'You're responsible for Alan Black's death too, and John Smith.'

Elewald cackled. 'Don't forget the sheep,' he said as he walked around the room, puffing out his chest. 'Everything is going according to plan. It needed to look like the killings only happened when the new Lord of Goldsborough was in residence. That the murders were all his doing. To reveal him as the true monster.' Elewald picked up a branding iron and began to caress it. 'People will consider Lyndhurst's death to be divine retribution.' He looked up at the ceiling. 'Then, finally, I will have it, the source of the river. The one thing my family has coveted for years, but only I am clever enough to secure it.'

'That is never going to happen,' Angeline cried.

Elewald threw down the branding iron in temper and sparks flew. 'Don't challenge me, girl!' he raged as he grappled to find his whip.

Angeline tried to swallow but her throat had closed up with fear as she realised Elewald was so deranged she would never be able to reason with him. He walked towards her, whip in one hand as he stroked her hair with the other.

'People will come looking for me,' she whispered once more.

'There will be nothing anyone can do about it when you are my wife.' He smiled. 'Very soon, you will be begging for death, just as my first wife did.'

Angeline could not stop a whimper escape from her lips. His rancid breath covered her face as his mouth contorted with rage.

'When I'm bored with you,' he sighed, 'I will feed you to my dogs. I will watch them tear you limb from limb.'

Desperation turned to anger as something deep inside Angeline finally snapped. 'Go to hell!' she spat as she squeezed her eyes shut, anticipating his next move.

He grabbed her hair and pulled so hard that her breath almost stopped. 'You need to be taught a lesson, my girl. You're just like your mother. Too headstrong for your own good.'

'You're insane,' she cried as she glanced up at the stars, silently begging for help. Angeline thought she saw a shadow pass over the grille in the ceiling. She felt faint. She must be hallucinating.

'Oh, my pretty, I'm going to have such fun with you.' Without thought, Angeline raised a knee, found his groin and jerked upwards hard. With a howl, Elewald crumpled in agony. Immediately she regretted the impulse, filled with dread at the revenge that would be exacted.

Suddenly, Elewald leapt upon her and caught her by the throat.

'Don't you dare!' came a familiar voice. Angeline blinked frantically, hoping she wasn't dreaming.

'Take your hand away from her,' said the voice in a measured, almost calm tone.

From the corner of her eye, Angeline identified his silhouette and began to sob with relief. William walked slowly into view. Elewald stared at him, shocked.

'You! No, it can't be! Where's my hound?' he shouted. The creatures in the cage started to bark savagely at the change in their master's demeanour.

'Gone to the devil,' William replied.

'No. I don't believe you. Not my beautiful boy. You couldn't have.'

William took a step closer, never taking his pistol away from its mark. 'Step away from her, Elewald. Now,' he shouted over the din.

Elewald's eyes flitted between Angeline and William, trying to work out his next move. She saw the whip twitch in his right hand. It was a gesture to the hounds, who became passive again.

'So, you're going to shoot me in cold blood, eh, just like you did your brother,' Elewald hissed.

'That was self-defence.' William said. 'I had no choice. Everyone knows it.'

'Do they now? That's not what I heard.' Elewald stroked Angeline's neck. 'Bringing down a man with a gun is not the same as snuffing out a life with your bare hands.' His voice was feverish. 'Purification can only come when a man is directly in touch with death.'

Angeline's eyes darted from man to man.

Elewald sighed. 'I can feel her pulse beat.'

'Move away, man. That's my last warning.'

At that, Elewald made his move and cracked his whip with full force, aiming at William's pistol, which went off immediately, but Elewald anticipated well and dived underneath the shot. The noise terrified the monster hounds and they clawed ferociously at the cage. He cracked the whip again and it snaked around William's ankle, pulling him down. William tugged at it with all his strength, dragging Elewald towards him. They tussled with each other, rolling across the floor, smashing and beating each other in a frenzied attack that went on and on until both men were drenched in blood. William found his footing and scrambled to stand upright. He yanked Elewald up by his hair before delivering an almighty punch that dashed him to the ground. Elewald lay quite still, prostrate on the floor, blood oozing from his mouth. Red liquid mingled with the blue of the woad and dripped purple onto the floor. He did not move.

The creatures were going berserk inside their cage, jumping and frothing at the mouth.

'The keys!' Angeline shouted. 'Over there, on the rack.'

She faltered with weakness as William released her from the chains and she collapsed into his arms. 'You're safe now, Angeline,' he said, 'quite safe. He will never molest you again.' William kissed her carefully and felt her body sink into his. 'I love you so much. There, I've said it. I love you. Say you'll marry me, Angeline, please. I need to keep you safe.'

The caged animals suddenly became subdued. They cowered, sensing defeat and danger.

She stroked his bloodied and bruised face. 'Yes, of course I will. We belong together. I have always loved you. I think I've loved you from the very first time we met.'

As they embraced the dogs began to bark again and she glanced over William's shoulder to see Elewald loom up from the dead. She pulled away in fright as he wrapped his whip around William's throat.

'Run!' William croaked, desperately trying to force his fingers between his throat and the whip. 'Run!'

The dogs howled with renewed excitement.

Out of sheer panic she bolted, but once at the door Angeline looked back to see William on his knees, choking to death. She could not leave him to die. She had to try to save him. She caught sight of the keys that William had dropped, but she was looking for a branding iron. She picked one up and swiftly dealt a blow to the back of Elewald's head. It wasn't enough to knock him out but the blood spurted and he howled just like his dogs as he fell. William, seizing the opportunity, released the whip from his neck, jumped up, and turned to face Elewald. They struggled, but William had been severely weakened.

'Open the cage,' William commanded. Angeline hesitated. 'Open it.'

She clambered for the keys. As soon as she opened the cage door, William made one last huge effort and pushed Elewald's body hard with his foot. Elewald staggered backwards. William pushed again, using the full force of his body and Elewald shot into the cage. William grabbed the keys from Angeline and relocked it.

There was a moment of complete silence as humans and beasts readjusted to the new situation.

'Now, my beauties, keep calm,' Elewald whispered, standing perfectly still. But the creatures seemed to hear the fear in his voice. Their ears twitched. His blood dripped onto the cage floor in great blobs and their noses wrinkled. Then their heads cocked, as if realising he had no whip in his hand.

Angeline would never forget the tortured scream for as long as she lived. Burying her head in William's chest, the screaming and the mauling seemed to go on forever. She covered her ears with her hands, but could not block out the sound of flesh being ripped and devoured.

CHAPTER 35

He felt her slender arms holding onto his body for dear life as they rode away from Elewald's decaying edifice. William looked back at the tower, shining like silver in the greyness of the night. It appeared to grow out of the mist that clung tightly to the ground. It reminded him of the tower in his dream, all those months ago. Angeline had stood in front of it, calling for him to come to her. He trembled at the memory.

A dank, musty smell hung in the air as he picked his way through a tumbled-down stone wall and a stagnant swamp. William manoeuvred his horse stealthily around a huge dead tree lying on the ground. Angeline's head relaxed onto his broad back as they passed through the crumbling gateposts, riding homewards.

'How did you escape from the beast?' Angeline finally asked. 'I was certain you must be dead.'

'I managed to lunge for the burning torch that was lying on the ground. Its fur went up in flames,' he replied.

'And the reverend?' she asked.

William shook his head. 'I'm sorry, he didn't survive,' was all he could say.

Angeline sighed heavily. She had been hoping for a miracle. 'And Nikolaus, what of him?'

William looked up towards the horizon. 'I think you will find that is our Hungarian.' He pointed to the tiny lights coming towards them. 'Luckily, he only knocked himself out when he hit the ground.'

Eventually, Nikolaus came into view, followed by Eric Sweyne, who was leading a mob.

'Thank goodness you're both safe,' Nikolaus said, relief ringing in his voice. He looked around. 'And Elewald?'

'Dead,' William answered as Sweyne walked up to join them. 'You'll find what's left of him in the dungeon. Be very careful, Mr Sweyne,' warned William. 'There are more of those wretched creatures down there, caged up. They are savage monsters and must be destroyed.'

Sweyne nodded in acknowledgement and moved onwards with the men. Nikolaus looked up at Angeline. 'When I returned to the castle, I explained to the men that the vicar was dead and you had been abducted. I made it clear that Elewald was insane and I had no idea how many of those beasts he had bred. But they did not hesitate to come to your rescue, Angeline, not a single one.'

She smiled appreciatively. Then Nikolaus screwed up his nose and sniffed at her like a dog.

'You smell of it now. That vile, undead smell.' He fixed on a blue stain that was smeared over Angeline's dress.

'I think it's woad you can smell,' she replied.

Nikolaus looked at her, mystified.

'The woad plant is mixed with potash and urine, then fermented to make blue dye.' Angeline touched the blue and held her hand out to Nikolaus, who backed away. 'Ordinary folk can't smell anything in its final form, as the terrible smell evaporates, but you, with your special nose, probably can still detect it.'

'Fascinating,' said Nikolaus. 'Well, hopefully, that is the final piece of this very disturbing puzzle.' He turned his head again, distracted by a light hovering over Elewald's land.

They all saw an orange glow burning brightly as it mushroomed into the night sky. The rotting fortification, once the seat of the Elewald dynasty, was on fire.

'And let that be the end of this whole sordid affair,' William said. 'Come, let's leave this loathsome place, Angeline.' He squeezed her leg affectionately. 'We belong at Goldsborough.'

They rode on, leaving Nikolaus to organise the men. William thought about Angeline coming back to rescue him from Elewald. She would always be headstrong and a bit wild, but she was in his blood, as he knew he was in hers. They were bonded together by some unseen force.

'You did a very brave thing, Angeline, back there. You saved my life. If you had run, as I instructed, I would not be here now.'

'Do you promise never to scold me again, when I do not do as you tell, my lord?' she replied, somehow finding the energy to tease him a little.

He nodded. 'I promise.' He caressed her arms that were wrapped around him. 'That is the second time my life has been saved by a woman.'

'Really?'

'Yes. Her name was Theresa. She was brave and beautiful, just like you.'

'What happened to her?'

'Unfortunately, she was a casualty of war, like so many others.' He shook his head. 'Such a terrible waste.'

Angeline held onto him even tighter. 'Did you love her?'

'Yes, I did once.' His voice quivered. 'But I know she would have approved of you very much indeed.'

When Goldsborough Castle came into view, the stained glass windows in the towers twinkled above the treetops, enticing the traveller forward. It reminded William of the very first time he had laid eyes on the splendid sight. He remembered how his heart had thumped in anticipation. He had no idea then that Angeline even existed. How much had changed in such a short space of time. Now he wanted her on any terms. He had told her he loved her. Nothing left a man more vulnerable, yet nothing could bring more joy.

'I love you with all my heart,' he said to Angeline.

She snuggled up to him. 'And I, you.'

EPILOGUE

The vicar from the neighbouring parish came to administer the wedding, which had been organised with great haste, in just under a fortnight. Time enough for Lady Vivian and the Hurstbournes to dash up from London.

The bride was dressed in ivory silk and lace, encrusted with tiny seed pearls. Angeline hoped William would not ask where the fabric came from. Luckily her waist was not yet expanding and her tiredness had subsided, so there were no telltale signs of the baby she was carrying.

'What is William talking about? He has been with those men for an age and all his attention should be on you today,' said Lady Vivian as she sat with Angeline at the wedding celebration. 'Oh, I do despair of him,' she said crossly as Nikolaus and Annabel danced past.

Angeline laughed. 'I am perfectly happy, Lady Vivian. He is very excited about his new project. William is going to build a brewery. He has promised the local men that he will create employment for them, and I wholeheartedly approve.'

'A brewery?' Lady Vivian gasped. 'Oh please, no. We are not of the mercantile classes. What will they say in London?'

'Honestly, I don't care what they say. He is a good man doing the right thing.'

Lady Vivian sighed heavily. 'Well, it's jolly good you both have me to smooth your pathway back into fashionable society, but it won't be easy, you know. It will take a very long time.'

'I'm sure we'll manage,' replied Angeline smiling at Eric and Brigid canoodling in one corner, whilst Venetia Pembroke was being consoled by a prominent member of the local gentry over the death of her beloved Hugh in another.

'I'm sure you will,' replied Lady Vivian affectionately. 'I really should not complain, I know. In the end, everything has worked out for the best.' Lady Vivian stared at Angeline with astonishment etched on her face, as if some brilliant thought had just occurred to her. 'It's almost as if fate had a hand in this outcome.'

'Yes, perhaps.' Angeline smiled.

'Truly,' Lady Vivian continued, ' I shudder at the thought of what might have happened to us all if George was still alive.'

This was too good an opportunity to miss, so Angeline took her cue.

'Lady Vivian, there is something I've been meaning to ask you.'

'Hmm, what's that, dear?' asked Lady Vivian absentmindedly, busy trying to attract William's attention.

'What exactly did happen between William and his brother? How did George die?'

The dowager duchess looked aghast at the question. 'Why bring that up now?'

'I need to know. He's the one ghost I can't lay to rest, Elewald accused William of shooting George in order to obtain Goldsborough.'

Lady Vivian fiddled with her fan for a long time before answering. 'I did not see what happened that night, nor did

Nikolaus, come to that. It was the night of the Hurstbourne ball. There were six people in the room: two are dead. George, William's brother, and George's mistress.' Lady Vivian shuffled around on her seat and began to fan herself almost violently. 'The four still alive are William himself, Simon, Louisa and Sirkett, Simon's butler. They will all swear that William shot George in self-defence. That George, drunk as usual, fired the first shot which missed William, and hit his own mistress by mistake, killing her.' Lady Vivian lent over and spoke softly. 'There has always been a sniff of scandal about it because all the witnesses are so loyal to each other and it was just too convenient. But the whole of society has let it be because, truth be told, it was convenient for all of us.'

'How so?' Angeline asked, her brow furrowing.

'George was a liability to the entire British establishment. He had destroyed too many families, leading sons and heirs into a life of debauchery. Gambling and drinking their inheritance away, ruining their sisters.' Lady Vivian shivered and looked around. 'William, on the other hand, was of outstanding character. Both he and Simon were war heroes. No one would openly doubt their word,' she said. 'I, for one, wholeheartedly believe William's account of what happened that night, and so should you. William fired in self-defence.' Lady Vivian patted Angeline's arm. 'Trust me, William knew nothing about George winning Goldsborough until after George died. None of us did.'

Angeline became lost in thought. 'Thank God George did not inherit Goldsborough,' she finally said.

'I'll drink to that,' replied Lady Vivian, raising her glass of champagne from the side table. She looked at Angeline long and hard before deciding to continue. 'I'm going to tell you something I have never told anyone else.'

Angeline hung onto her words.

'William is not a murderer. But I believe George was.'

Angeline held her hand to her mouth.

'I can't prove it, of course, but I think he killed his own father in order to inherit.'

A shocked 'no' slipped from Angeline's lips.

'Do you remember the conversation we had about my brother when we were visiting Lyndhurst Manor?'

'Yes,' replied Angeline. 'You said he died from a riding accident, despite his wife believing he was the greatest horseman in the county.'

The old dowager sighed deeply. 'And that was the truth. My brother was an outstanding rider. I never believed it was an accident. It didn't make any sense, but George was desperate and had everything to gain. He had run out of money and his father had refused to give him any more. Only because there was not much more to give.'

Angeline shook her head in disbelief.

'Yes, everything has turned out for the very best,' Lady Vivian said. 'It's just such a shame that William has had to sacrifice his reputation. It meant everything to him. It was the one thing that separated him from his father and brother.'

Angeline felt a twinge of remorse and vowed to herself, then and there, to work tirelessly to restore William's position in society. It was the least she could do for the man she loved.

William held out his hand to her for the next dance.

'I did not think you liked to dance, sir,' Angeline said coyly.

'I will do anything that allows me to hold you in my arms, my darling,' he replied.

She looked into his eyes and almost swooned with overwhelming love for this man.

'Are you happy?' he asked her.

'Happier than I ever thought possible.' *Thank you, Coventina,* Angeline said to herself as he gathered her up and waltzed her around the room. For it was she who had sent him to her. Coventina, the weaver of fates and the bringer of dreams.